ADRIAN and the TREE of SECRETS

story by **HUBERT**
illustrations by **MARIE CAILLOU**

translated by **DAVID HOMEL**

Vancouver · Arsenal Pulp Press

ADRIAN AND THE TREE OF SECRETS
English language edition © 2014 by Arsenal Pulp Press

First published in French as *La Ligne Droite* by Hubert and Marie Caillou © 2013—Editions Glénat

ARSENAL PULP PRESS
Suite 202–211 East Georgia St.
Vancouver, BC V6A 1Z6
Canada
arsenalpulp.com

Cet ouvrage a bénéficié du soutien des Programmes d'aide à la publication de l'Institut français.

Printed and bound in the Republic of Korea

Library and Archives Canada Cataloguing in Publication:
Hubert, 1971–
[Ligne droite. English]
Adrian and the tree of secrets / story by Hubert ; illustrations
by Marie Caillou ; translated by David Homel.

Translation of: La ligne droite.
Issued in print and electronic formats.
ISBN 978-1-55152-556-3 (pbk.).—ISBN 978-1-55152-557-0 (epub)

1. Graphic novels. I. Homel, David, translator II. Caillou, Marie, 1971–,
illustrator III. Title.

PZ23.7.H83Ad 2014   j741.5'944   C2014-904513-1
                                                     C2014-904514-X

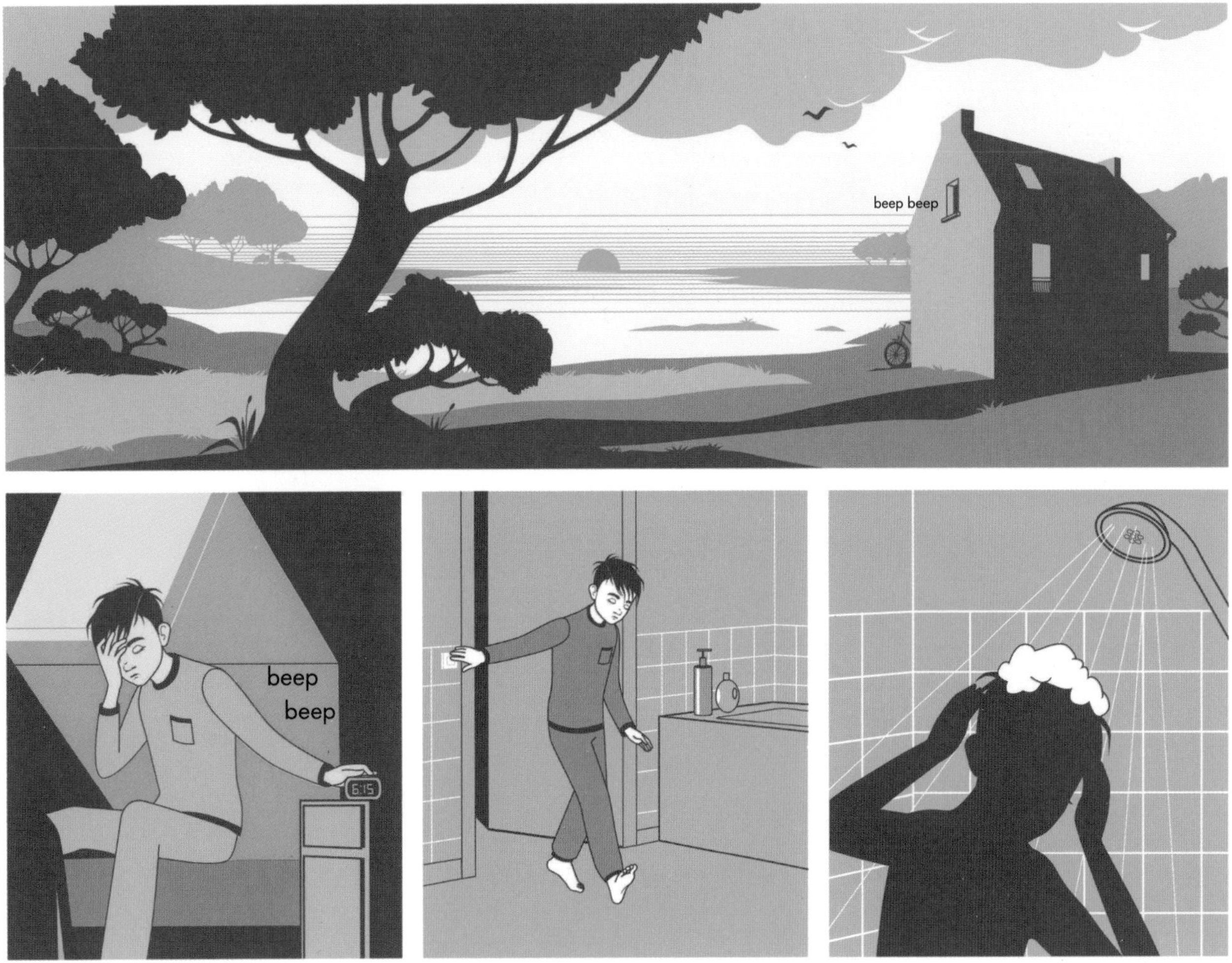
beep beep
beep
beep
6:15

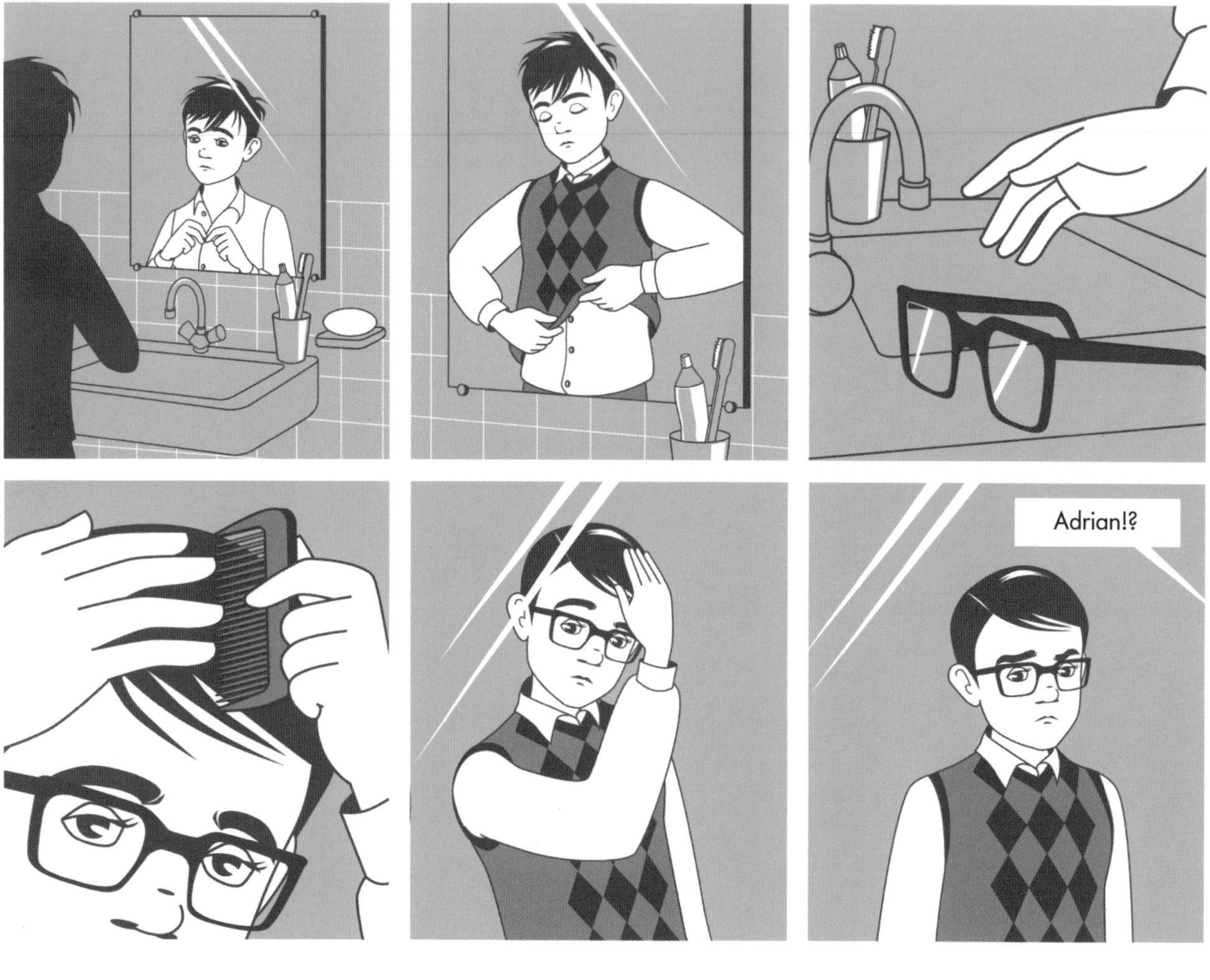
Adrian!?

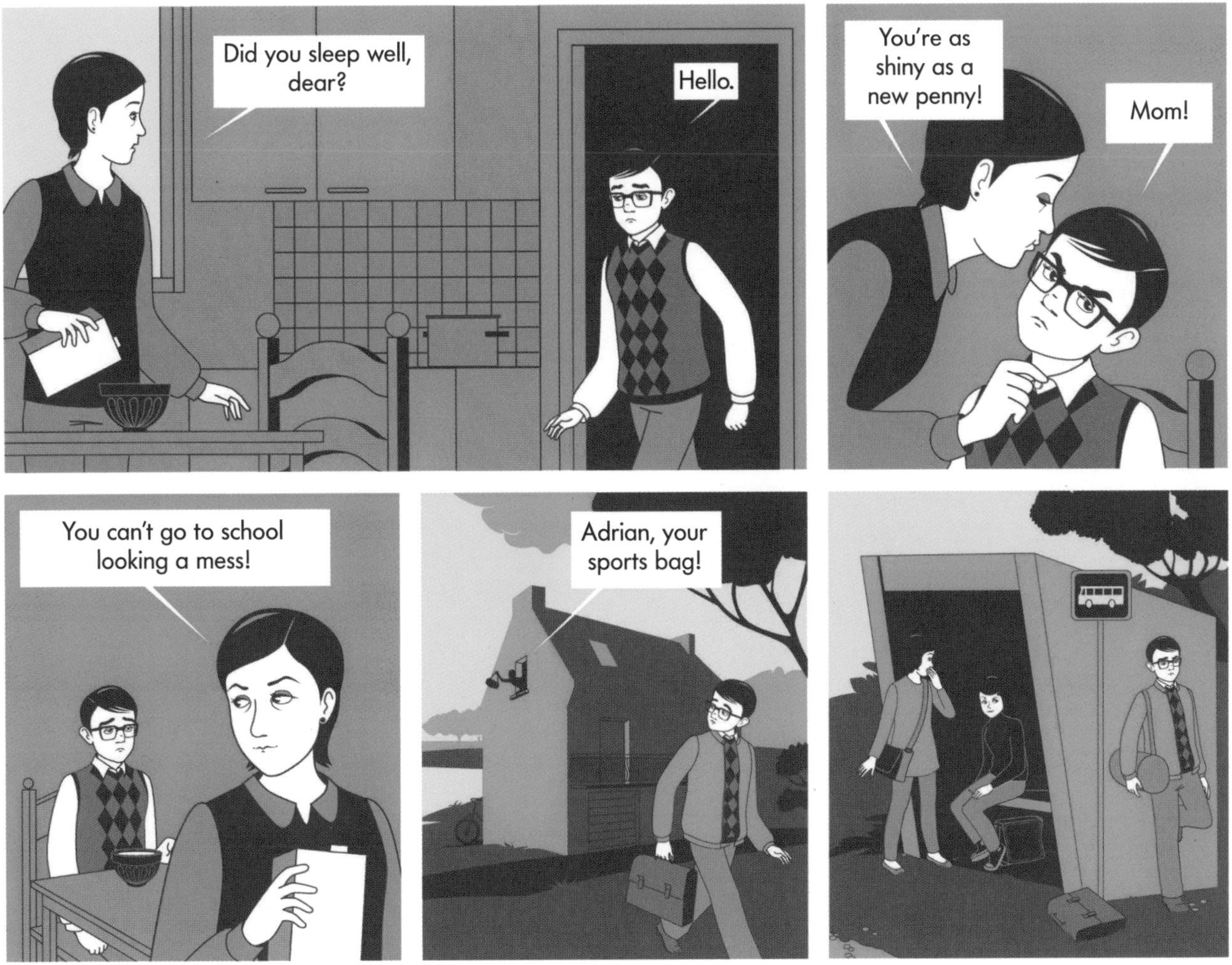
Did you sleep well, dear?
Hello.
You're as shiny as a new penny!
Mom!
You can't go to school looking a mess!
Adrian, your sports bag!

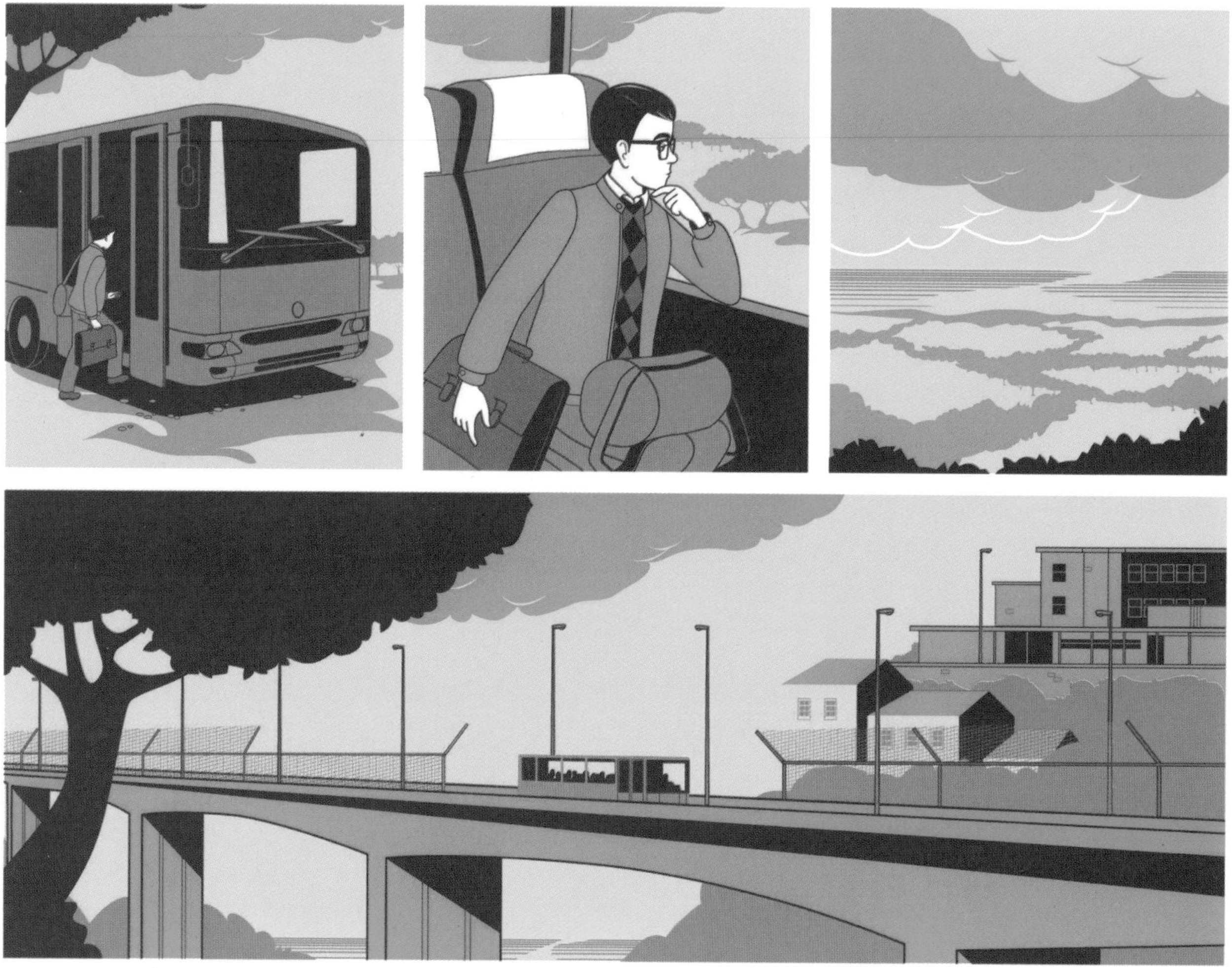

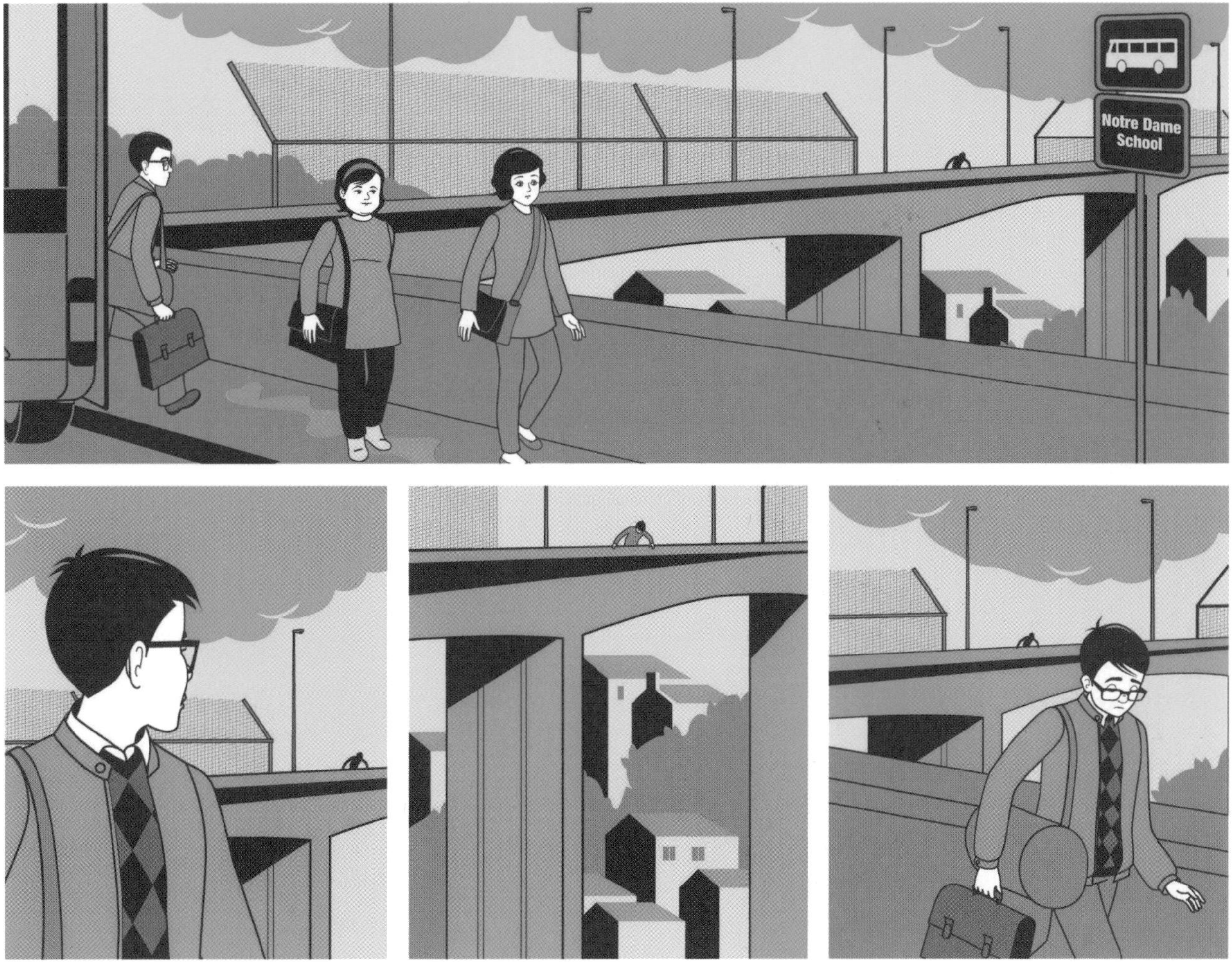
Notre Dame
School

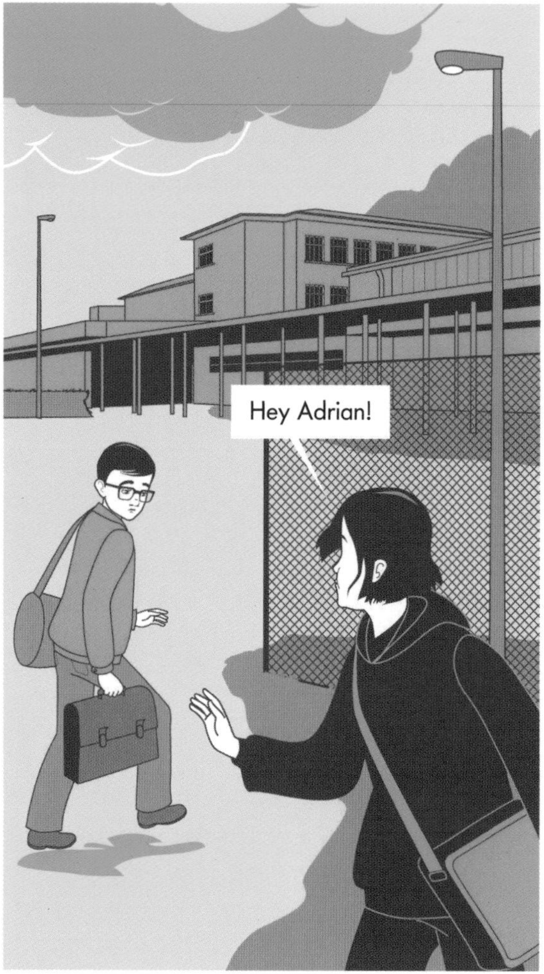
Hey Adrian!

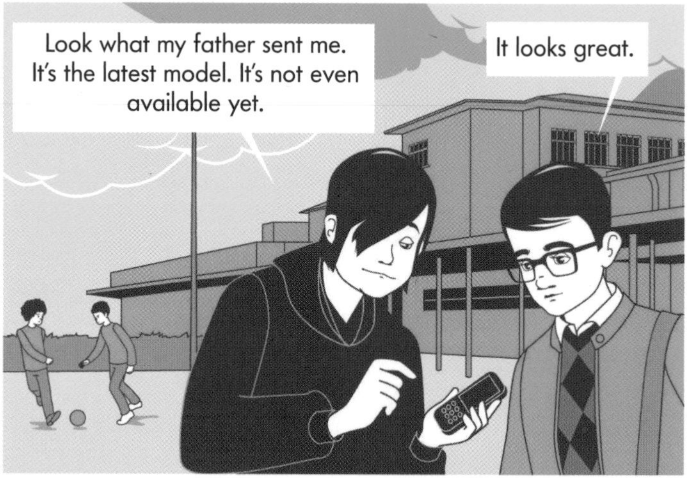
Look what my father sent me. It's the latest model. It's not even available yet.
It looks great.

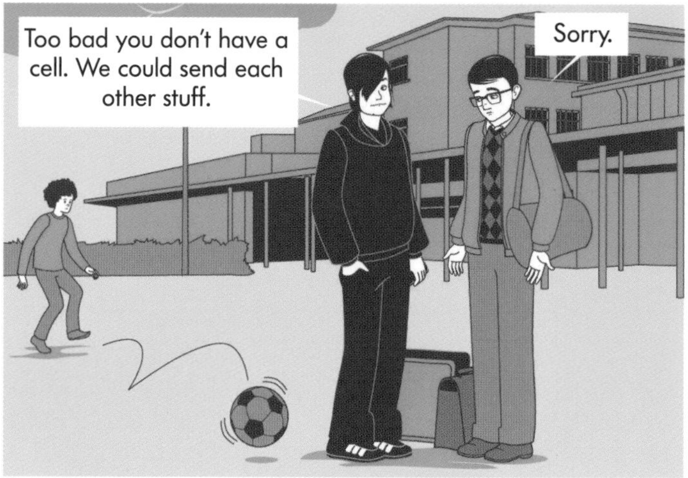
Too bad you don't have a cell. We could send each other stuff.
Sorry.

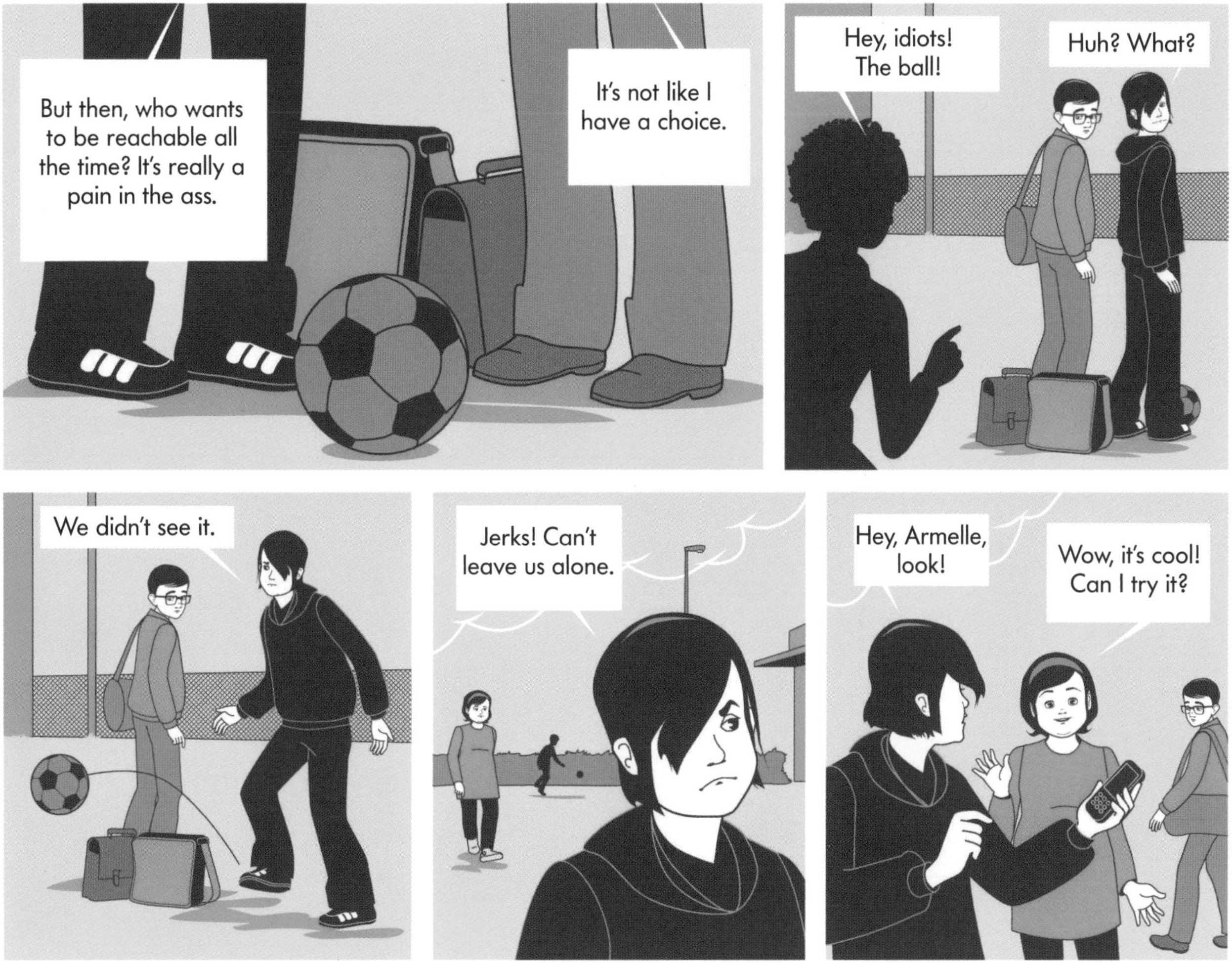
But then, who wants to be reachable all the time? It's really a pain in the ass.
It's not like I have a choice.
Hey, idiots! The ball!
Huh? What?
We didn't see it.
Jerks! Can't leave us alone.
Hey, Armelle, look!
Wow, it's cool! Can I try it?

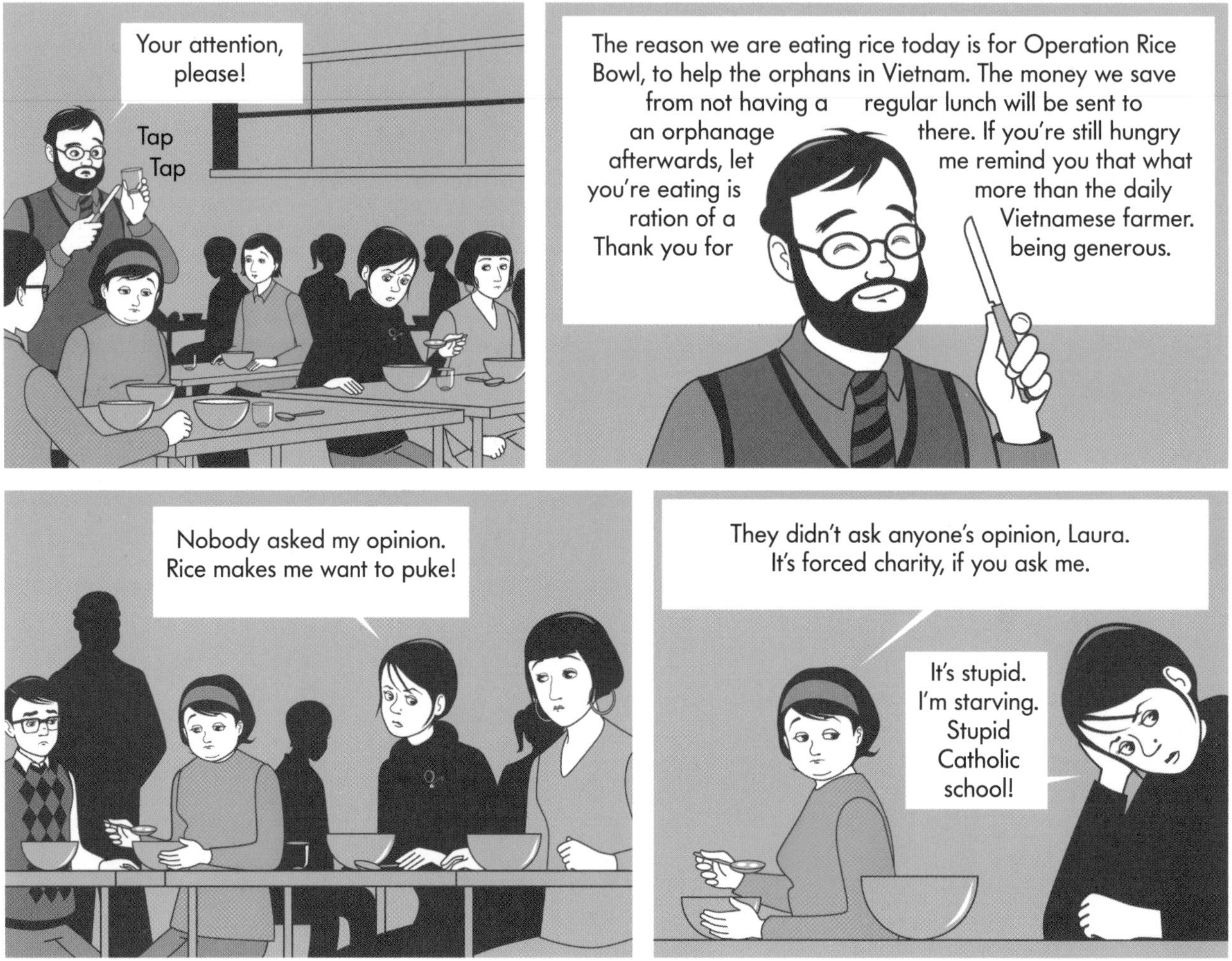
Your attention, please!
Tap Tap
The reason we are eating rice today is for Operation Rice Bowl, to help the orphans in Vietnam. The money we save from not having a regular lunch will be sent to an orphanage there. If you're still hungry afterwards, let me remind you that what you're eating is more than the daily ration of a Vietnamese farmer. Thank you for being generous.
Nobody asked my opinion. Rice makes me want to puke!
They didn't ask anyone's opinion, Laura. It's forced charity, if you ask me.
It's stupid. I'm starving. Stupid Catholic school!

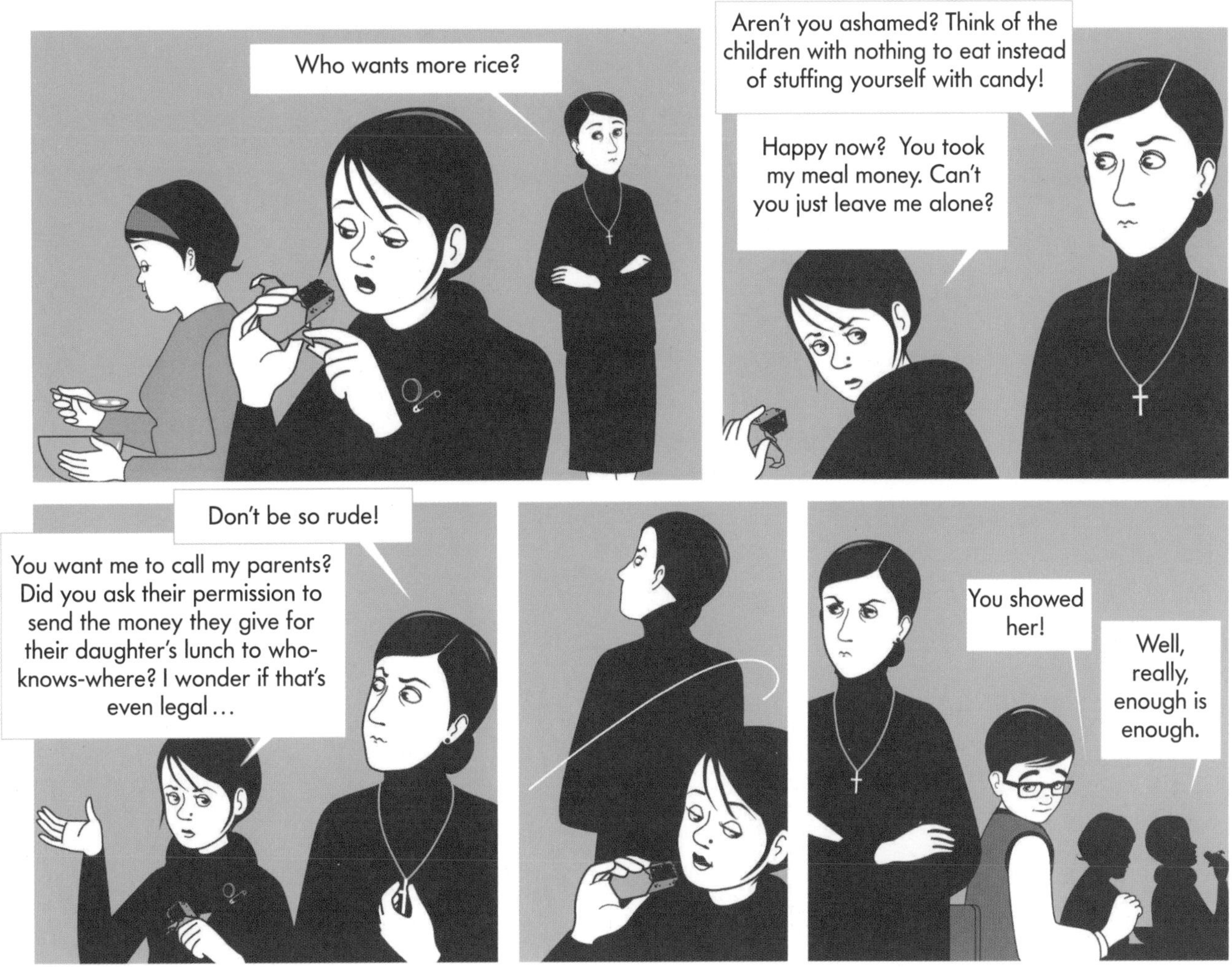
Who wants more rice?
Aren't you ashamed? Think of the children with nothing to eat instead of stuffing yourself with candy!
Happy now? You took my meal money. Can't you just leave me alone?
Don't be so rude!
You want me to call my parents? Did you ask their permission to send the money they give for their daughter's lunch to who-knows-where? I wonder if that's even legal . . .
You showed her!
Well, really, enough is enough.

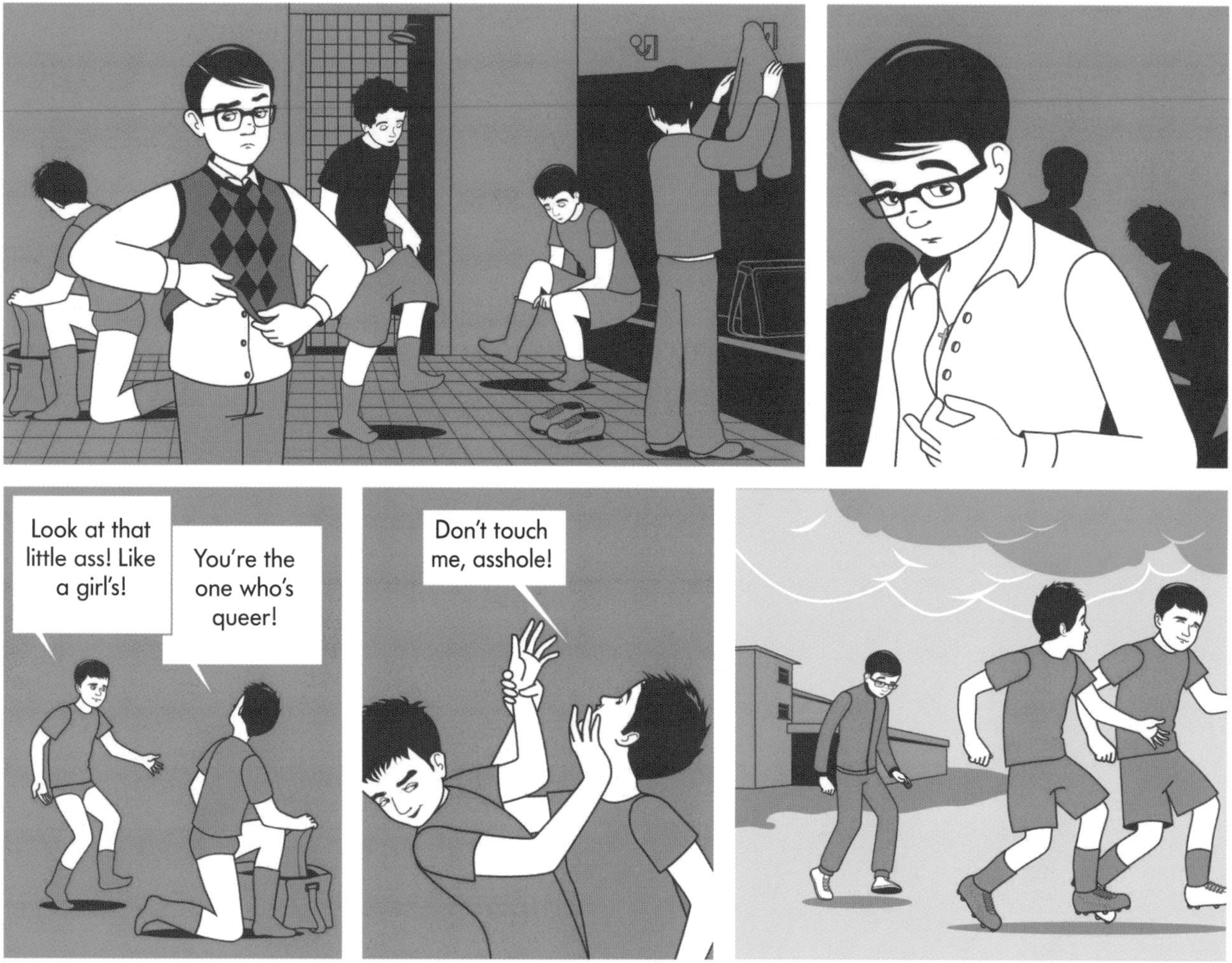
Look at that little ass! Like a girl's!
You're the one who's queer!
Don't touch me, asshole!

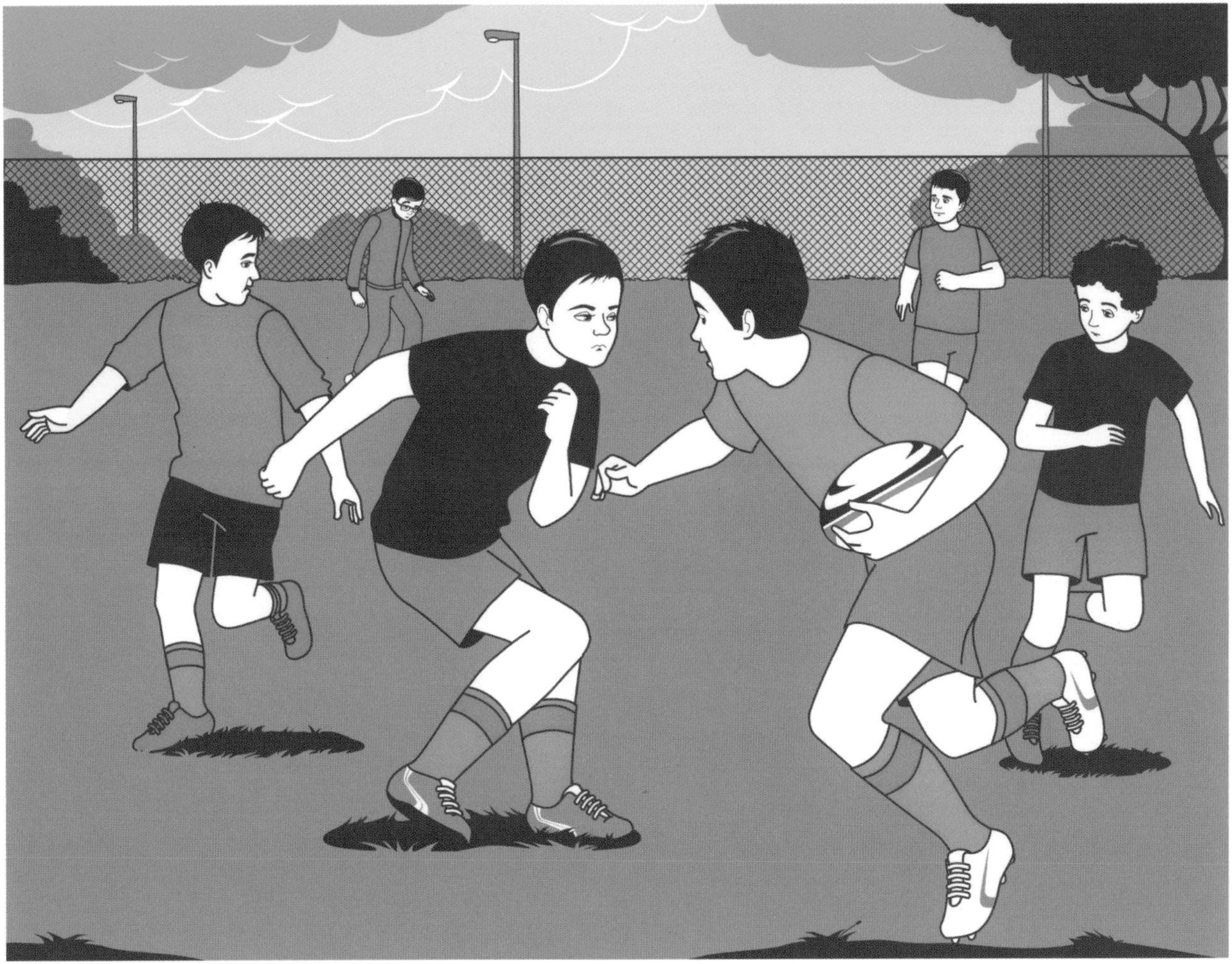

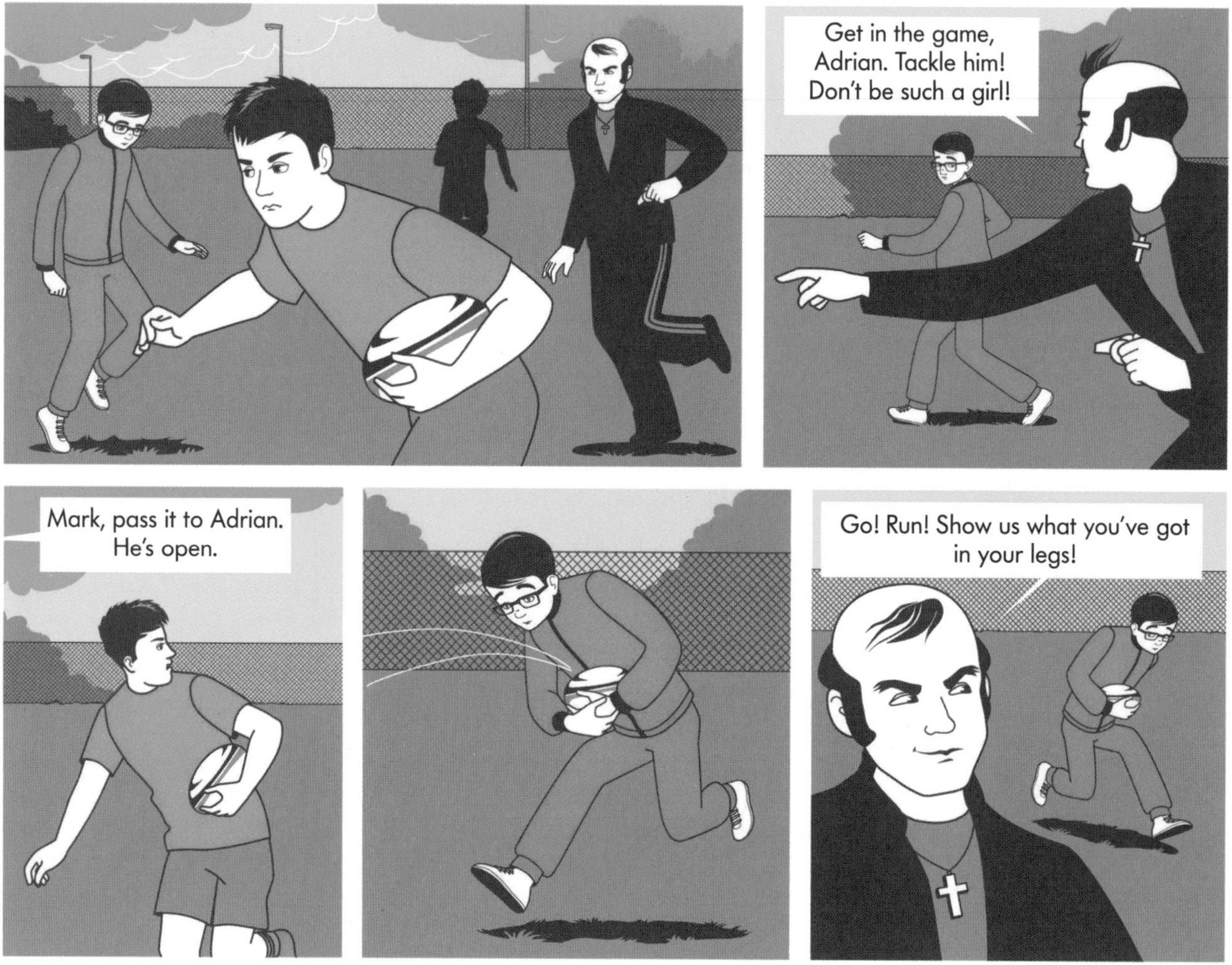
Get in the game, Adrian. Tackle him! Don't be such a girl!
Mark, pass it to Adrian. He's open.
Go! Run! Show us what you've got in your legs!

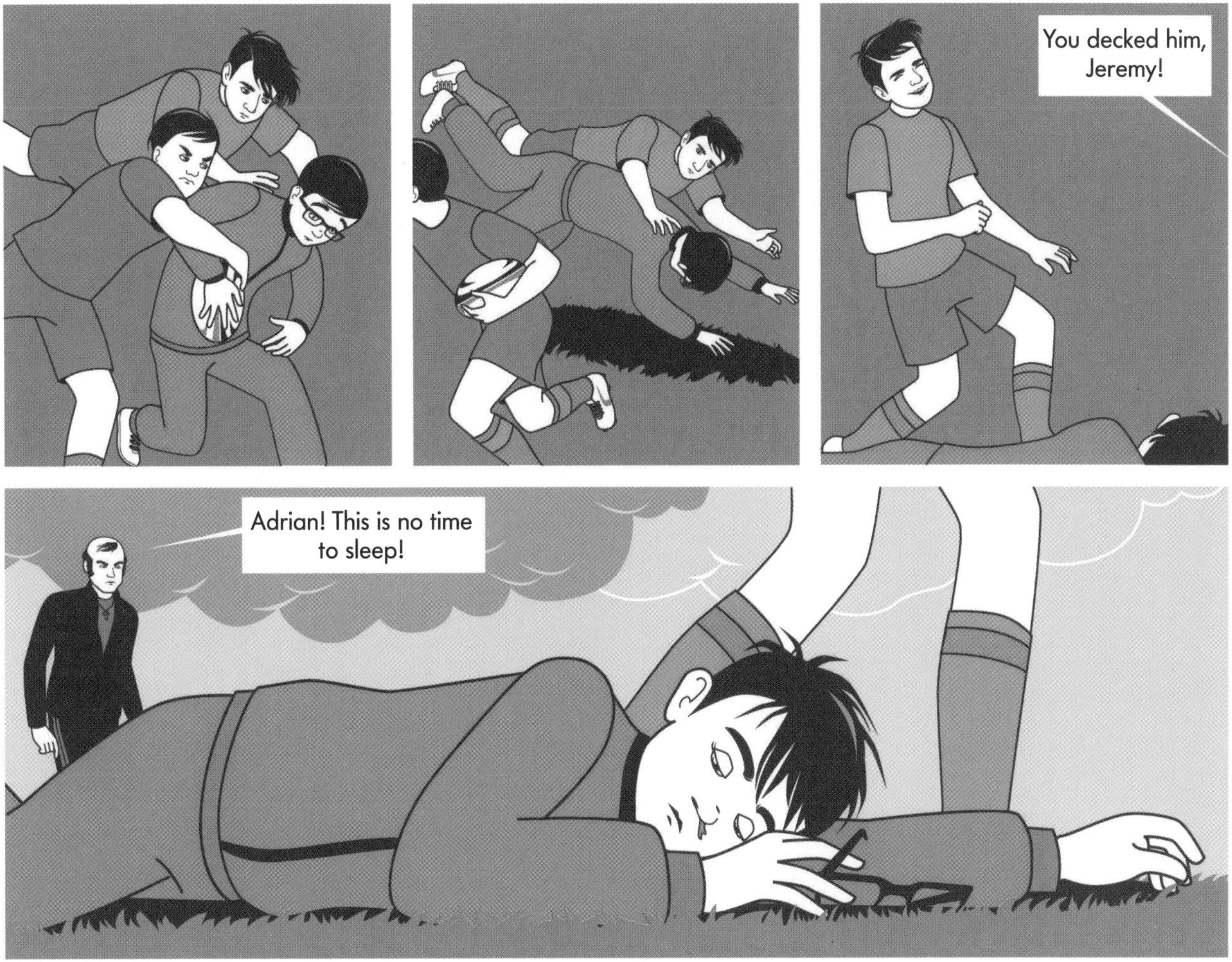
You decked him, Jeremy!
Adrian! This is no time to sleep!

Adrian!
SLAP

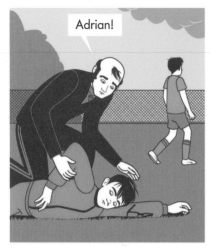

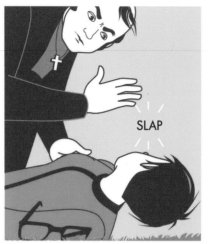

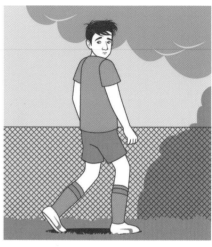

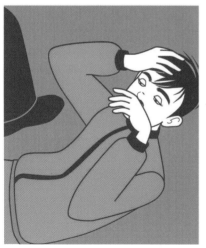

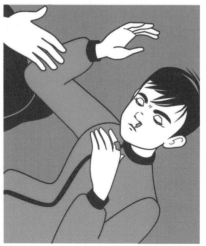

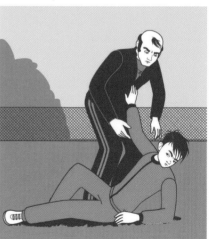

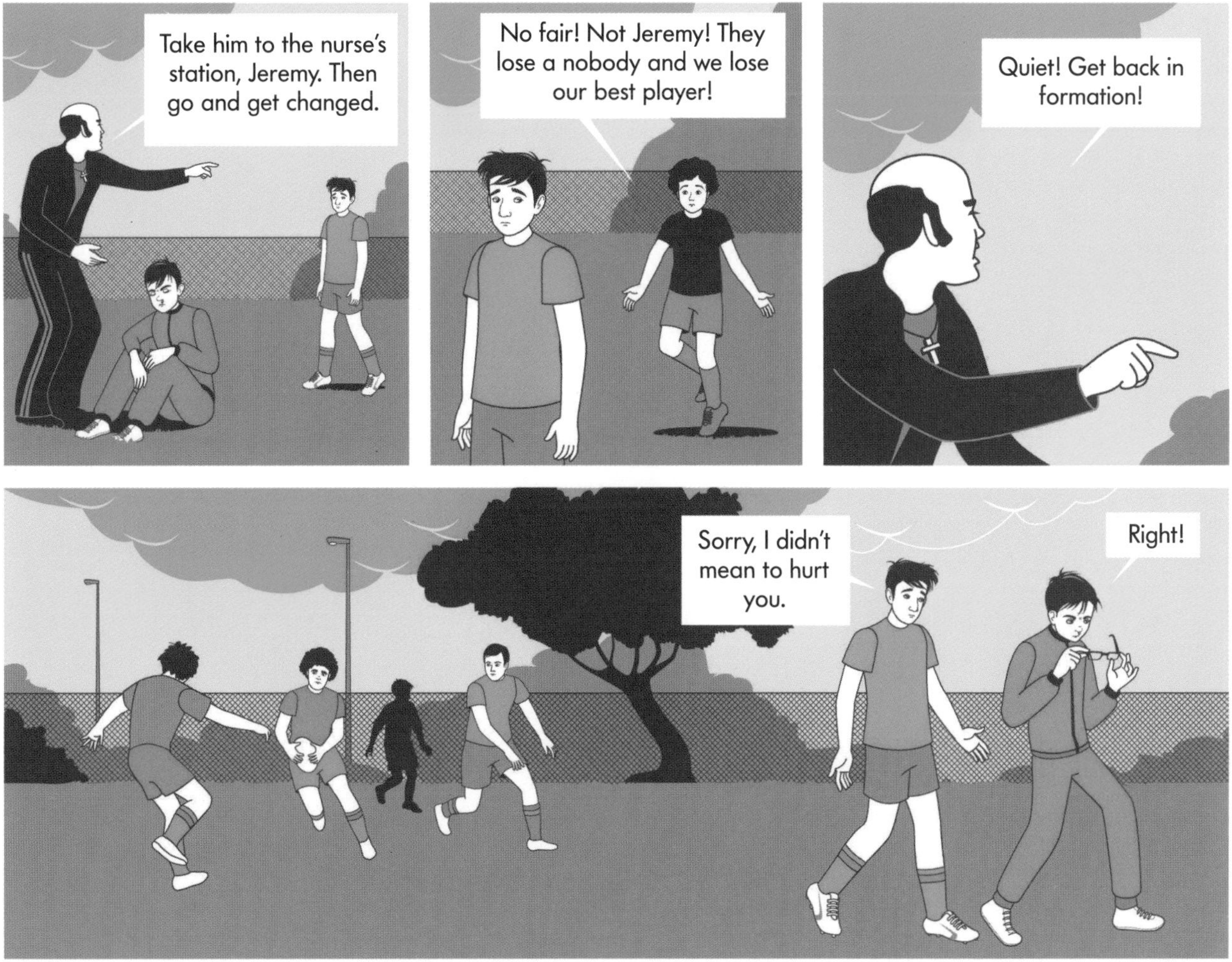
Take him to the nurse's station, Jeremy. Then go and get changed.
No fair! Not Jeremy! They lose a nobody and we lose our best player!
Quiet! Get back in formation!
Sorry, I didn't mean to hurt you.
Right!

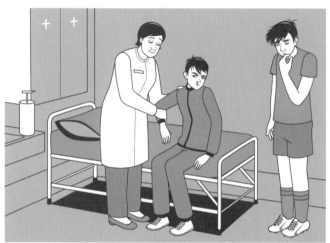

Who's the brute who did this to you?

He did.

I hope you're happy.

It was an accident! We were playing rugby.

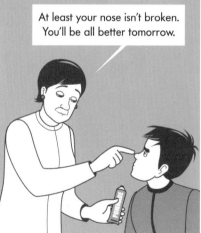

At least your nose isn't broken. You'll be all better tomorrow.

It would be a shame to spoil such a pretty face!

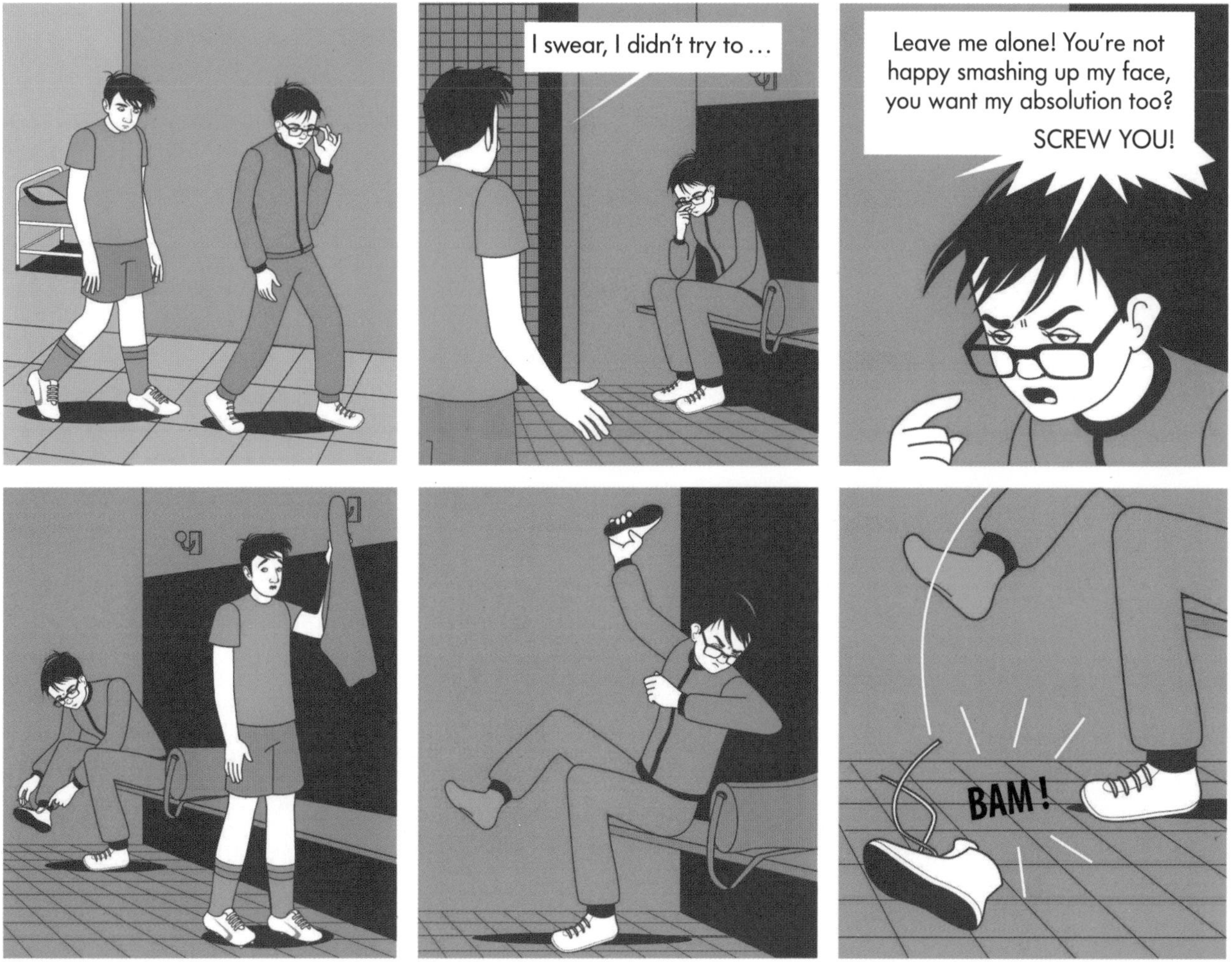
I swear, I didn't try to . . .
Leave me alone! You're not happy smashing up my face, you want my absolution too?
SCREW YOU!
BAM!

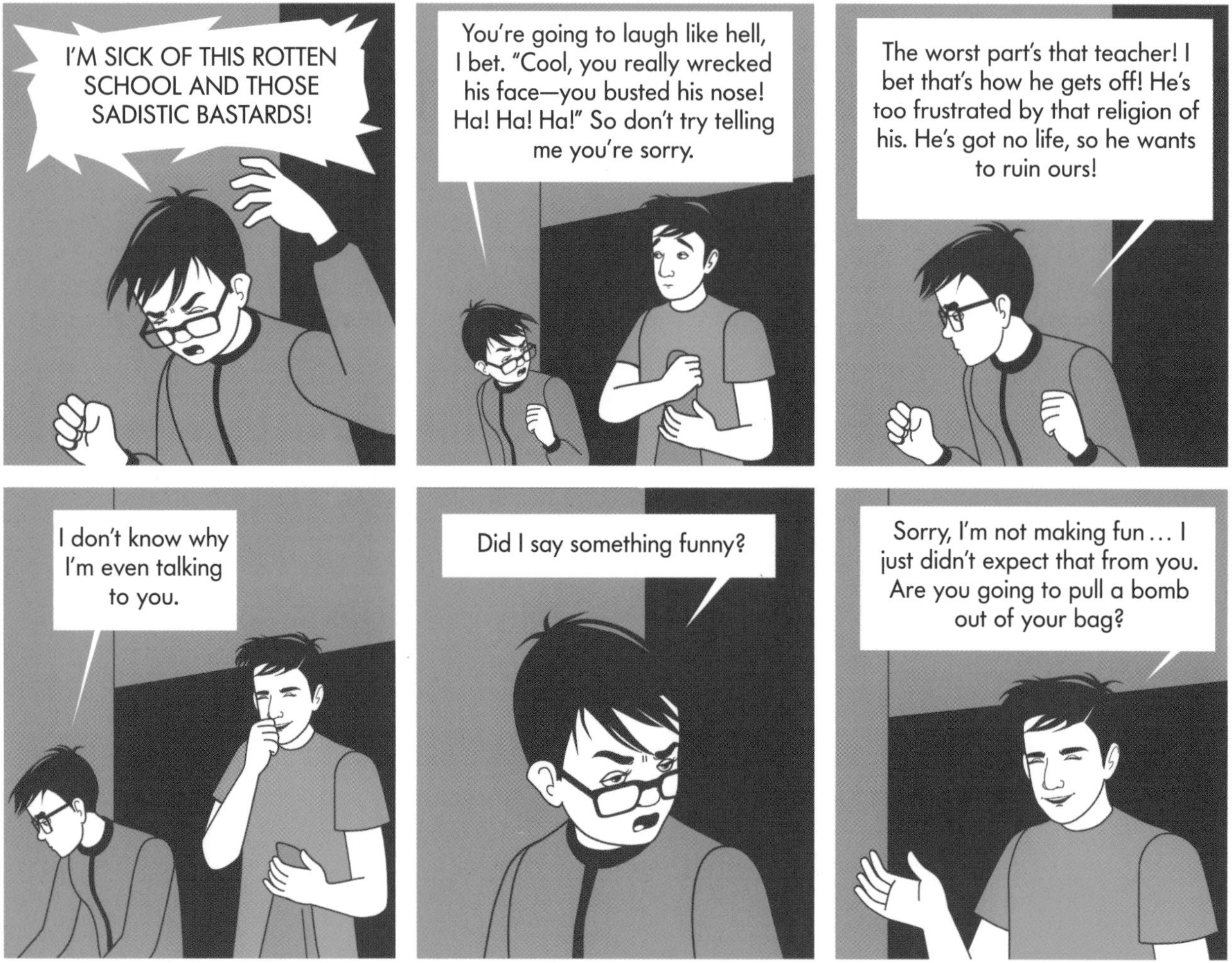
I'M SICK OF THIS ROTTEN SCHOOL AND THOSE SADISTIC BASTARDS!
You're going to laugh like hell, I bet. "Cool, you really wrecked his face—you busted his nose! Ha! Ha! Ha!" So don't try telling me you're sorry.
The worst part's that teacher! I bet that's how he gets off! He's too frustrated by that religion of his. He's got no life, so he wants to ruin ours!
I don't know why I'm even talking to you.
Did I say something funny?
Sorry, I'm not making fun . . . I just didn't expect that from you. Are you going to pull a bomb out of your bag?

I should have kept my mouth shut.

I won't tell anyone there's a terrorist in the school. What happened to the mama's boy with the argyle sweater and the parted hair?

He doesn't exist. It's just a cover...

...a survival mechanism, really.

And here I thought you were a boring guy.

Thanks. Because I'm not?

No. You're strange. And not that obvious.

And you're not as bull-headed as you look.

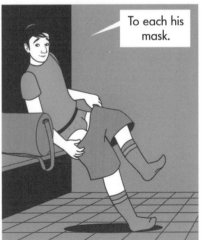

To each his mask.

You're not changing?
Yeah... Sure.
PLOP

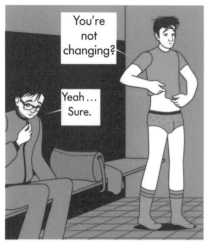

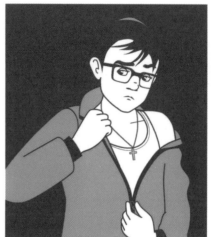

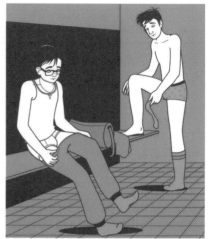

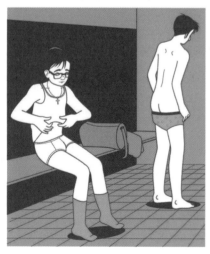

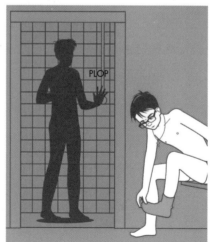

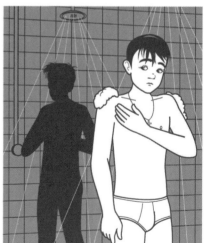

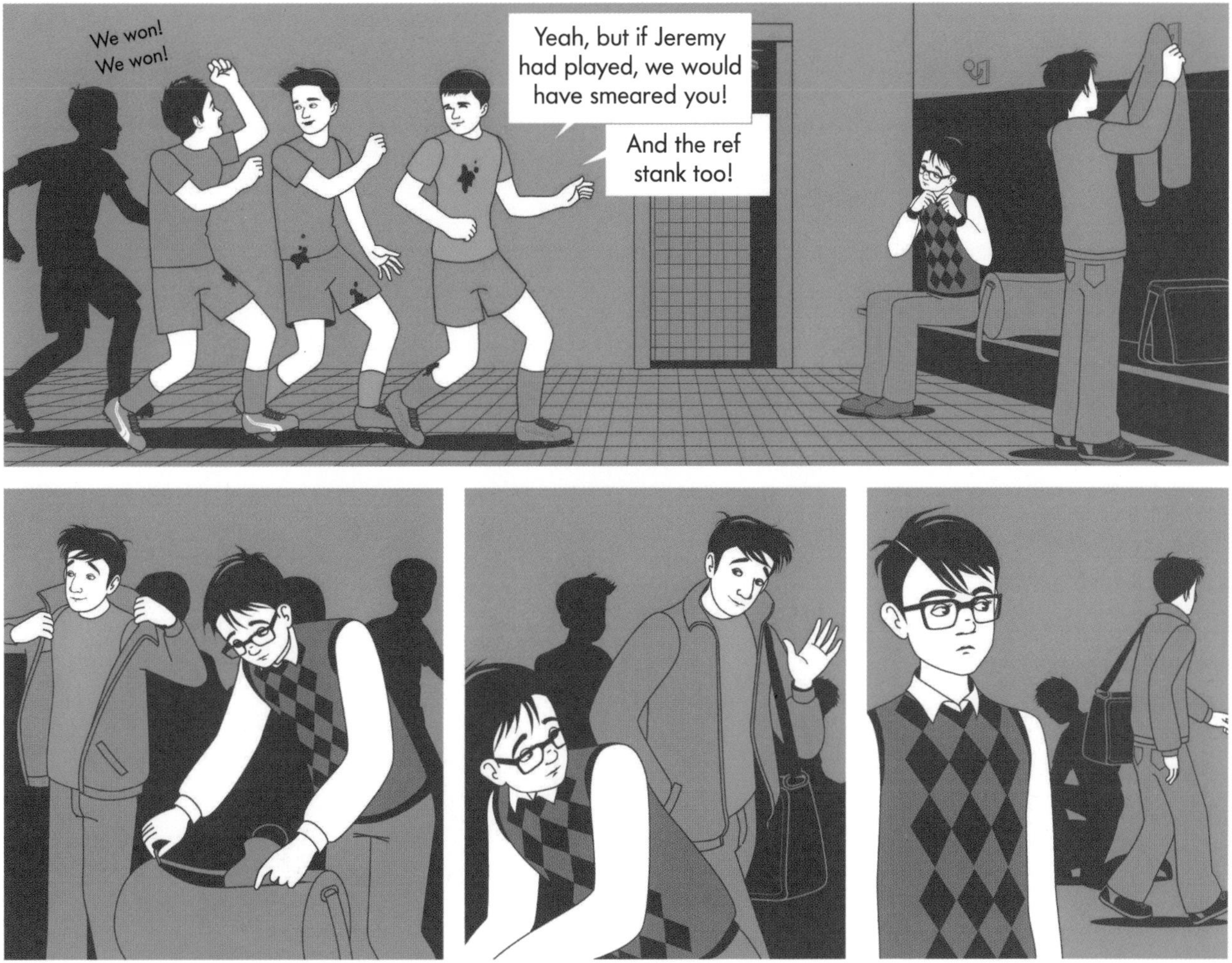
We won!
We won!
Yeah, but if Jeremy had played, we would have smeared you!
And the ref stank too!

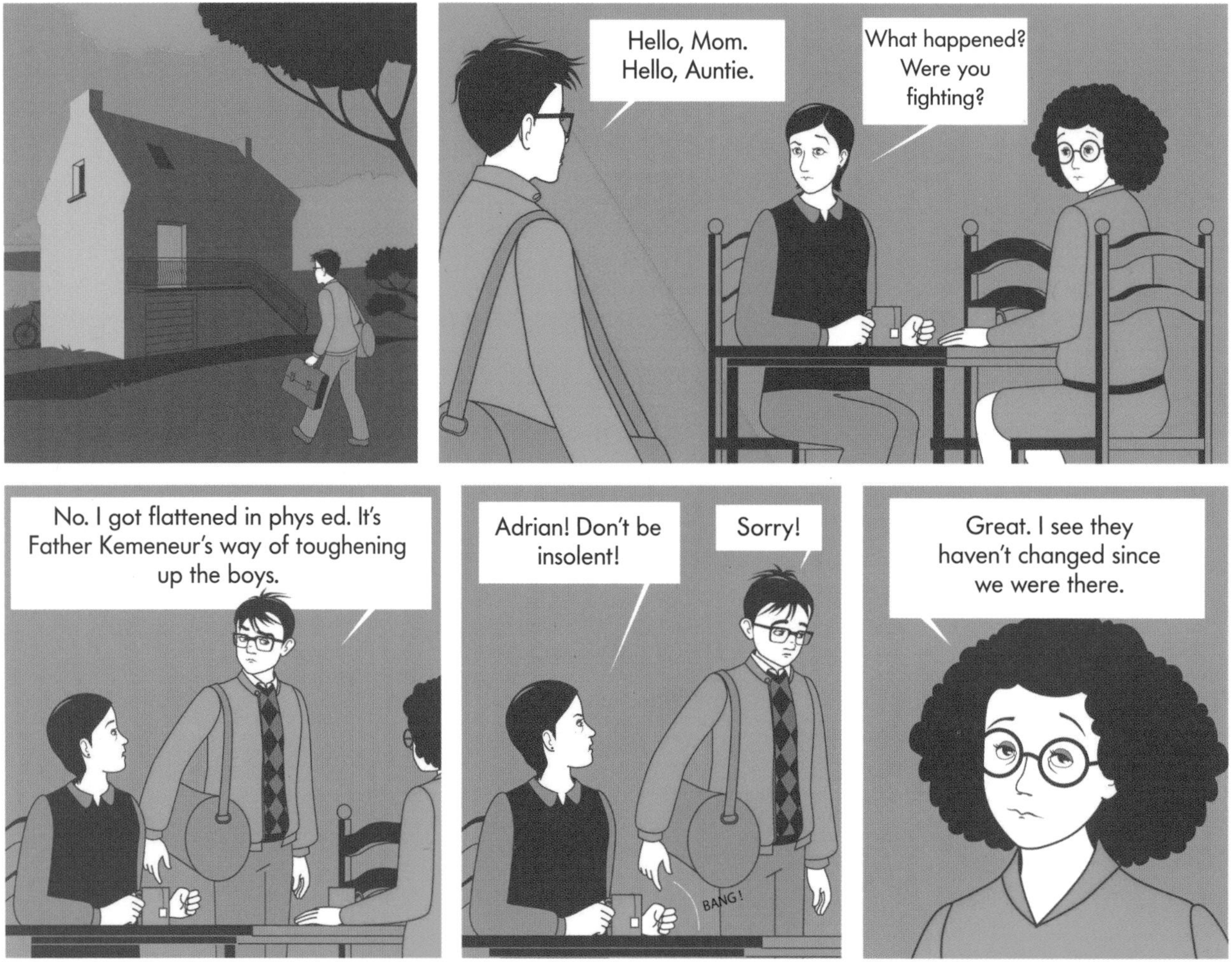
Hello, Mom.
Hello, Auntie.
What happened? Were you fighting?
No. I got flattened in phys ed. It's Father Kemeneur's way of toughening up the boys.
Adrian! Don't be insolent!
Sorry!
BANG!
Great. I see they haven't changed since we were there.

Father Abgrall asked me to have a word with you …

Ah. I wondered why you invited me.

The parish received your estimate, and it's too high.

Come on, now! I have to make a living.

You're not the only stained-glass artist.

Sure, but they don't get their own sister to tell them to lower their price.

They'll tell you the same thing! That's what it costs. If it's too much for the parish, they should try a simpler option.

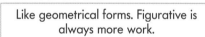

Like geometrical forms. Figurative is always more work.

But it's for a chapel.

Some very pretty abstract designs have been made for churches. The Soulages windows in Conques, for example. I'll show you.

Adrian, can you walk the dog?

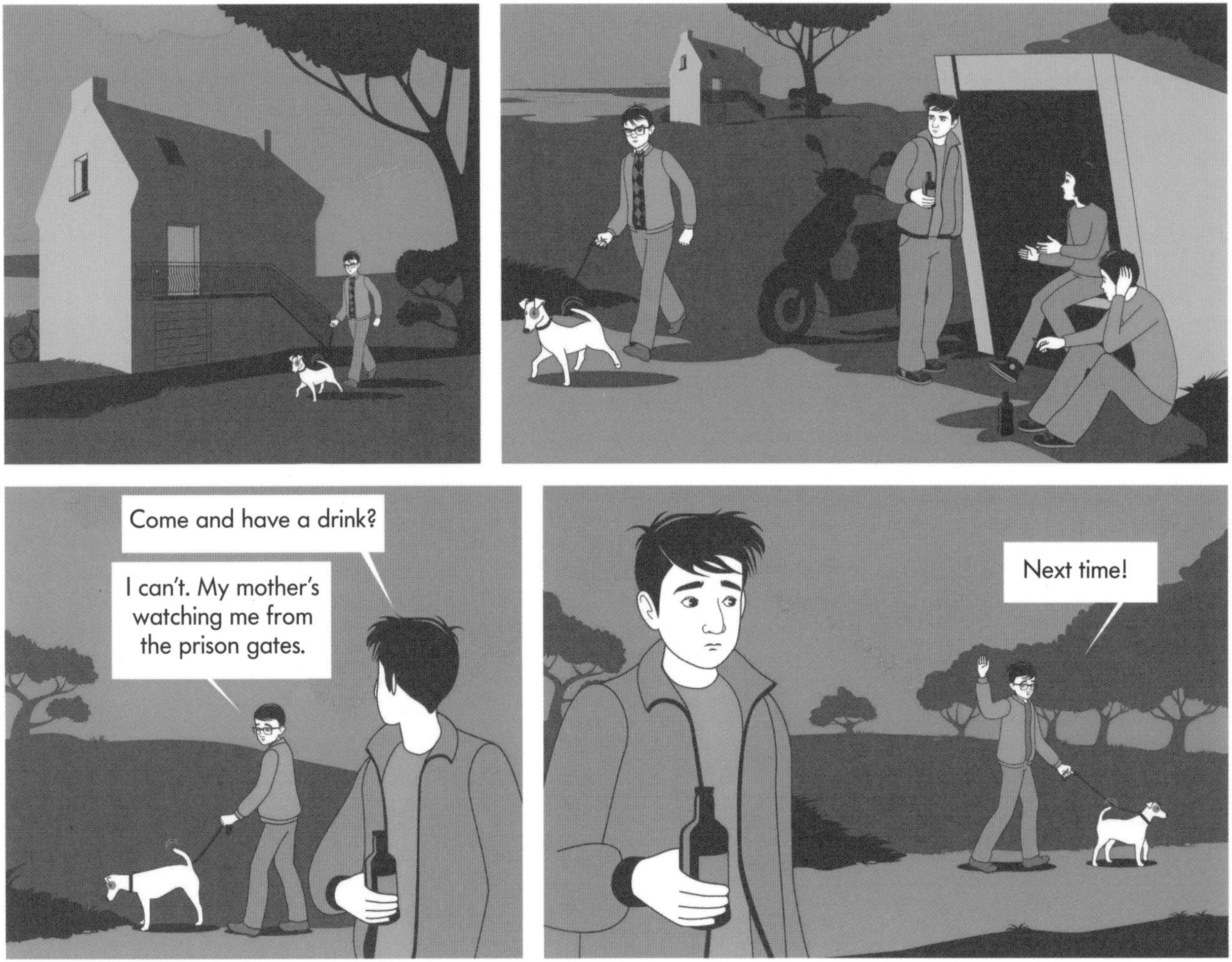
Come and have a drink?
I can't. My mother's watching me from the prison gates.
Next time!

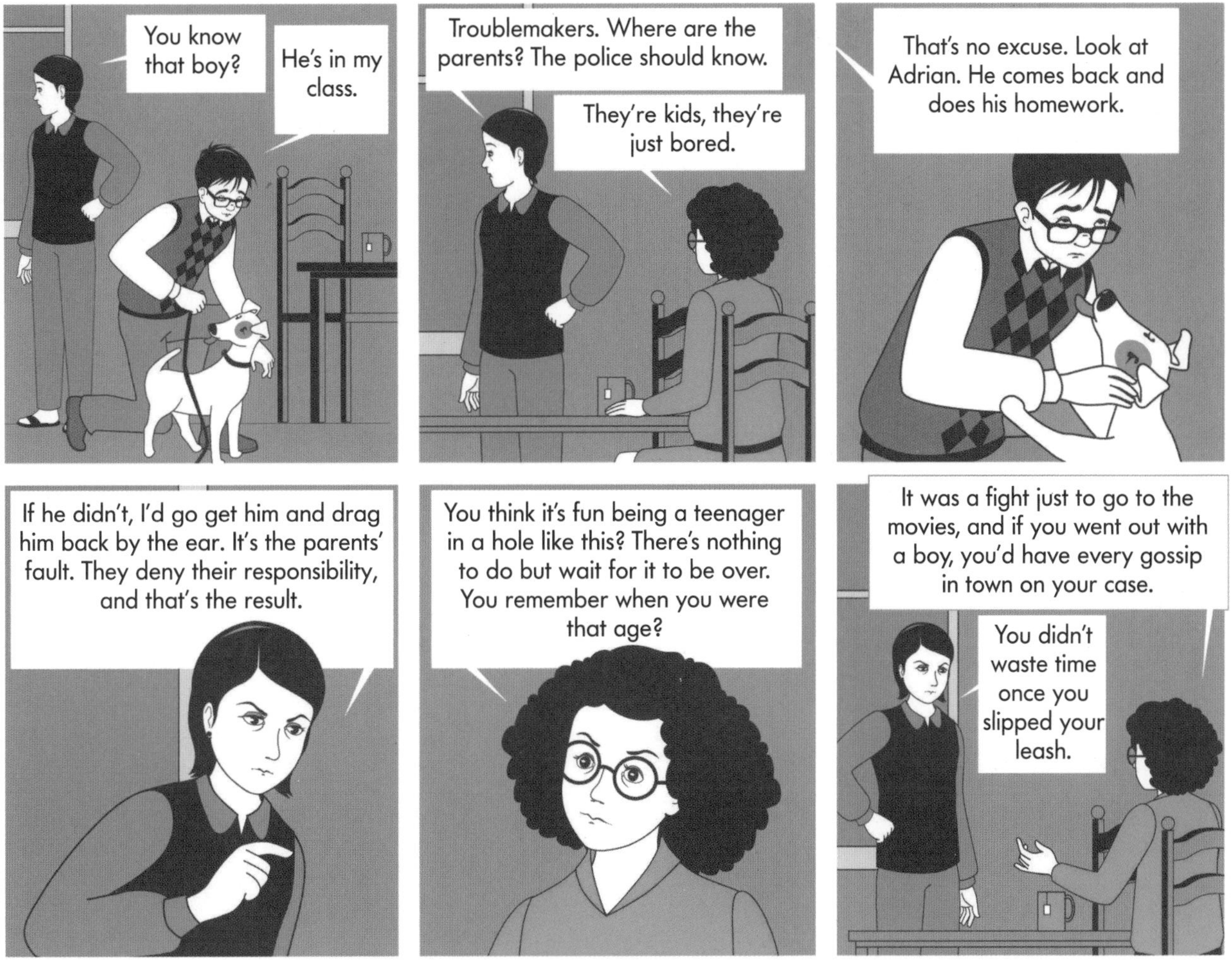
You know that boy?
He's in my class.
Troublemakers. Where are the parents? The police should know.
They're kids, they're just bored.
That's no excuse. Look at Adrian. He comes back and does his homework.
If he didn't, I'd go get him and drag him back by the ear. It's the parents' fault. They deny their responsibility, and that's the result.
You think it's fun being a teenager in a hole like this? There's nothing to do but wait for it to be over. You remember when you were that age?
It was a fight just to go to the movies, and if you went out with a boy, you'd have every gossip in town on your case.
You didn't waste time once you slipped your leash.

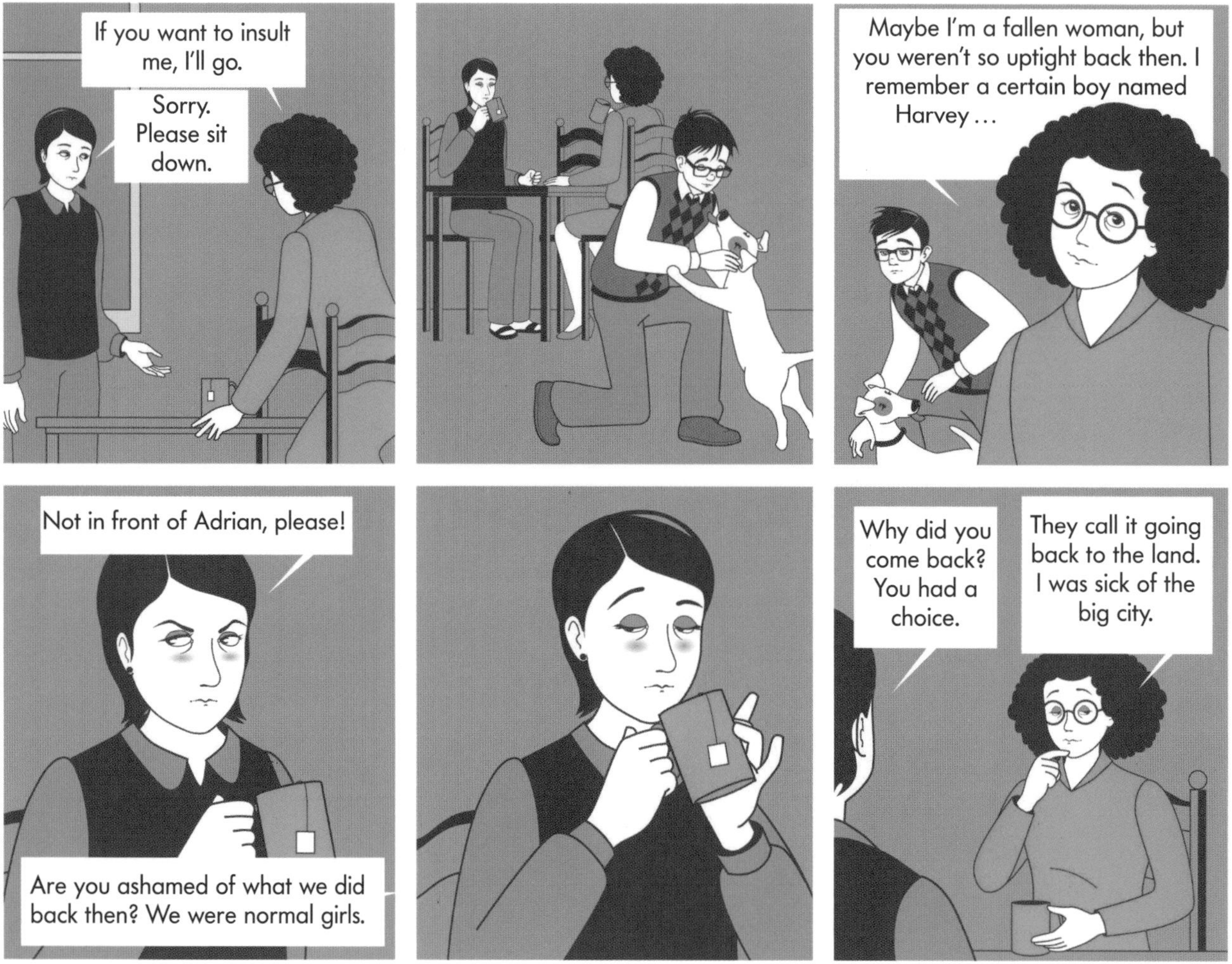
If you want to insult me, I'll go.
Sorry. Please sit down.
Maybe I'm a fallen woman, but you weren't so uptight back then. I remember a certain boy named Harvey . . .
Not in front of Adrian, please!
Are you ashamed of what we did back then? We were normal girls.
Why did you come back? You had a choice.
They call it going back to the land. I was sick of the big city.

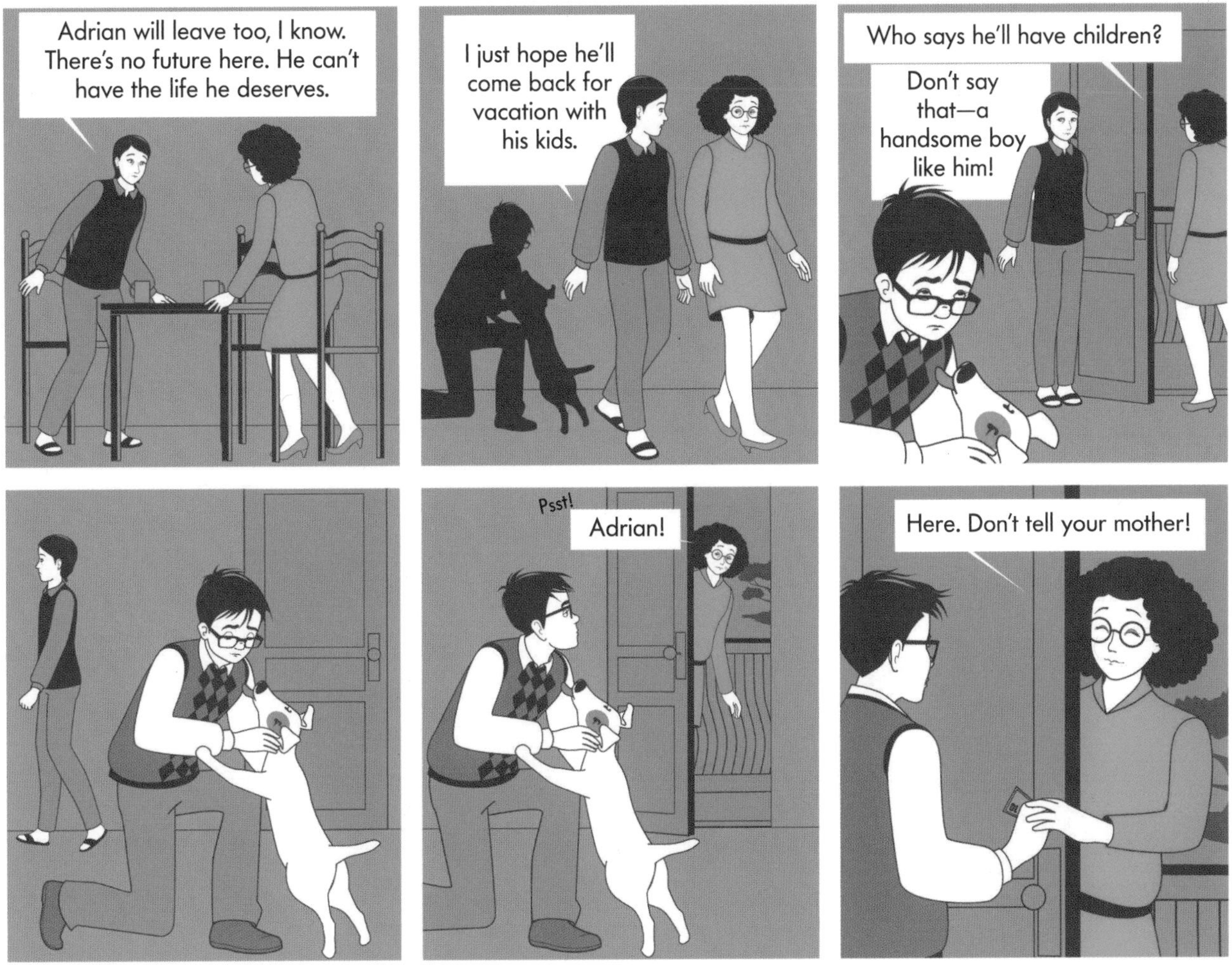

Adrian will leave too, I know. There's no future here. He can't have the life he deserves.
I just hope he'll come back for vacation with his kids.
Who says he'll have children?
Don't say that—a handsome boy like him!
Psst!
Adrian!
Here. Don't tell your mother!

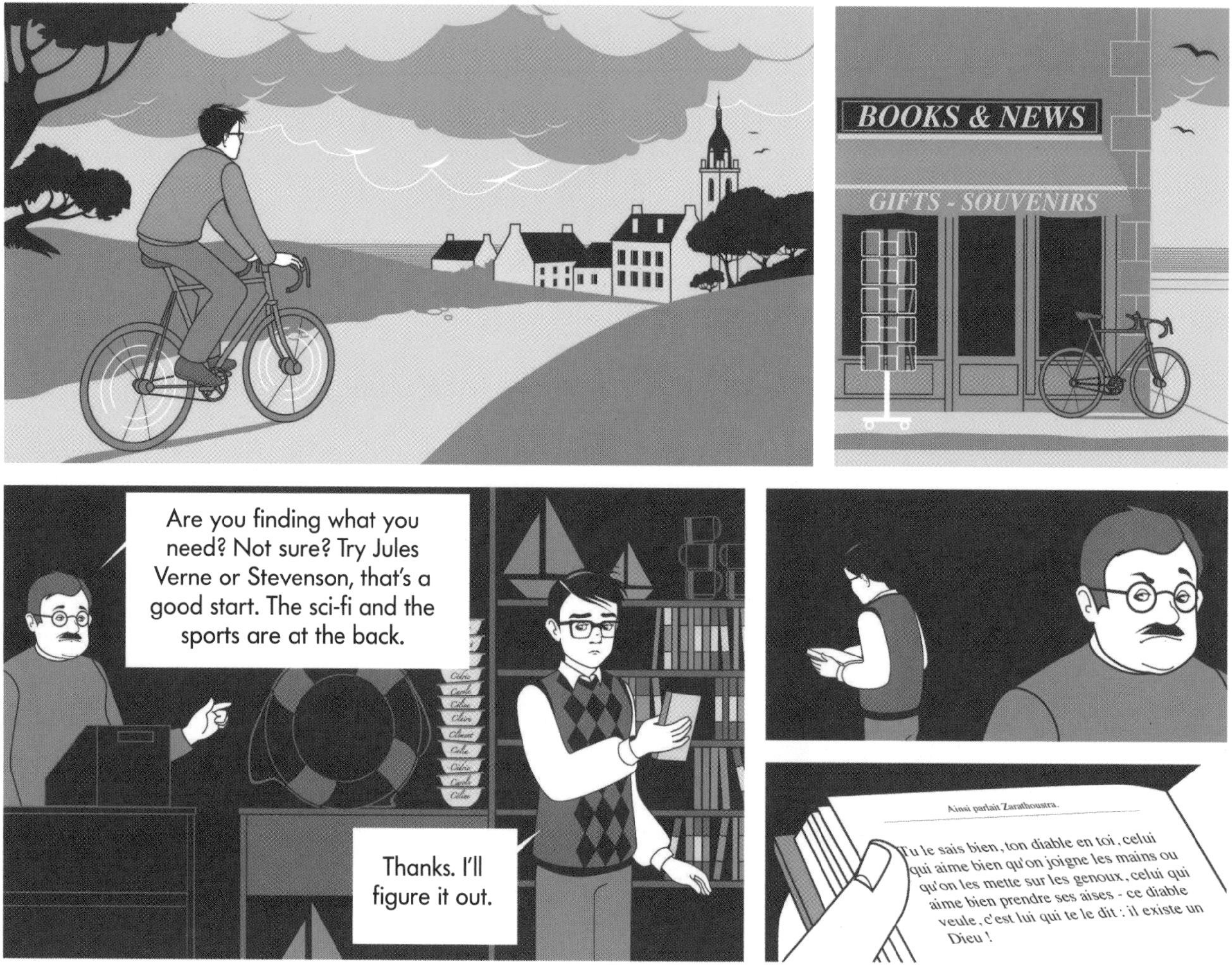
BOOKS & NEWS
GIFTS - SOUVENIRS
Are you finding what you need? Not sure? Try Jules Verne or Stevenson, that's a good start. The sci-fi and the sports are at the back.
Thanks. I'll figure it out.
Ainsi parlait Zarathoustra.
Tu le sais bien, ton diable en toi, celui qui aime bien qu'on joigne les mains ou qu'on les mette sur les genoux, celui qui aime bien prendre ses aises - ce diable veule, c'est lui qui te le dit : il existe un Dieu !

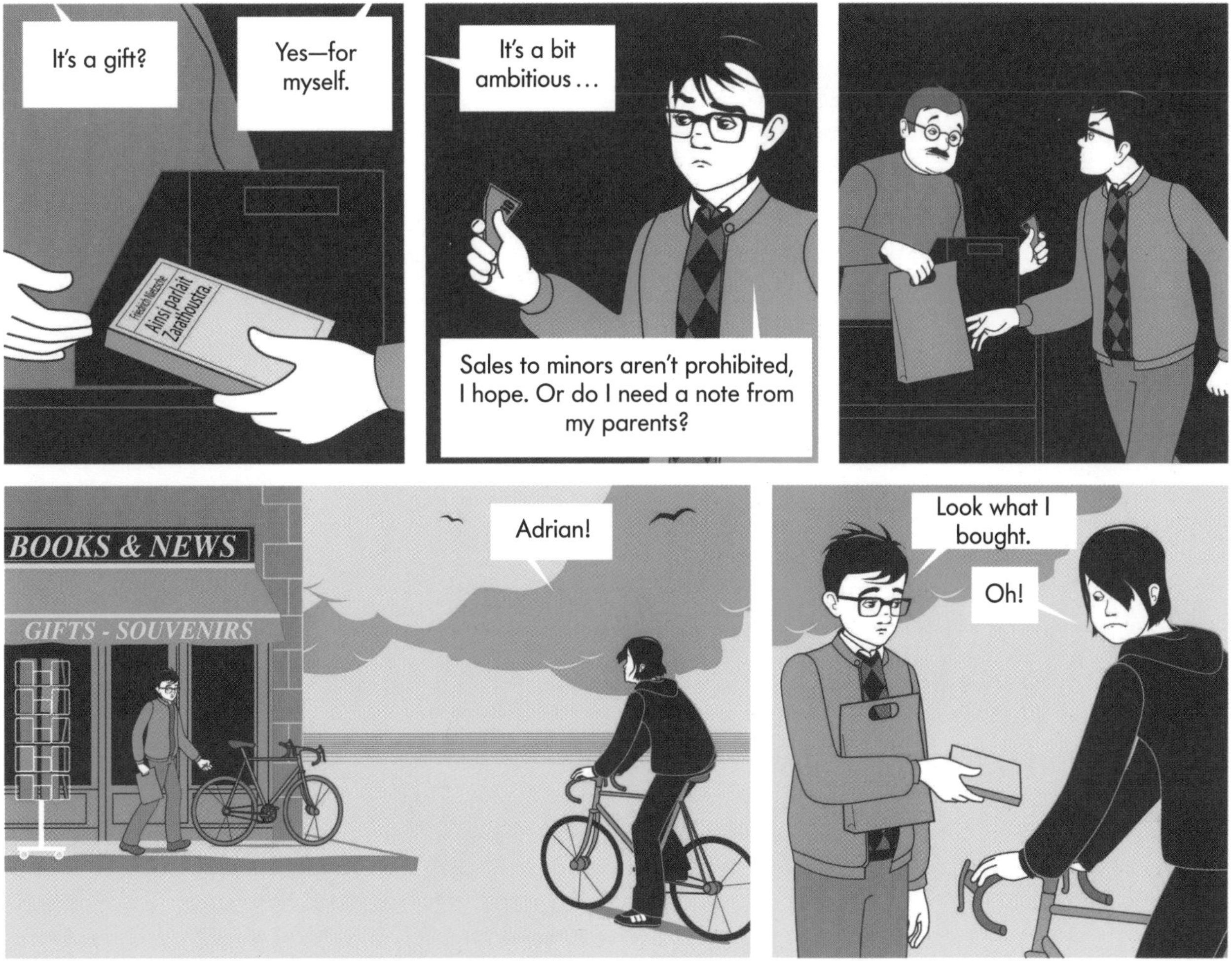
It's a gift?
Yes—for myself.
Friedrich Nietzsche
Ainsi parlait Zarathoustra.
It's a bit ambitious . . .
Sales to minors aren't prohibited, I hope. Or do I need a note from my parents?
BOOKS & NEWS
GIFTS - SOUVENIRS
Adrian!
Look what I bought.
Oh!

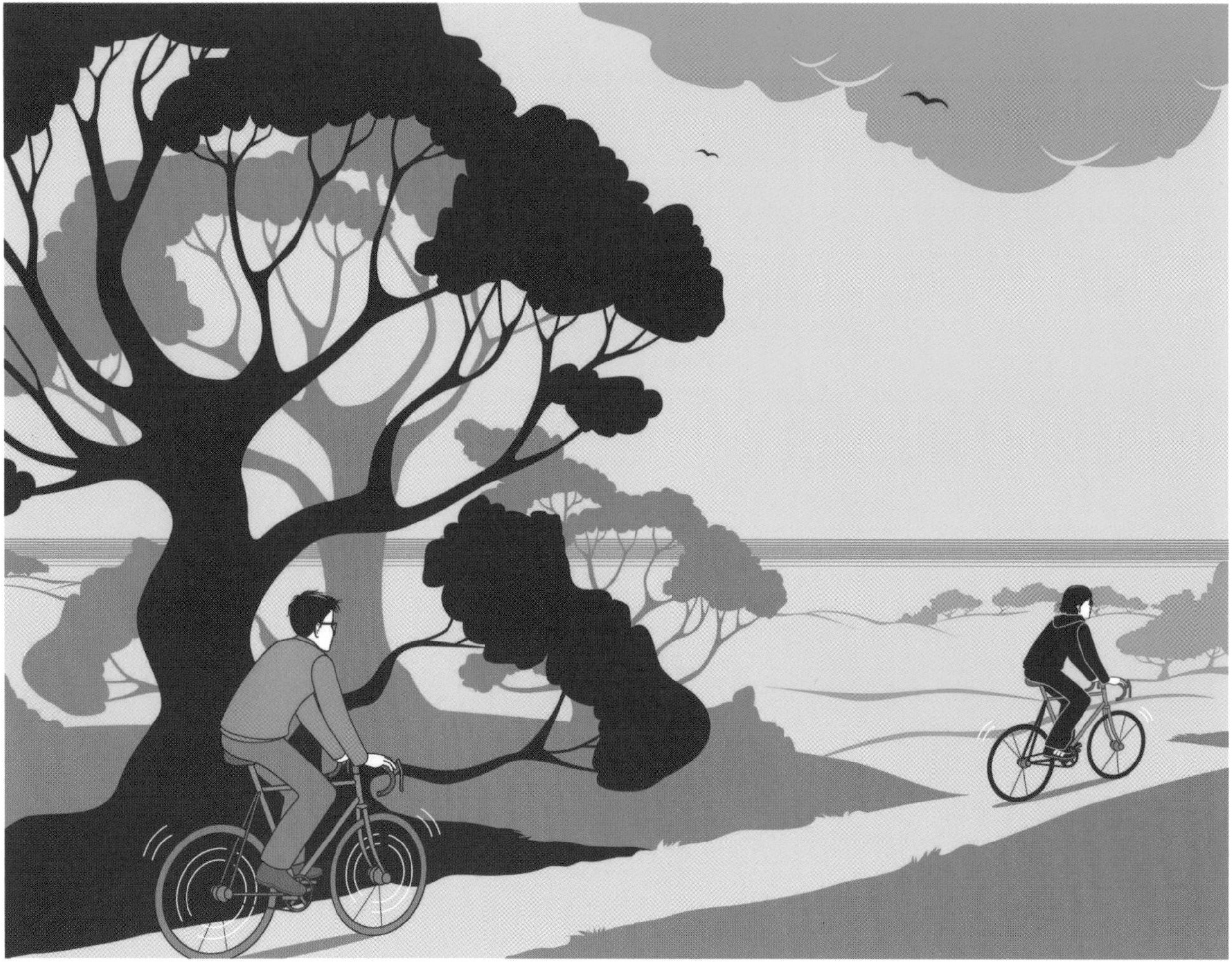

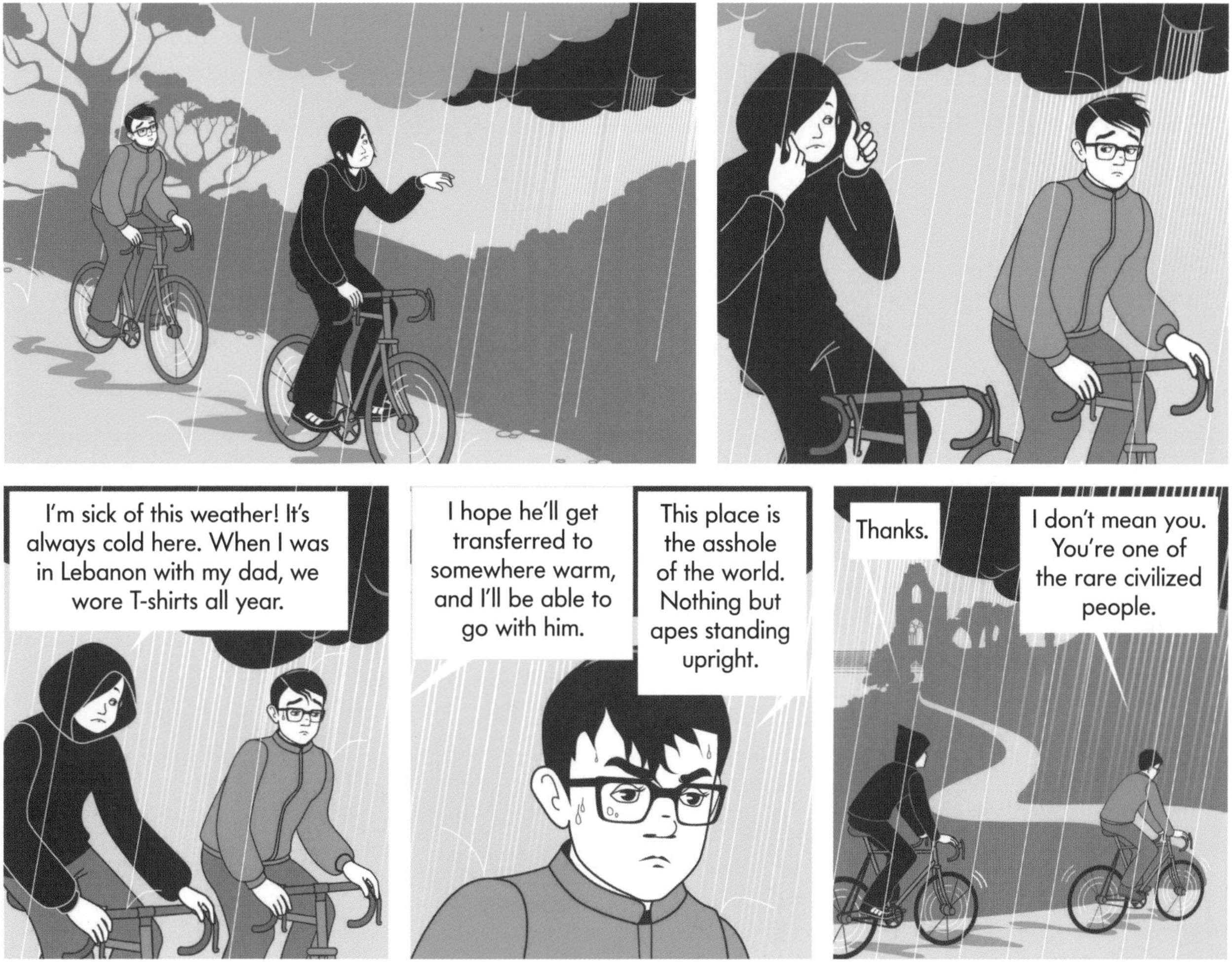
I'm sick of this weather! It's always cold here. When I was in Lebanon with my dad, we wore T-shirts all year.
I hope he'll get transferred to somewhere warm, and I'll be able to go with him.
This place is the asshole of the world. Nothing but apes standing upright.
Thanks.
I don't mean you. You're one of the rare civilized people.

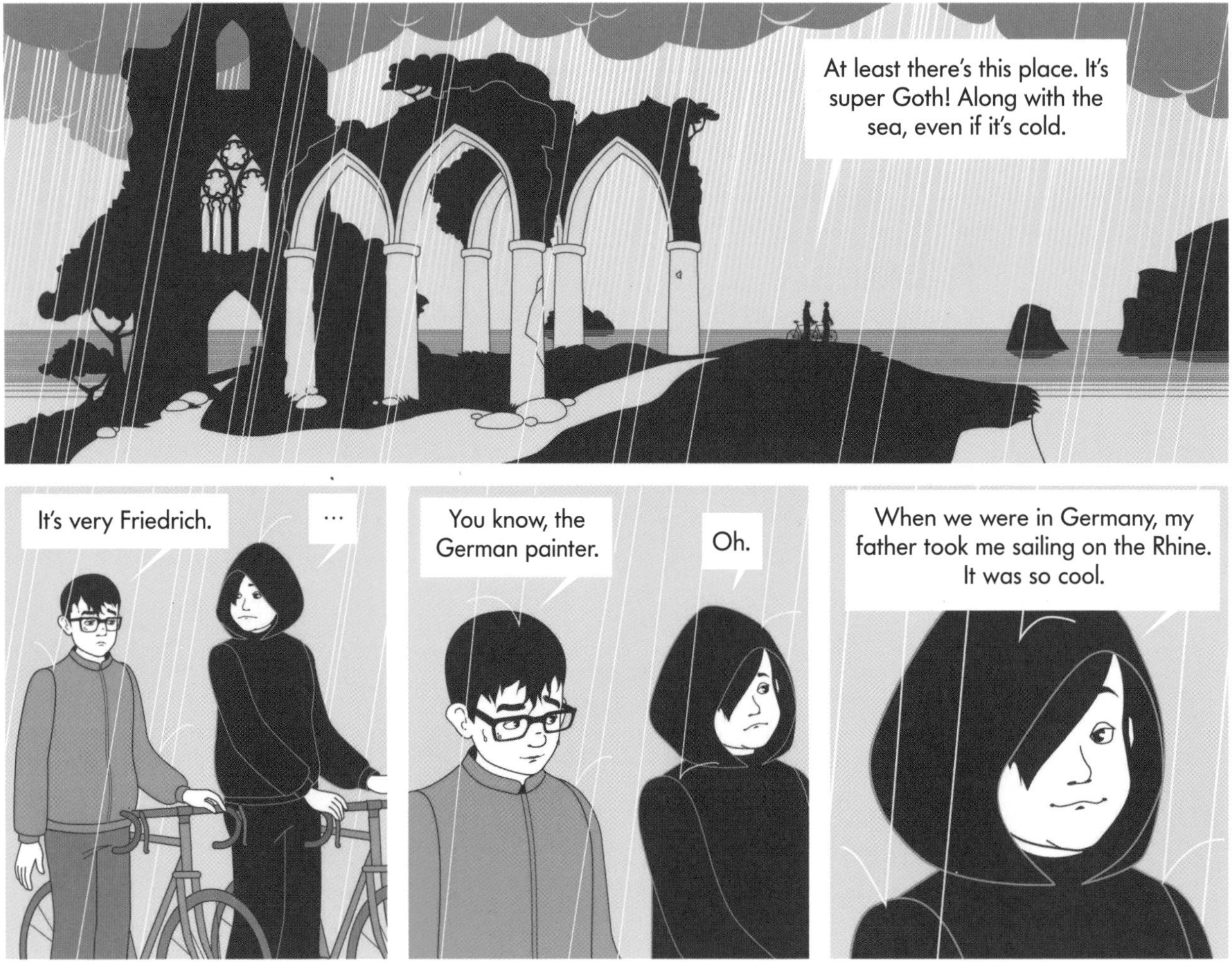
At least there's this place. It's super Goth! Along with the sea, even if it's cold.
It's very Friedrich.
...
You know, the German painter.
Oh.
When we were in Germany, my father took me sailing on the Rhine. It was so cool.

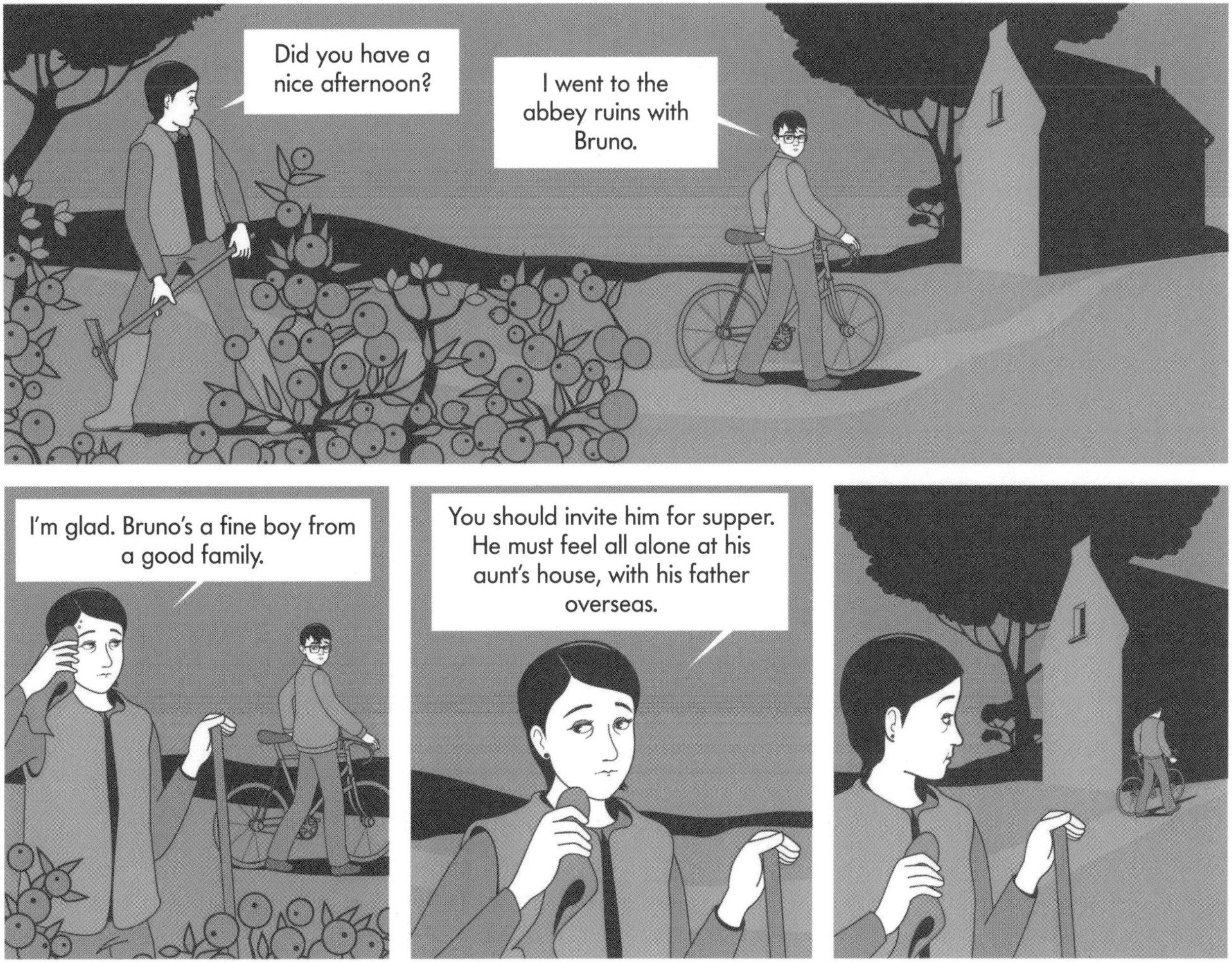
Did you have a nice afternoon?
I went to the abbey ruins with Bruno.
I'm glad. Bruno's a fine boy from a good family.
You should invite him for supper. He must feel all alone at his aunt's house, with his father overseas.

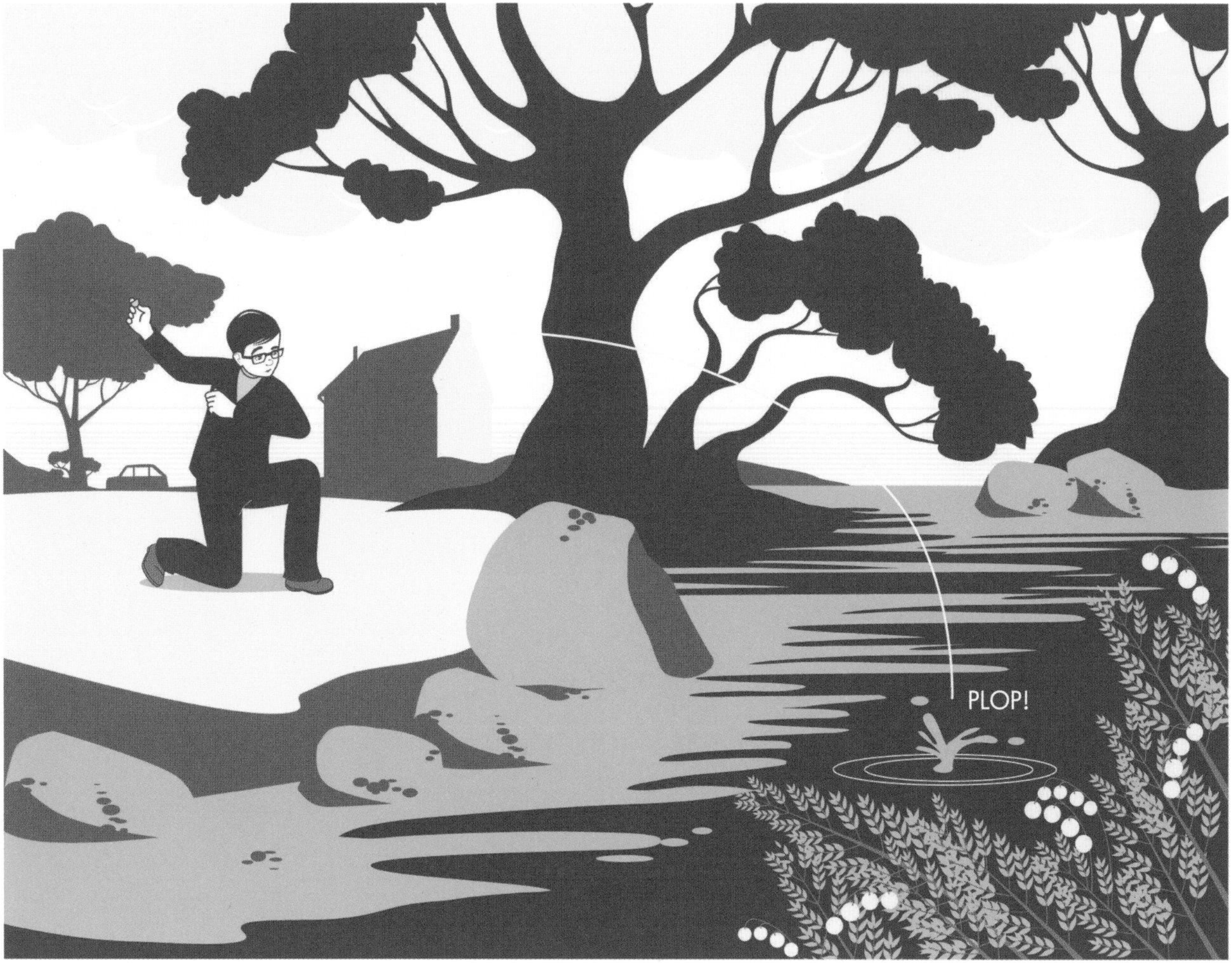
PLOP!

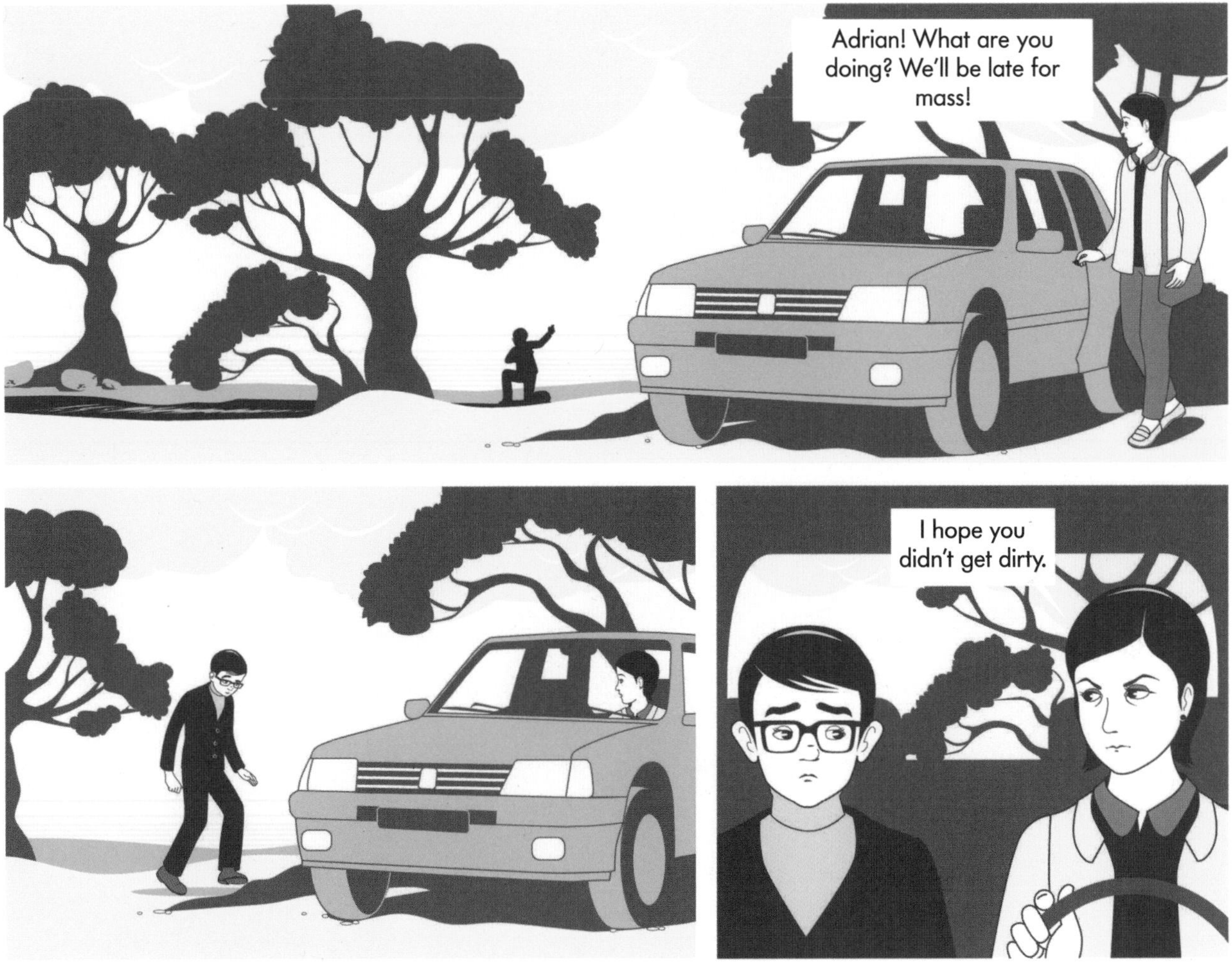
Adrian! What are you doing? We'll be late for mass!
I hope you didn't get dirty.

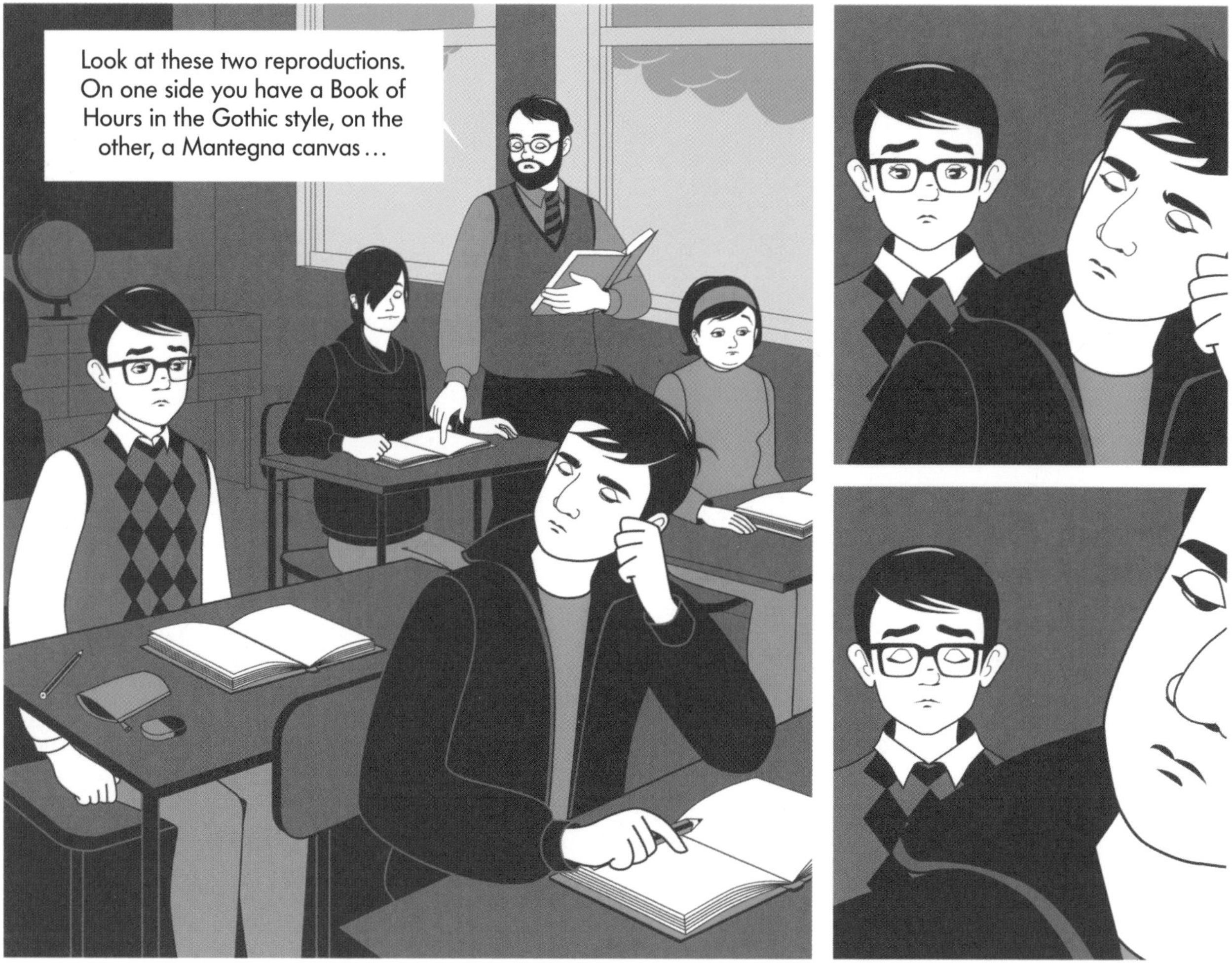
Look at these two reproductions. On one side you have a Book of Hours in the Gothic style, on the other, a Mantegna canvas…

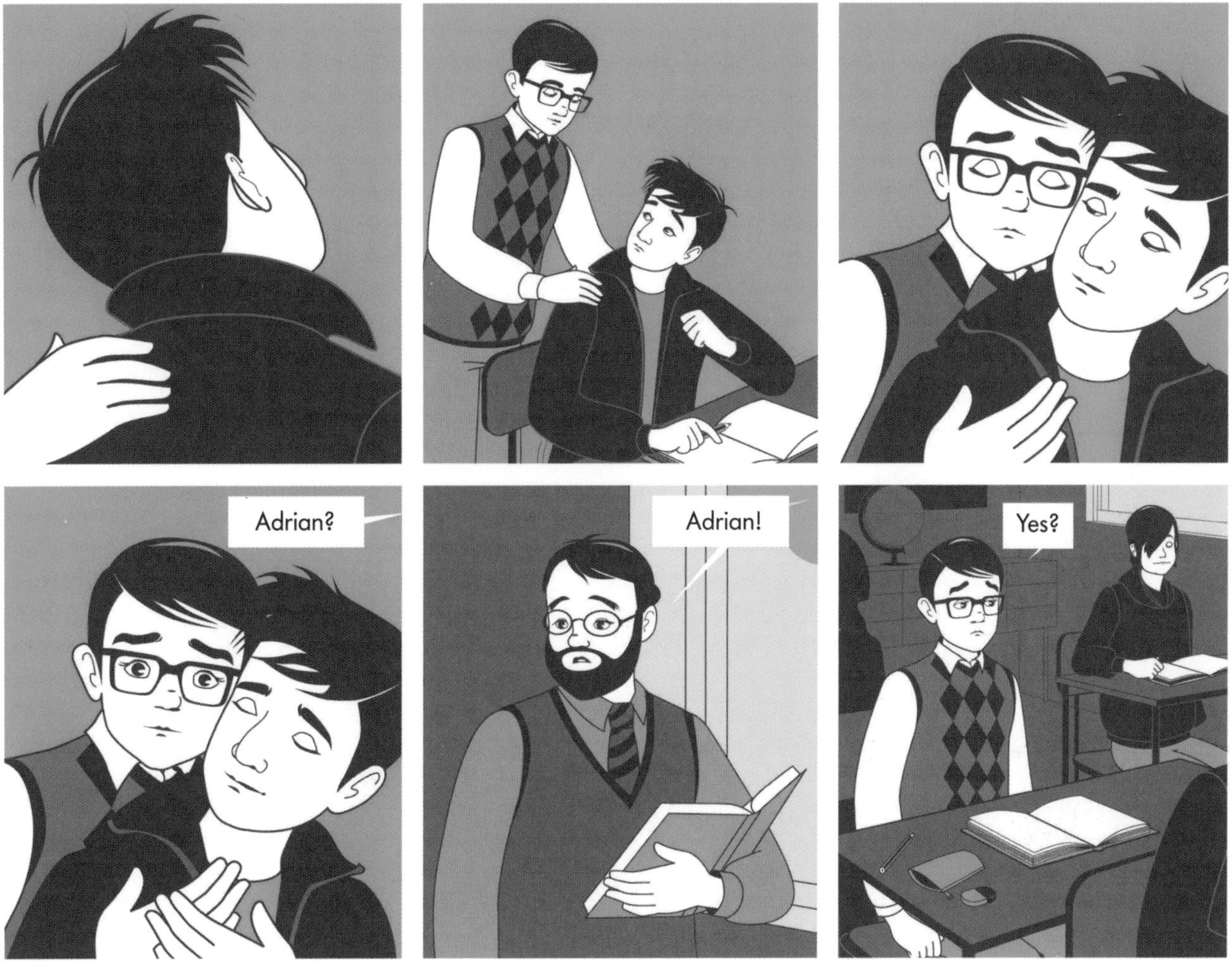
Adrian?
Adrian!
Yes?

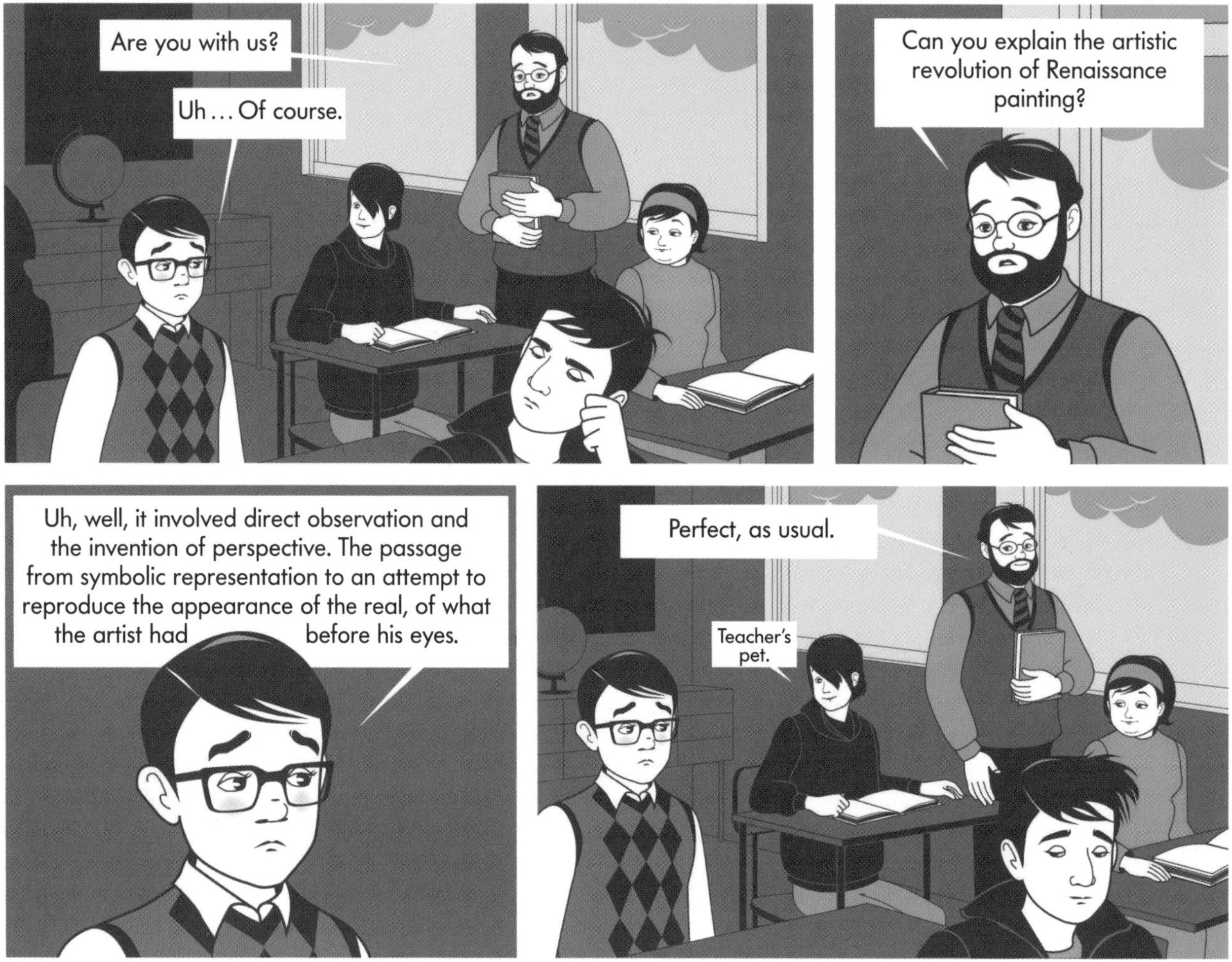
Are you with us?
Uh . . . Of course.
Can you explain the artistic revolution of Renaissance painting?
Uh, well, it involved direct observation and the invention of perspective. The passage from symbolic representation to an attempt to reproduce the appearance of the real, of what the artist had before his eyes.
Perfect, as usual.
Teacher's pet.

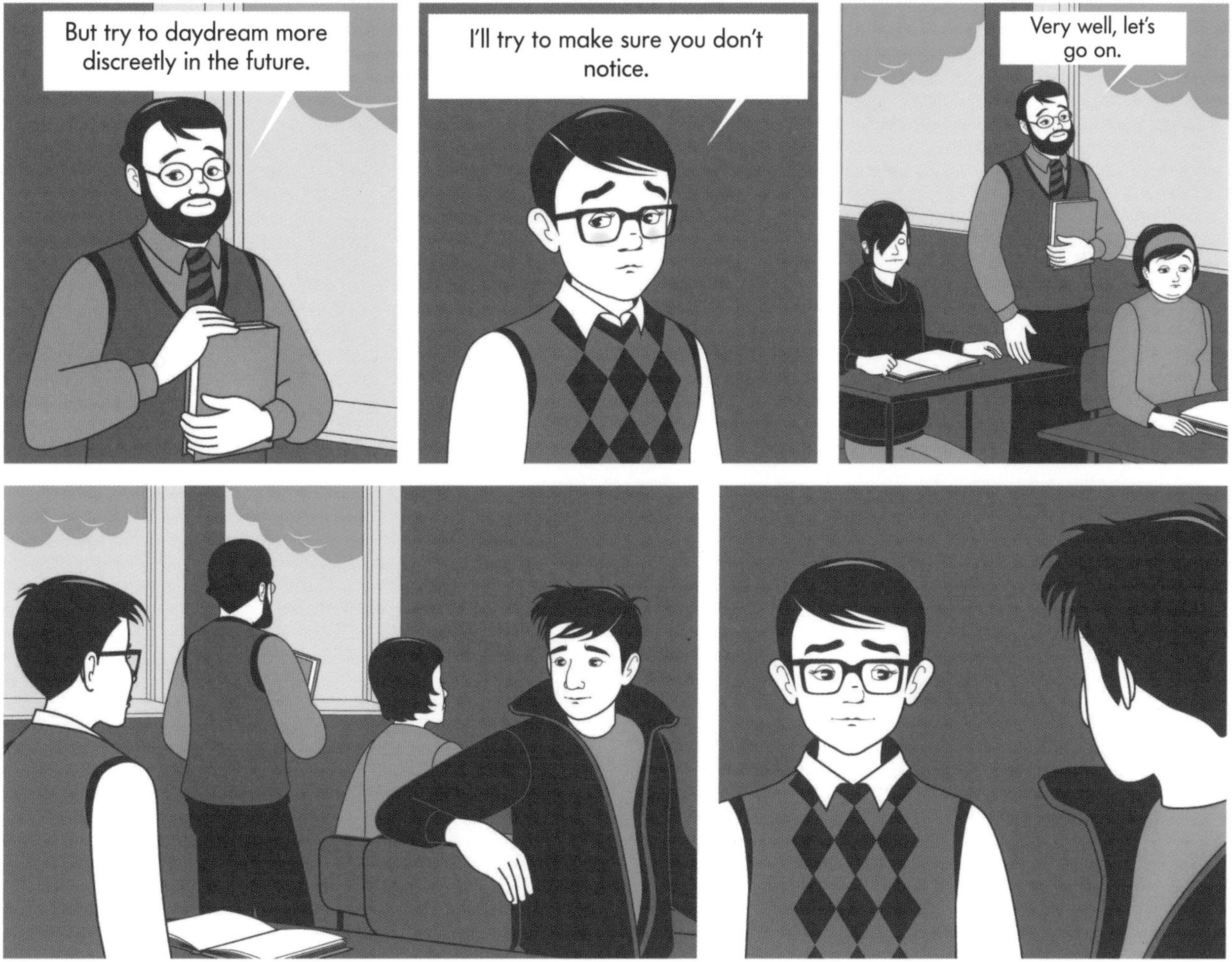
But try to daydream more discreetly in the future.
I'll try to make sure you don't notice.
Very well, let's go on.

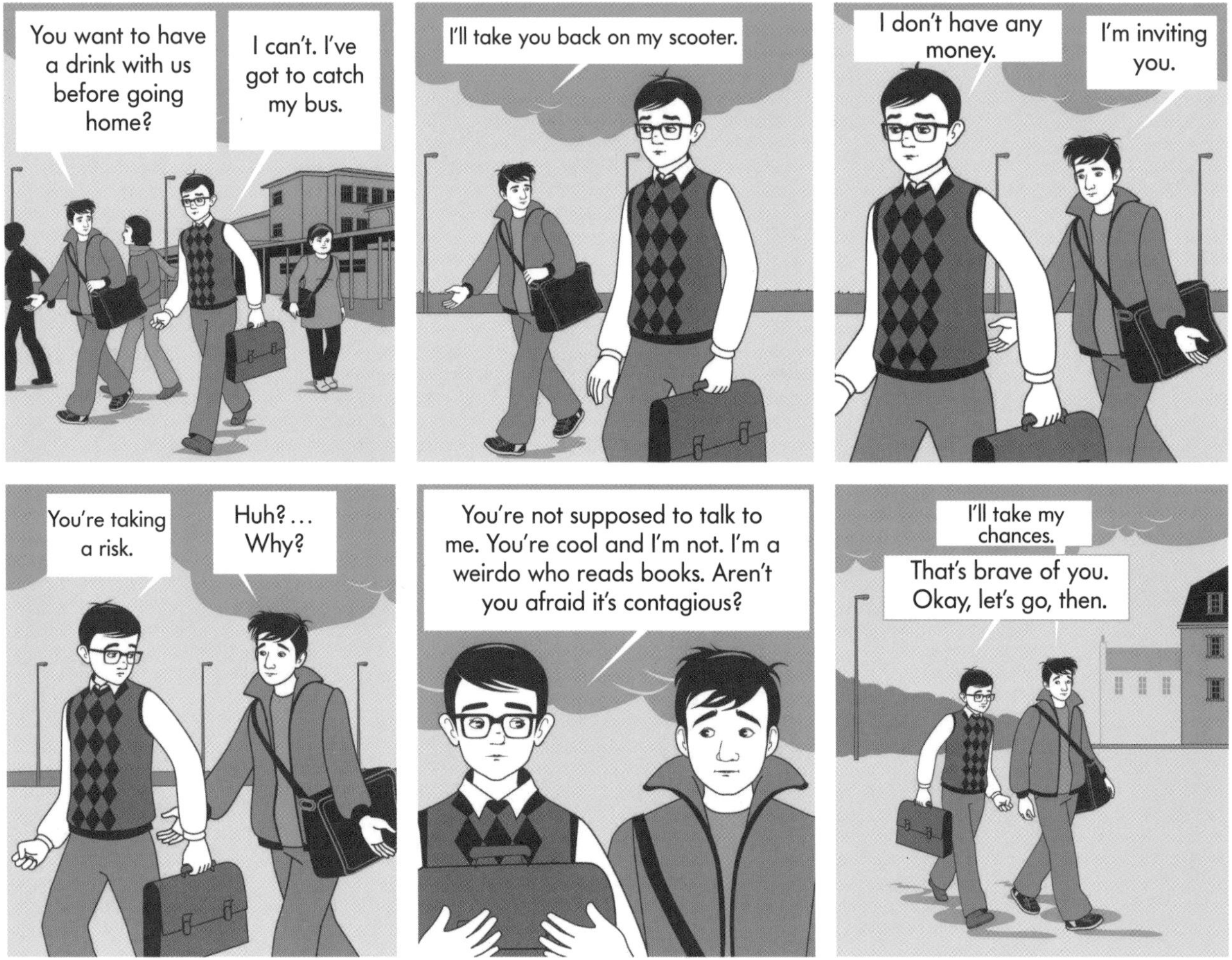

You want to have a drink with us before going home?
I can't. I've got to catch my bus.
I'll take you back on my scooter.
I don't have any money.
I'm inviting you.
You're taking a risk.
Huh?... Why?
You're not supposed to talk to me. You're cool and I'm not. I'm a weirdo who reads books. Aren't you afraid it's contagious?
I'll take my chances.
That's brave of you. Okay, let's go, then.

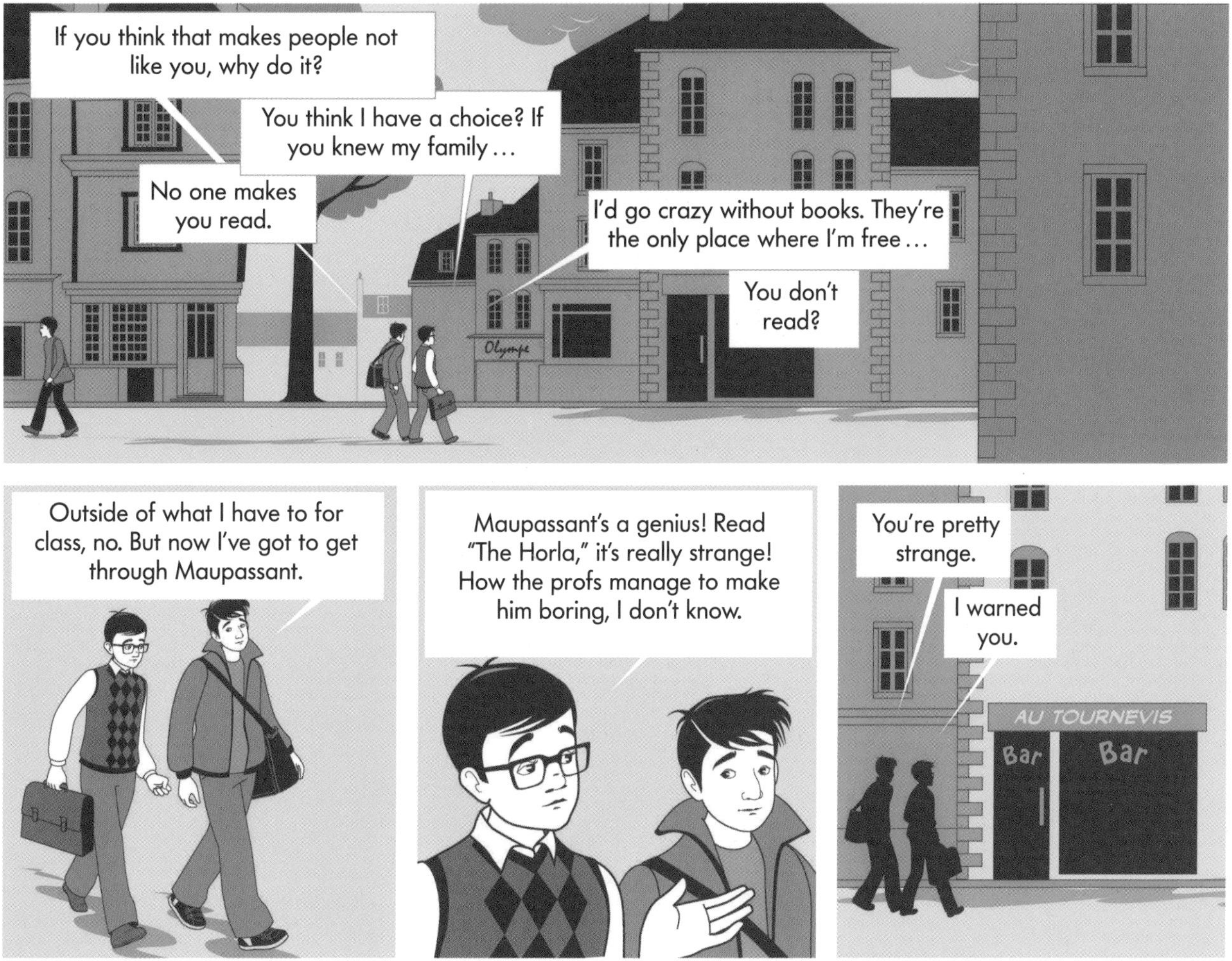
If you think that makes people not like you, why do it?
You think I have a choice? If you knew my family…
No one makes you read.
I'd go crazy without books. They're the only place where I'm free…
You don't read?
Olympe
Outside of what I have to for class, no. But now I've got to get through Maupassant.
Maupassant's a genius! Read "The Horla," it's really strange! How the profs manage to make him boring, I don't know.
You're pretty strange.
I warned you.
AU TOURNEVIS
Bar
Bar

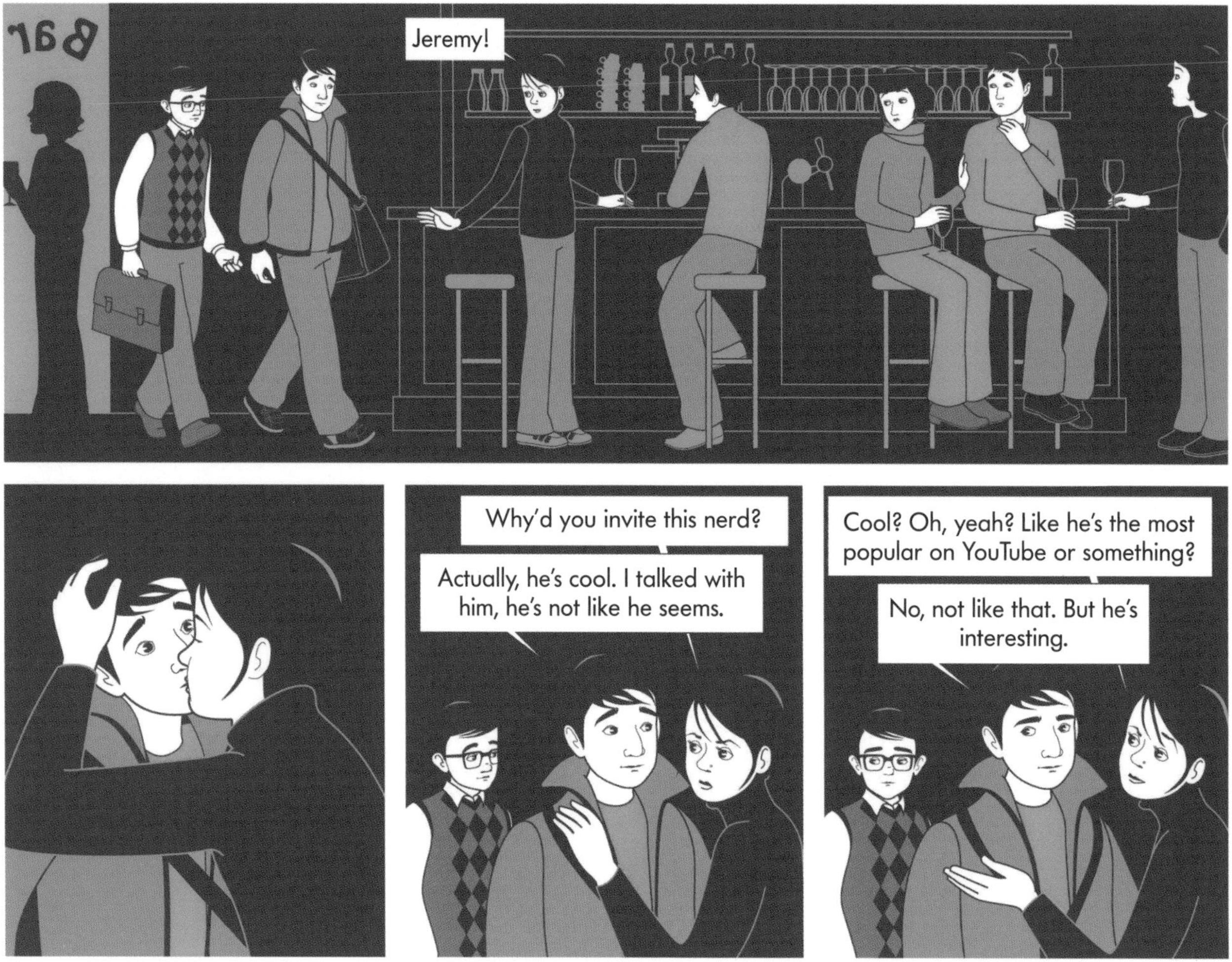
Bar
Jeremy!
Why'd you invite this nerd?
Actually, he's cool. I talked with him, he's not like he seems.
Cool? Oh, yeah? Like he's the most popular on YouTube or something?
No, not like that. But he's interesting.

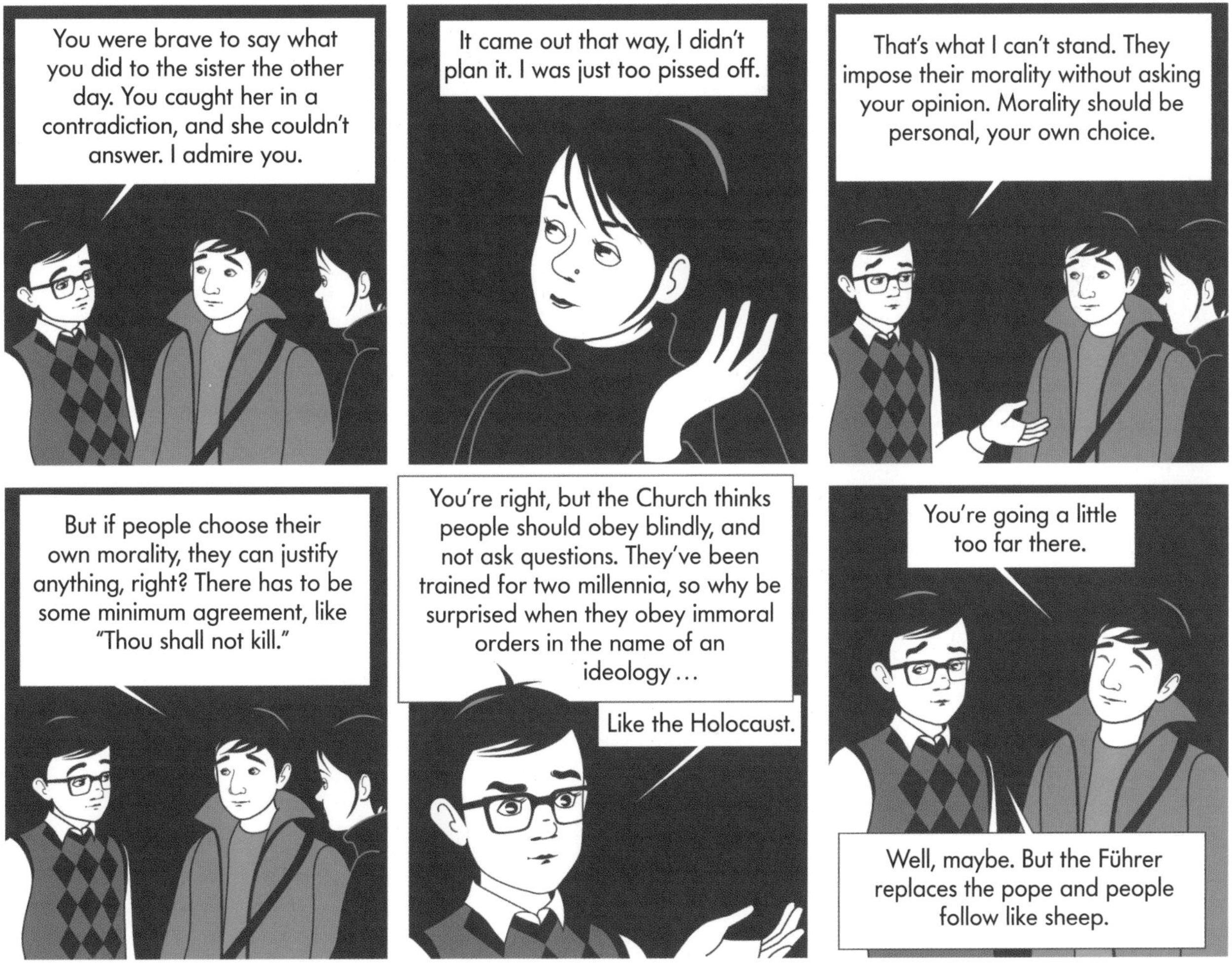
You were brave to say what you did to the sister the other day. You caught her in a contradiction, and she couldn't answer. I admire you.
It came out that way, I didn't plan it. I was just too pissed off.
That's what I can't stand. They impose their morality without asking your opinion. Morality should be personal, your own choice.
But if people choose their own morality, they can justify anything, right? There has to be some minimum agreement, like "Thou shall not kill."
You're right, but the Church thinks people should obey blindly, and not ask questions. They've been trained for two millennia, so why be surprised when they obey immoral orders in the name of an ideology …
Like the Holocaust.
You're going a little too far there.
Well, maybe. But the Führer replaces the pope and people follow like sheep.

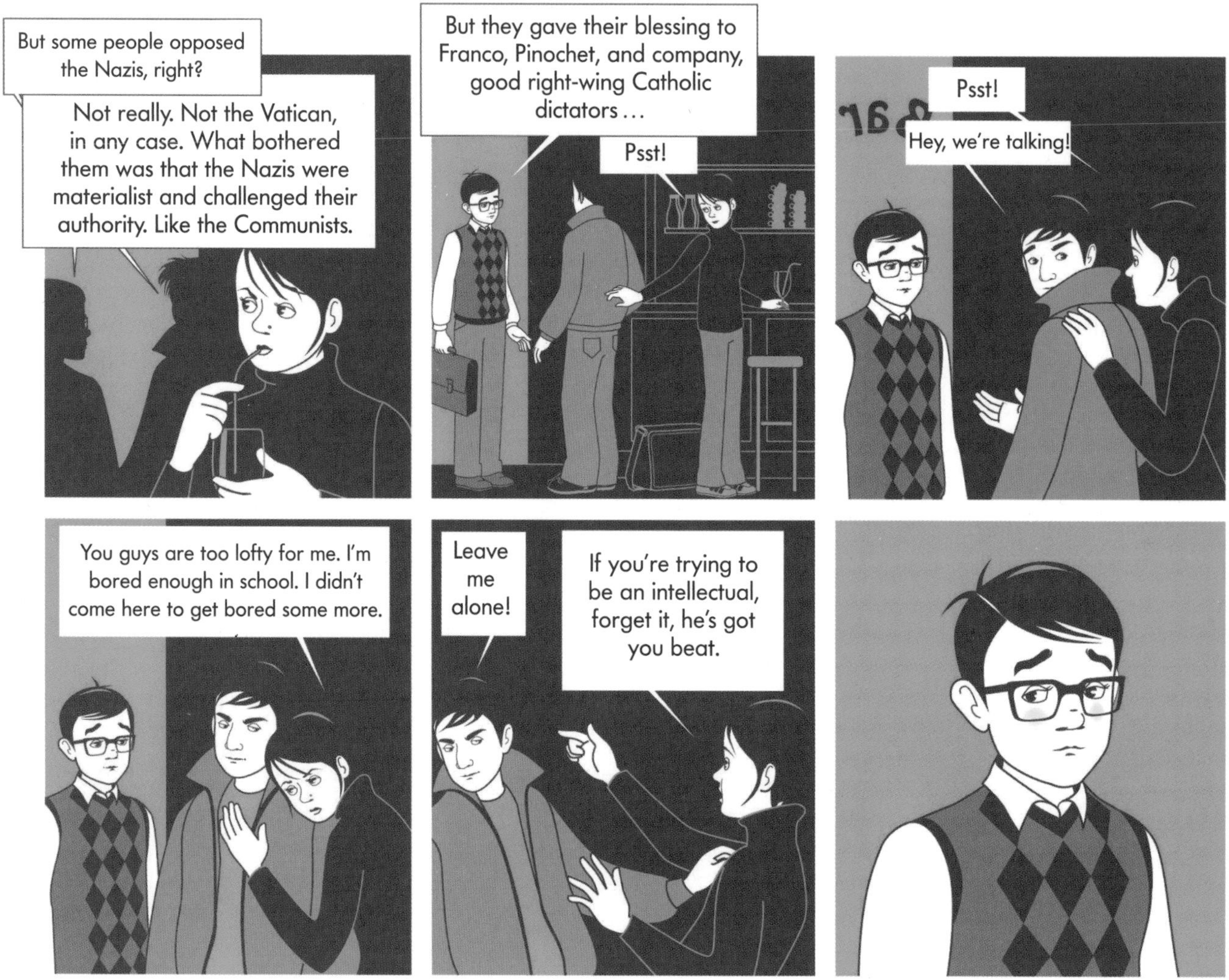
But some people opposed the Nazis, right?
Not really. Not the Vatican, in any case. What bothered them was that the Nazis were materialist and challenged their authority. Like the Communists.
But they gave their blessing to Franco, Pinochet, and company, good right-wing Catholic dictators . . .
Psst!
Psst!
Hey, we're talking!
You guys are too lofty for me. I'm bored enough in school. I didn't come here to get bored some more.
Leave me alone!
If you're trying to be an intellectual, forget it, he's got you beat.

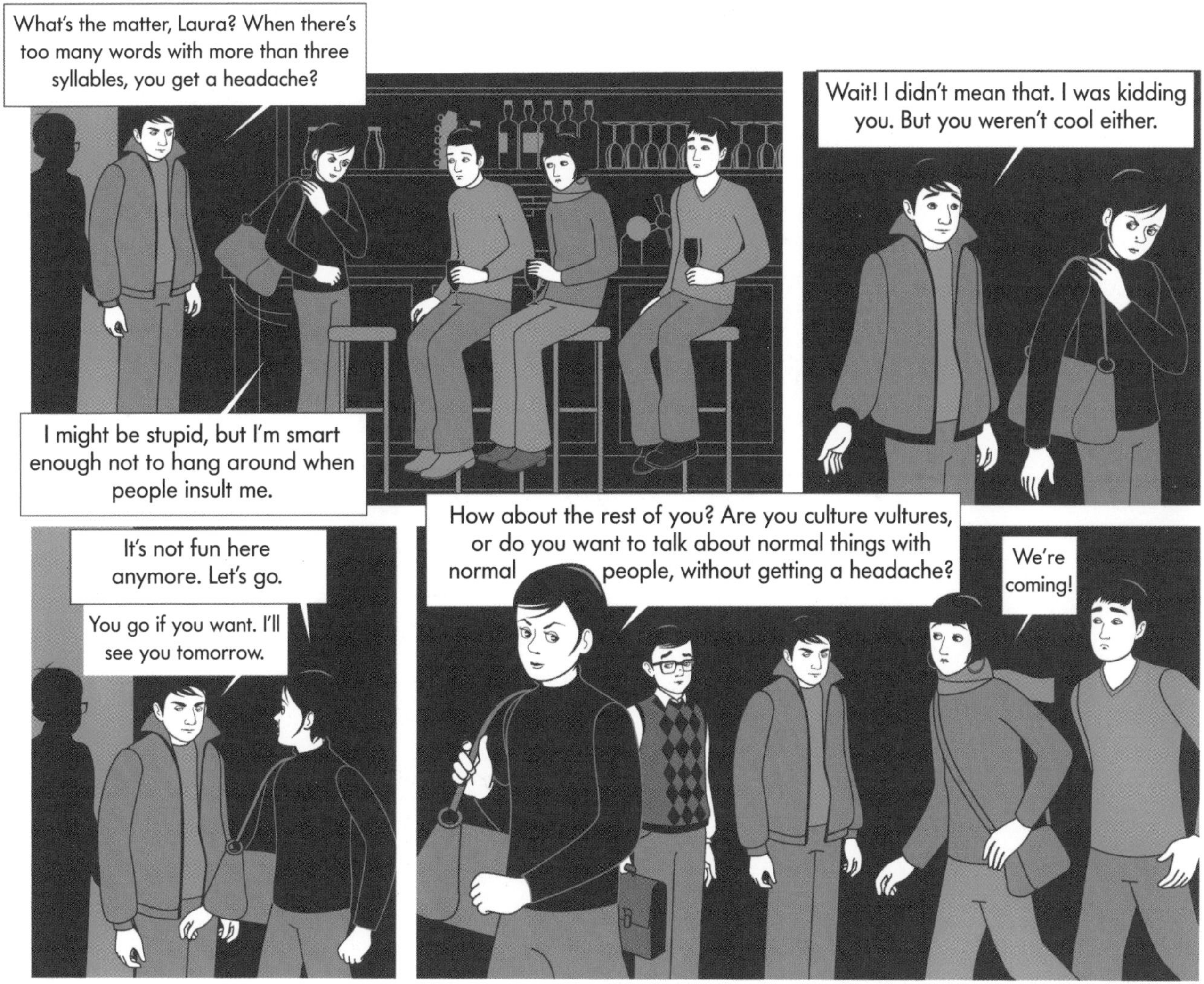

What's the matter, Laura? When there's too many words with more than three syllables, you get a headache?
I might be stupid, but I'm smart enough not to hang around when people insult me.
Wait! I didn't mean that. I was kidding you. But you weren't cool either.
It's not fun here anymore. Let's go.
You go if you want. I'll see you tomorrow.
How about the rest of you? Are you culture vultures, or do you want to talk about normal things with normal people, without getting a headache?
We're coming!

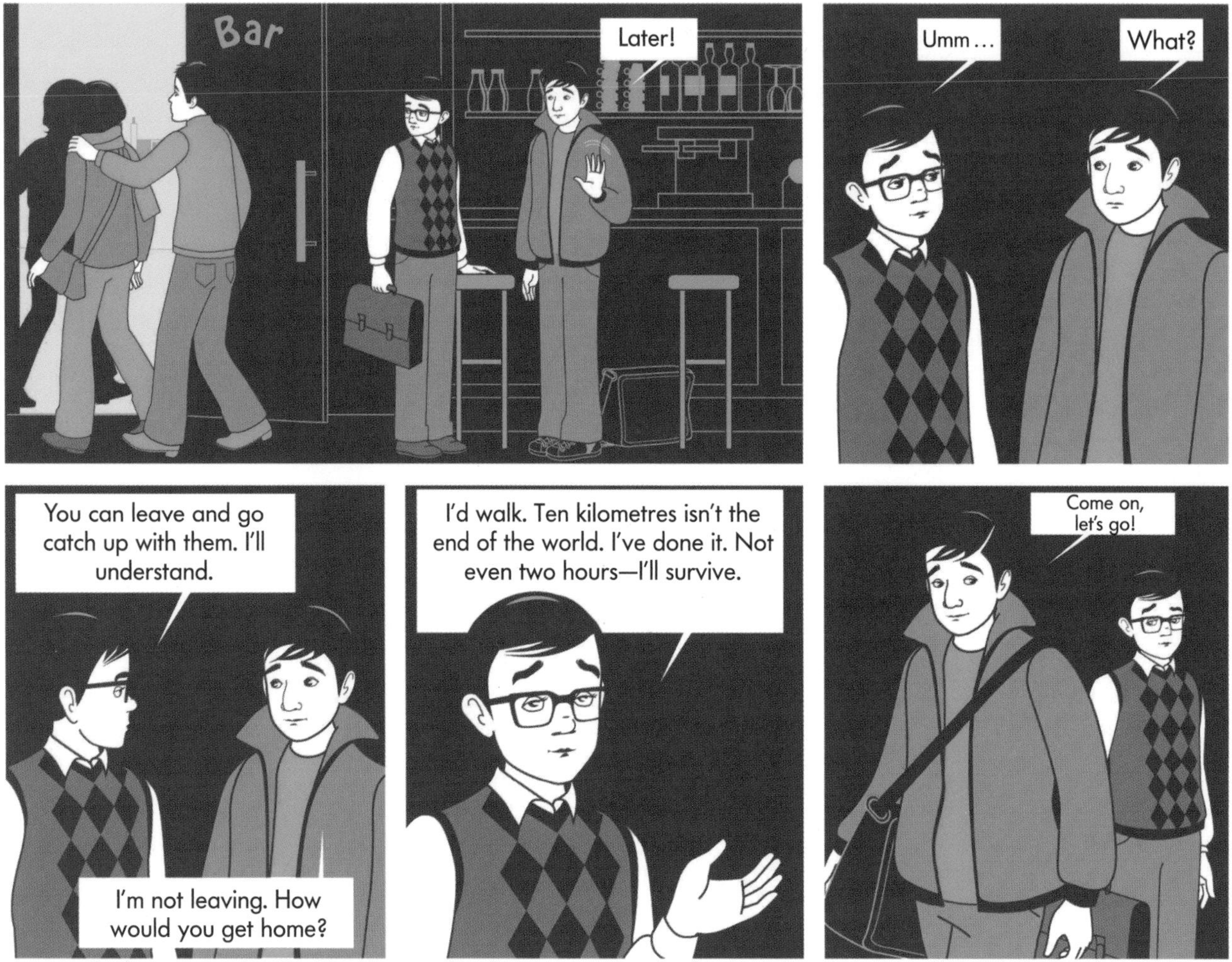
Bar
Later!
Umm …
What?
You can leave and go catch up with them. I'll understand.
I'm not leaving. How would you get home?
I'd walk. Ten kilometres isn't the end of the world. I've done it. Not even two hours—I'll survive.
Come on, let's go!

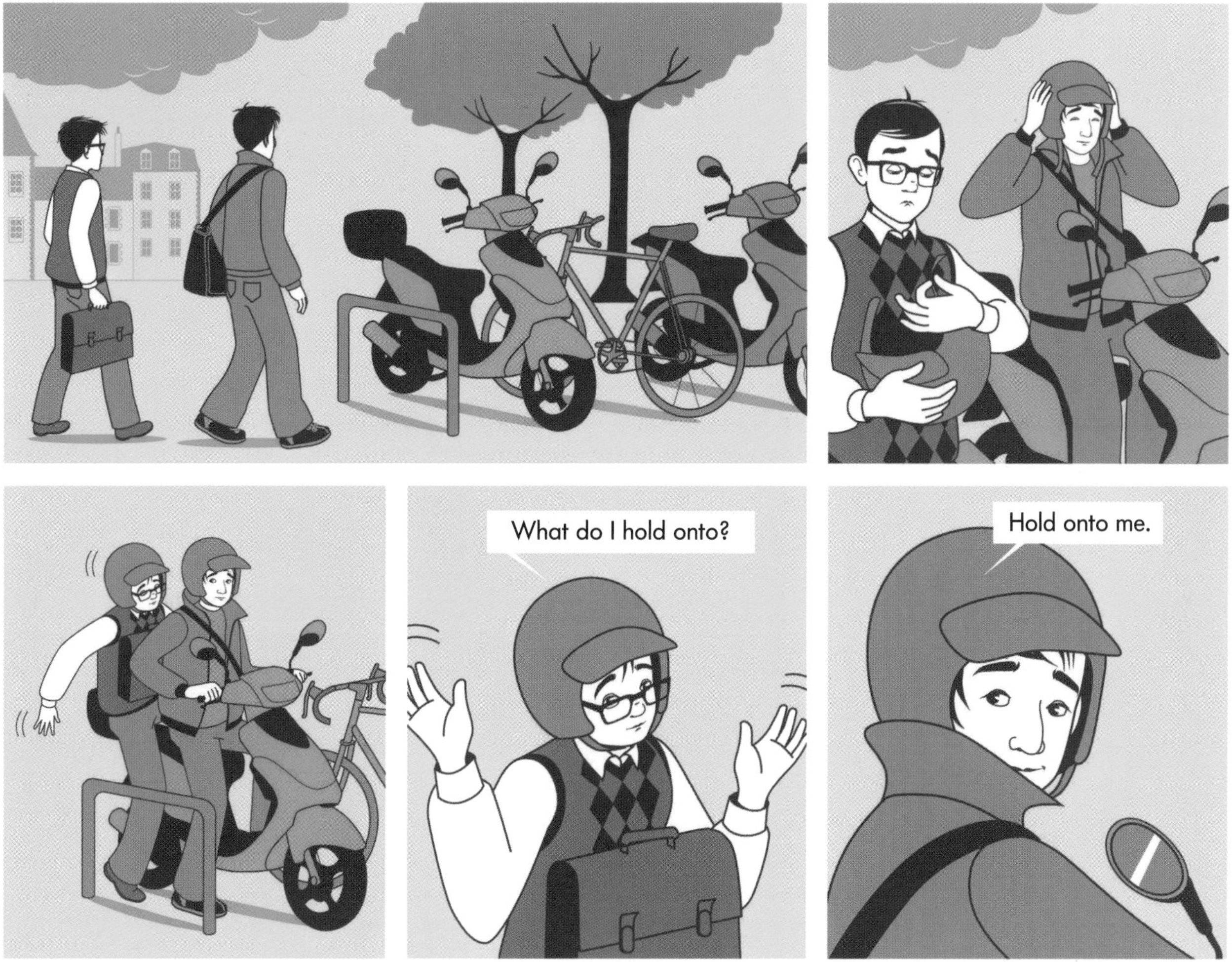
What do I hold onto?
Hold onto me.

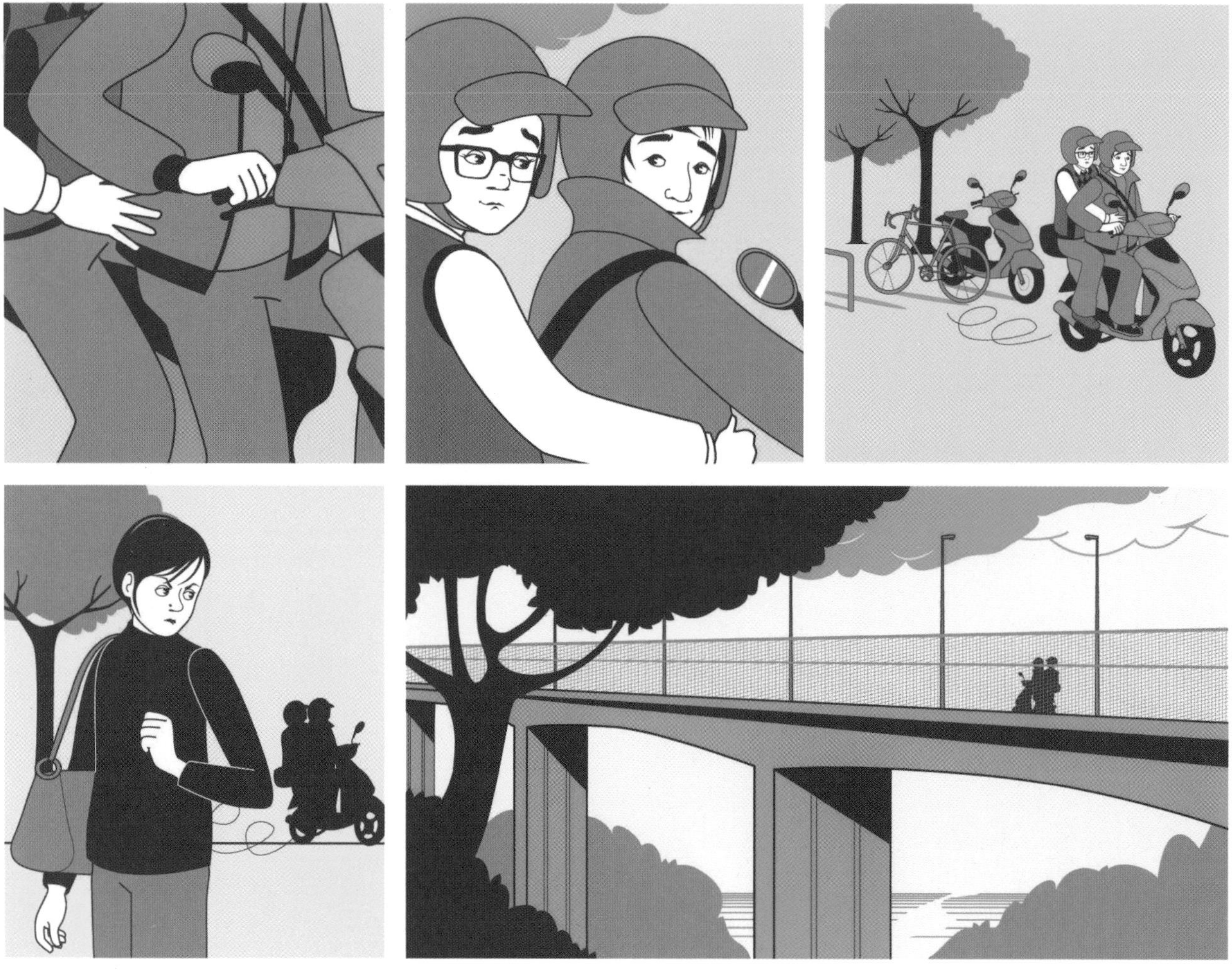

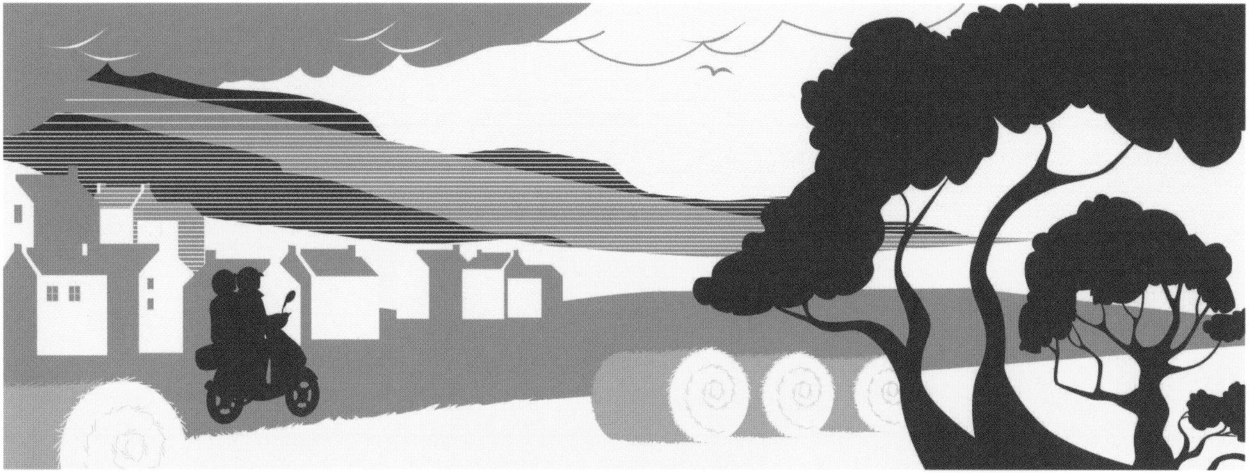

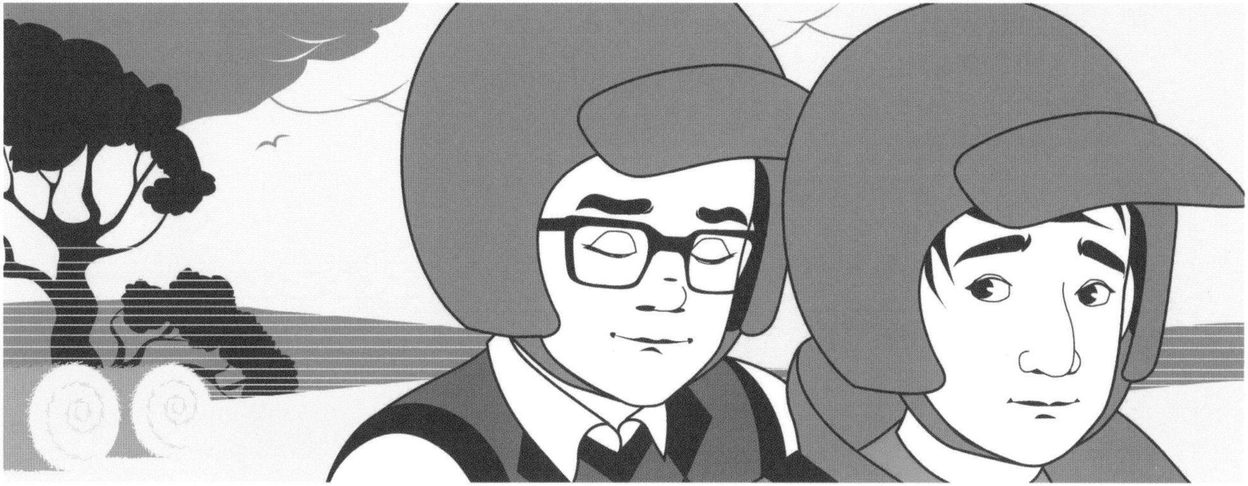

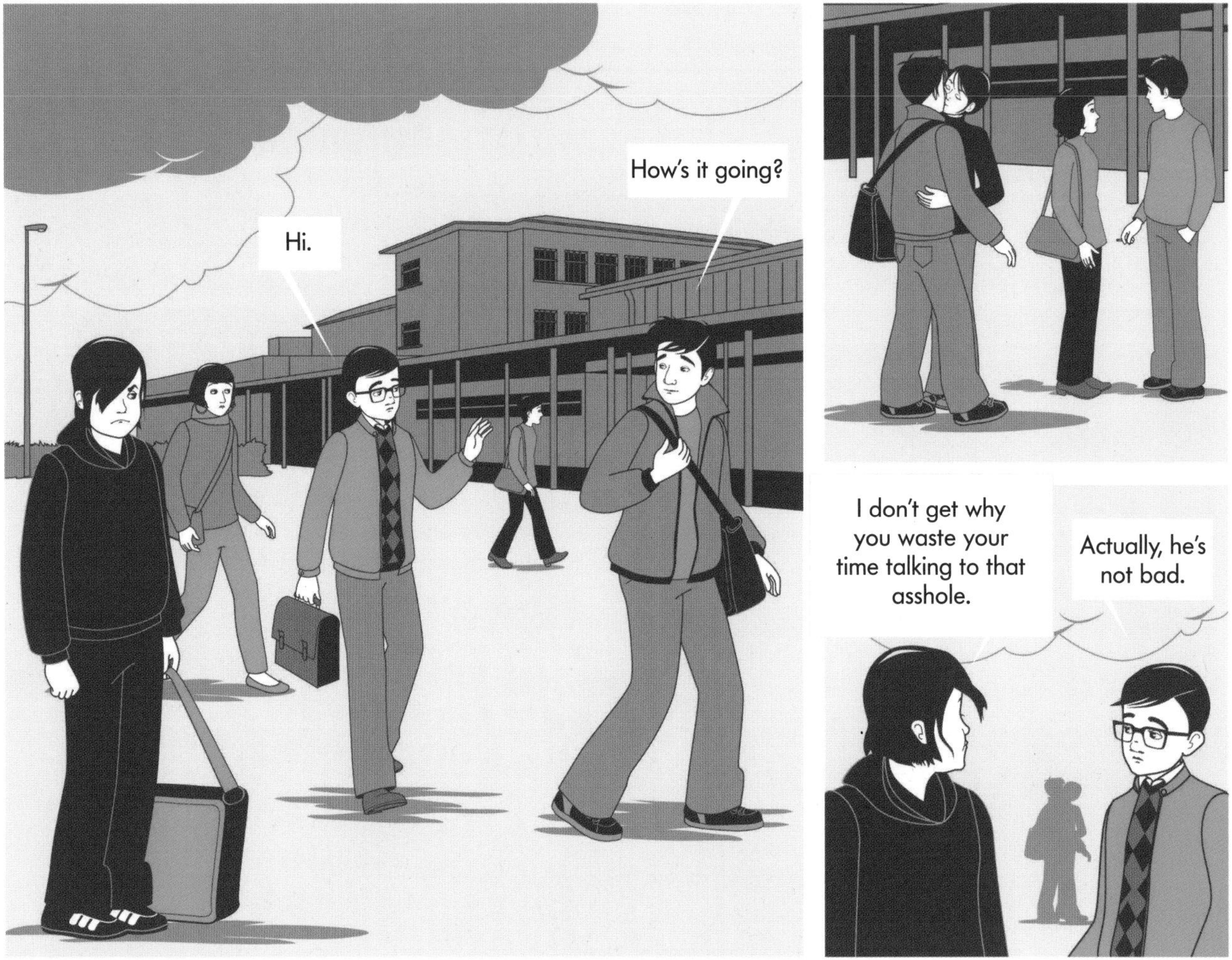
Hi.
How's it going?
I don't get why you waste your time talking to that asshole.
Actually, he's not bad.

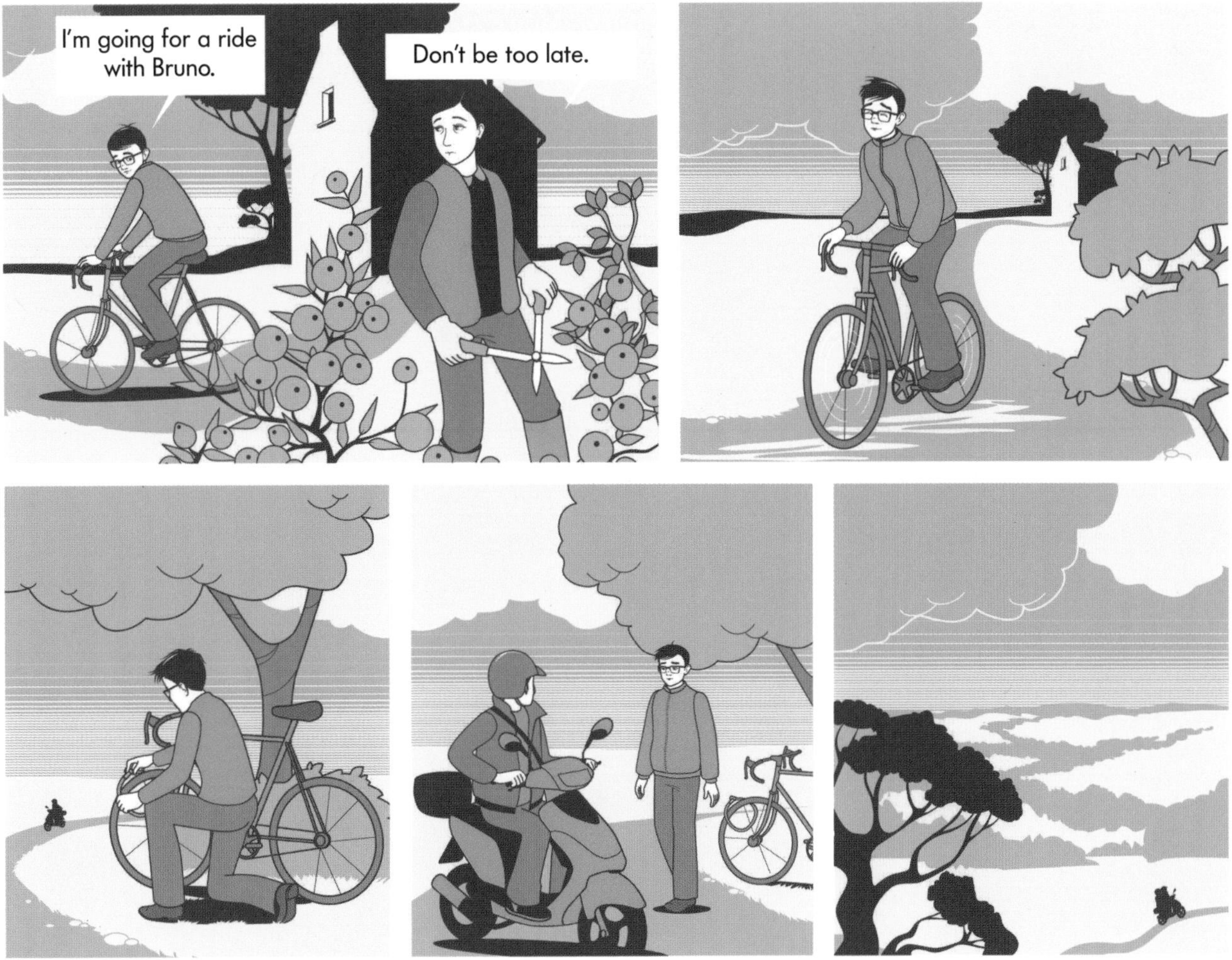
I'm going for a ride with Bruno.
Don't be too late.

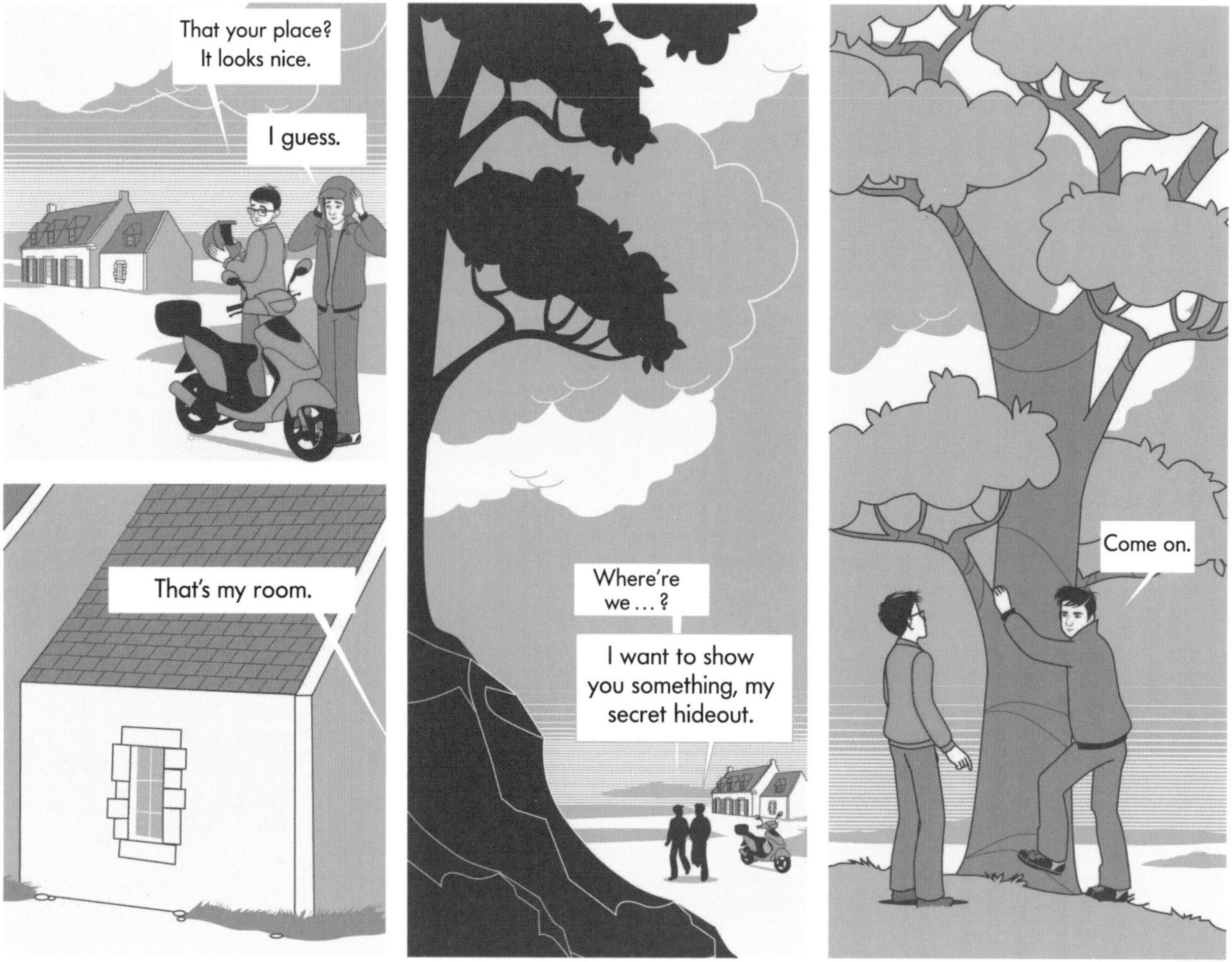
That your place? It looks nice.
I guess.
That's my room.
Where're we ... ?
I want to show you something, my secret hideout.
Come on.

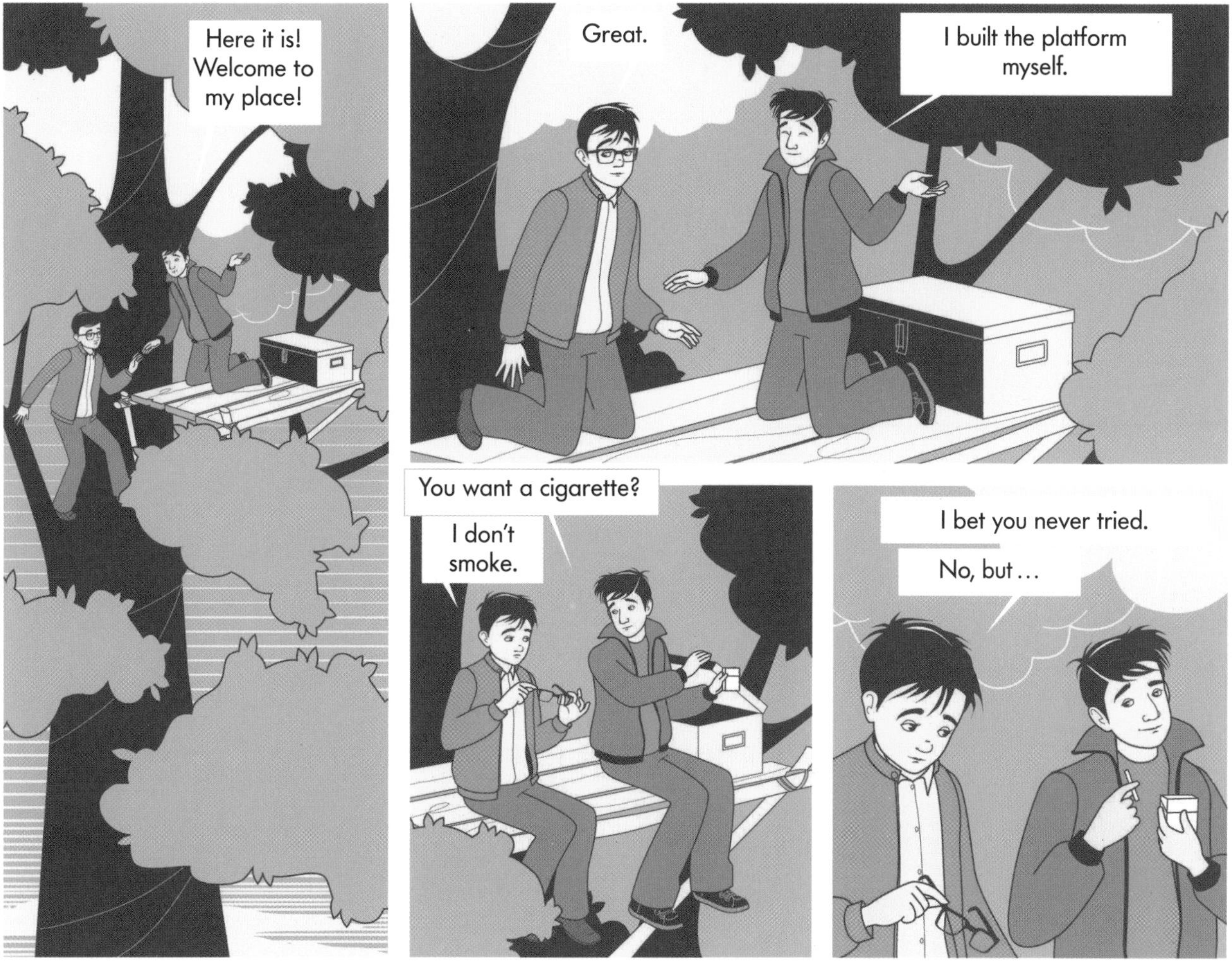
Here it is! Welcome to my place!
Great.
I built the platform myself.
You want a cigarette?
I don't smoke.
I bet you never tried.
No, but…

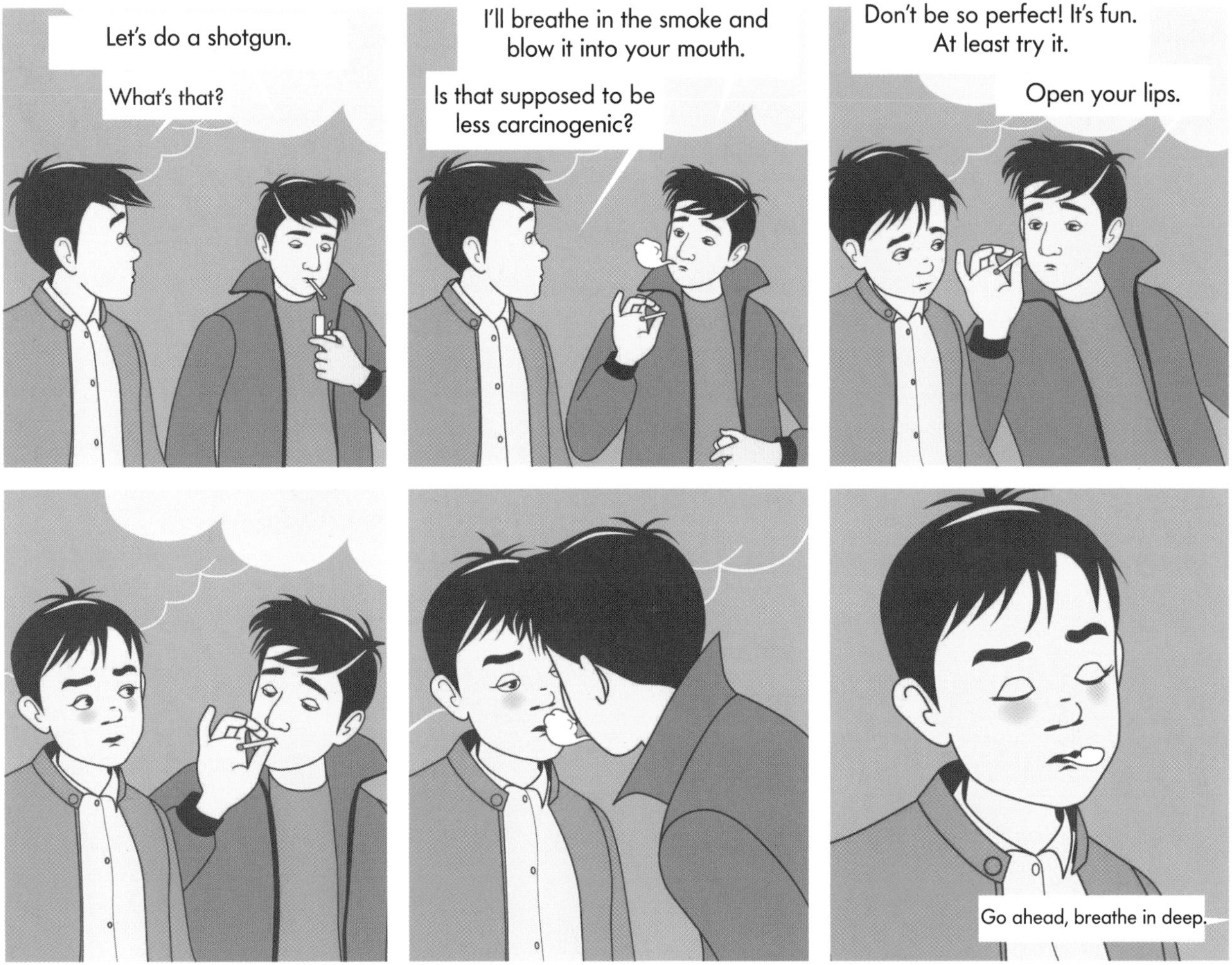

Let's do a shotgun.
What's that?
I'll breathe in the smoke and blow it into your mouth.
Is that supposed to be less carcinogenic?
Don't be so perfect! It's fun. At least try it.
Open your lips.
Go ahead, breathe in deep.

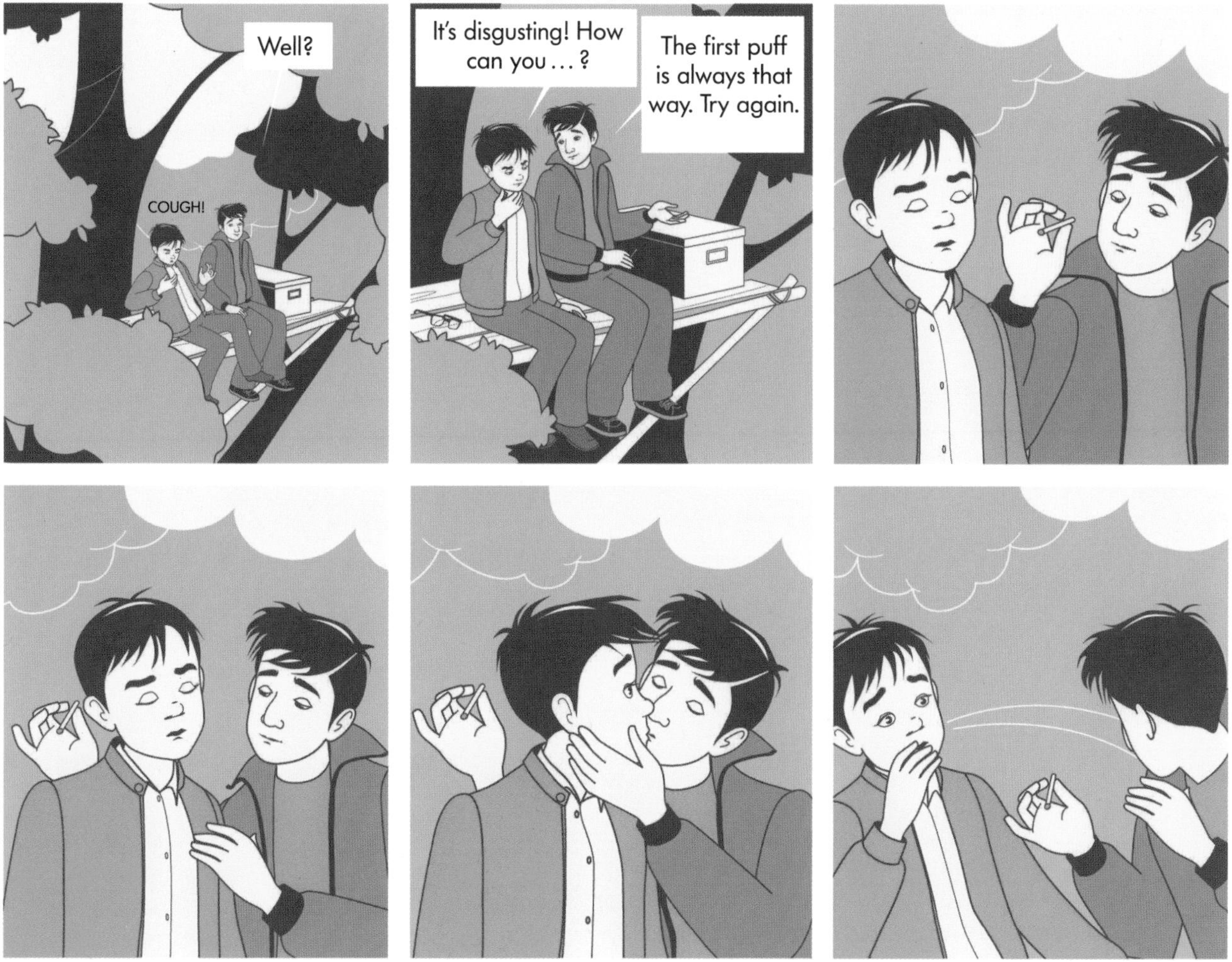
Well?
COUGH!
It's disgusting! How can you . . . ?
The first puff is always that way. Try again.

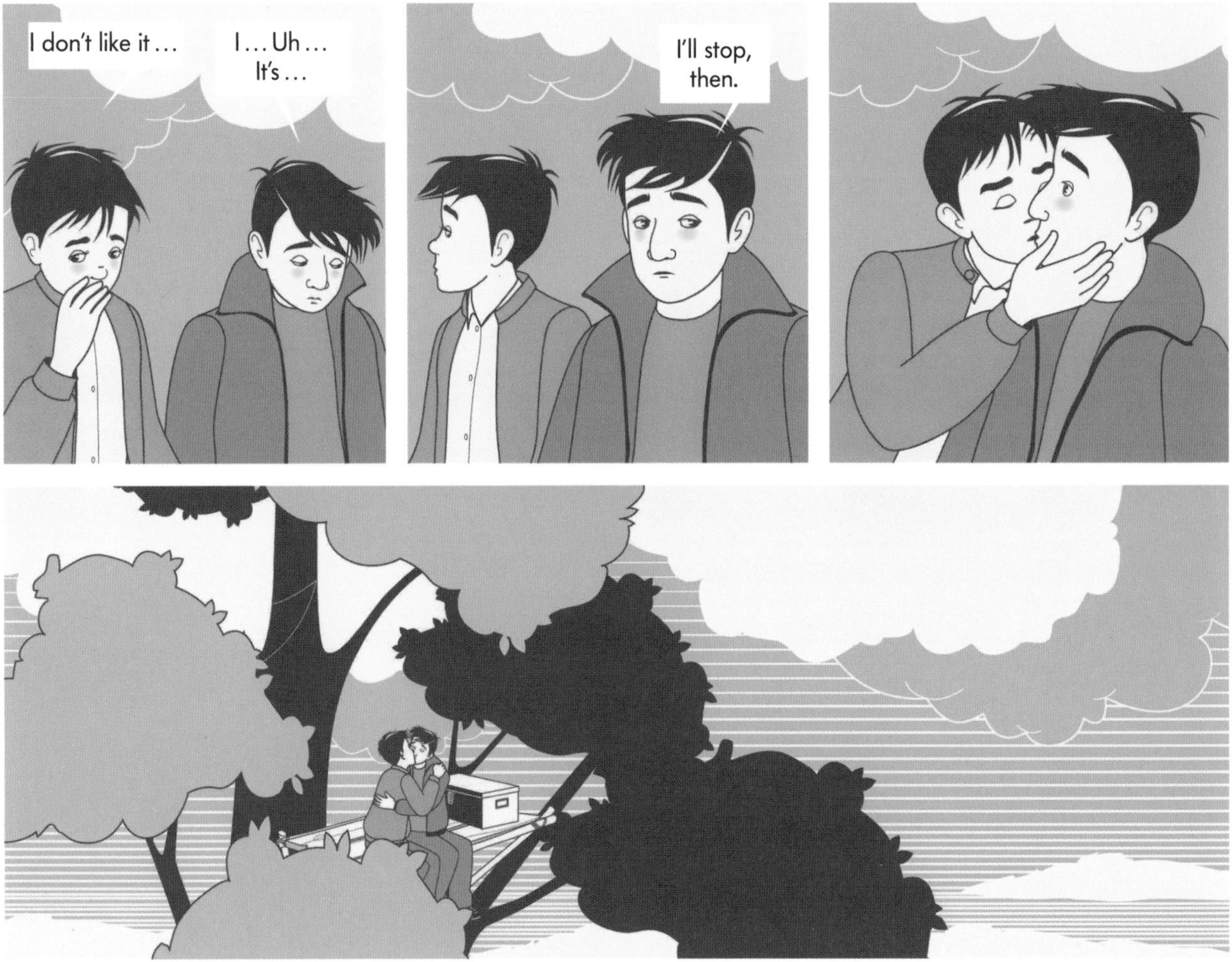
I don't like it . . .
I . . . Uh . . . It's . . .
I'll stop, then.

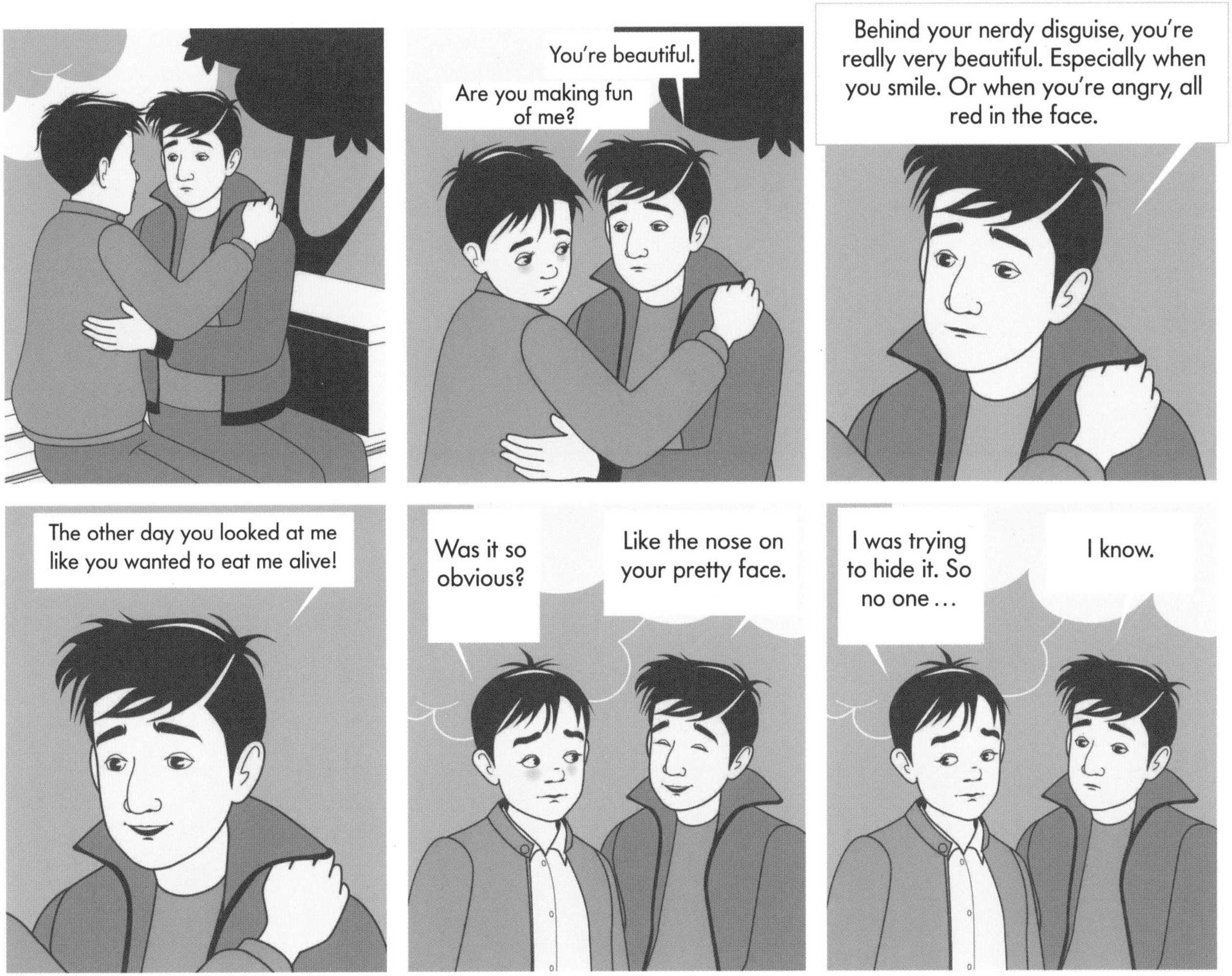
Are you making fun of me?
You're beautiful.
Behind your nerdy disguise, you're really very beautiful. Especially when you smile. Or when you're angry, all red in the face.
The other day you looked at me like you wanted to eat me alive!
Was it so obvious?
Like the nose on your pretty face.
I was trying to hide it. So no one …
I know.

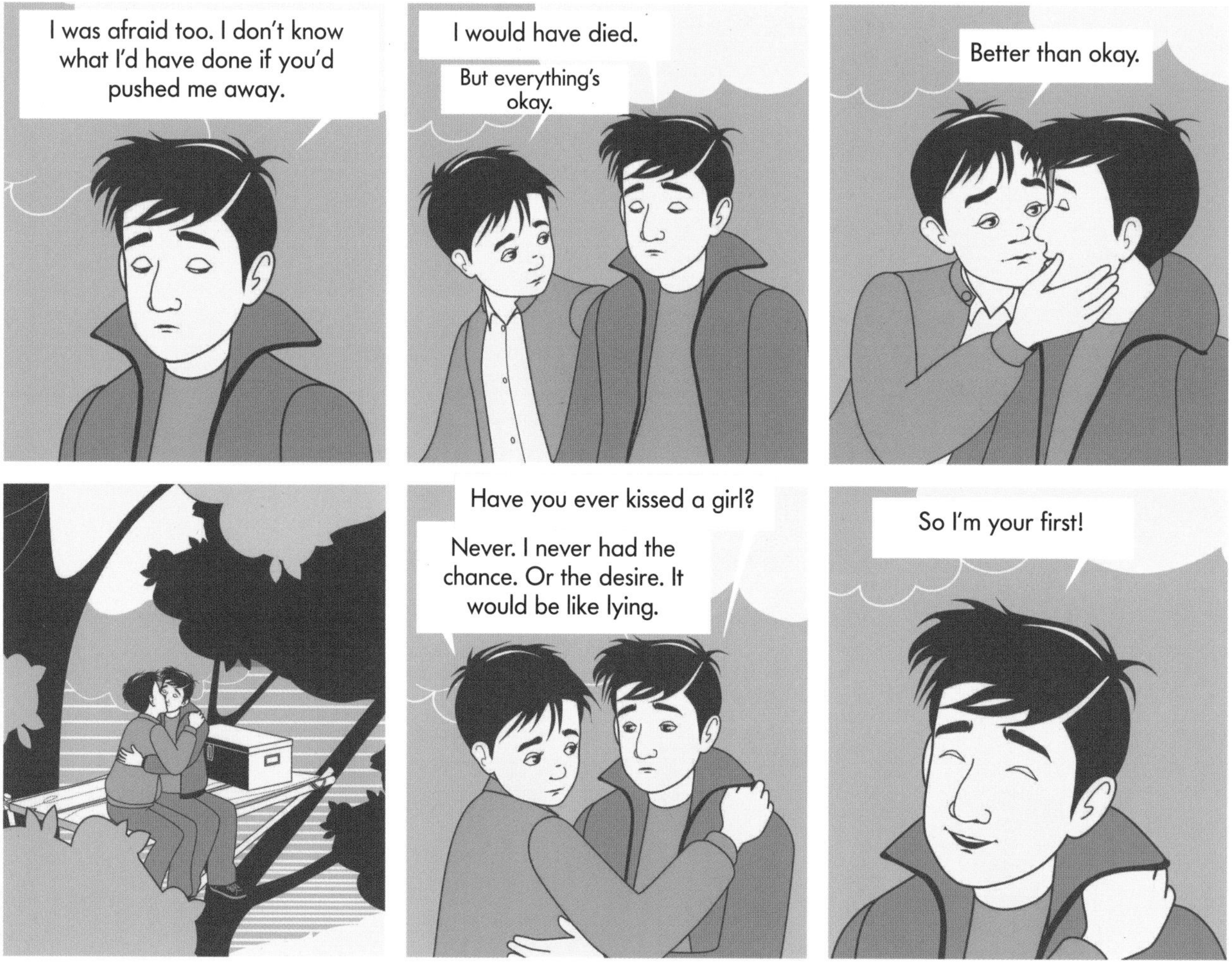
I was afraid too. I don't know what I'd have done if you'd pushed me away.
I would have died.
But everything's okay.
Better than okay.
Have you ever kissed a girl?
Never. I never had the chance. Or the desire. It would be like lying.
So I'm your first!

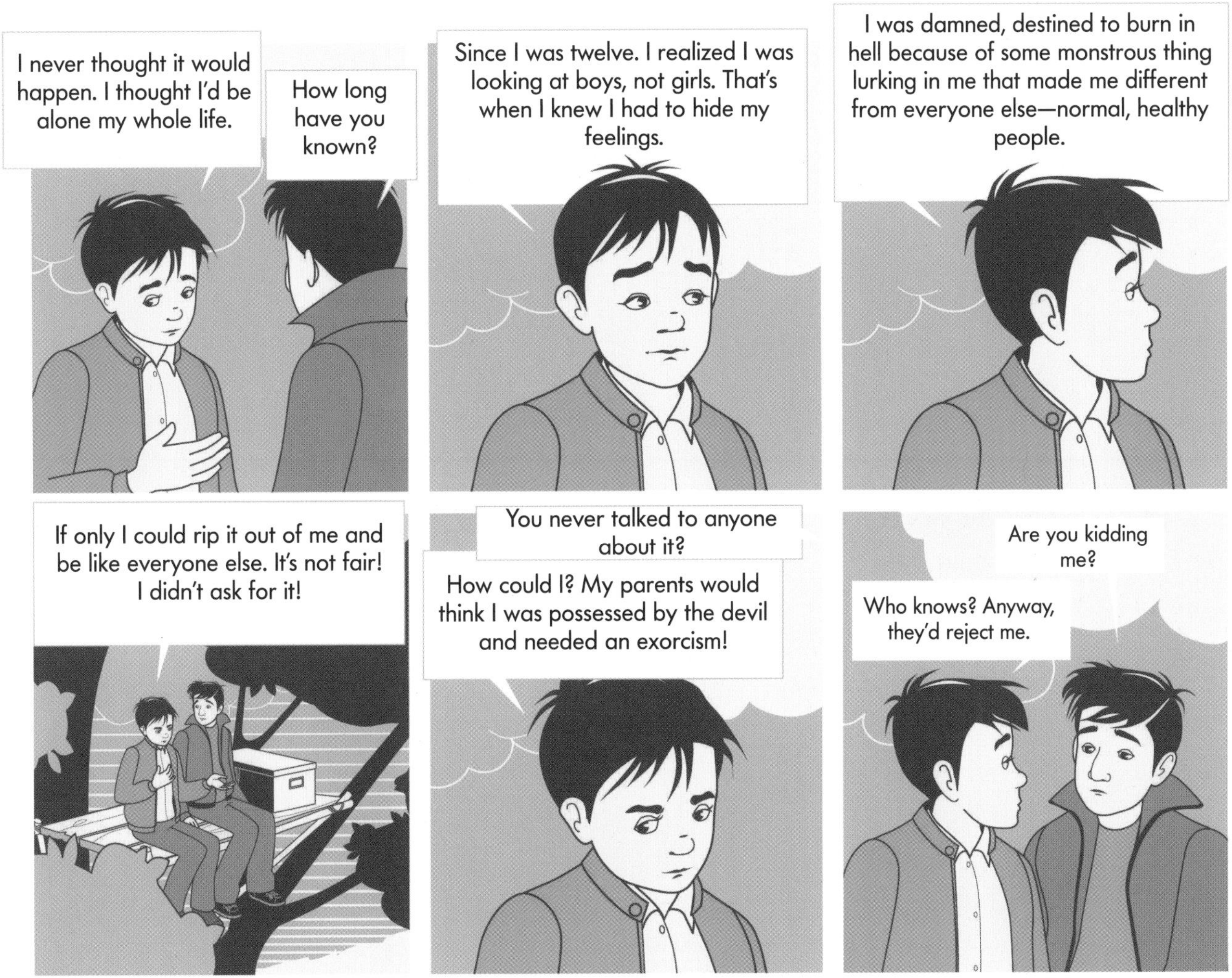
I never thought it would happen. I thought I'd be alone my whole life.
How long have you known?
Since I was twelve. I realized I was looking at boys, not girls. That's when I knew I had to hide my feelings.
I was damned, destined to burn in hell because of some monstrous thing lurking in me that made me different from everyone else—normal, healthy people.
If only I could rip it out of me and be like everyone else. It's not fair! I didn't ask for it!
You never talked to anyone about it?
How could I? My parents would think I was possessed by the devil and needed an exorcism!
Are you kidding me?
Who knows? Anyway, they'd reject me.

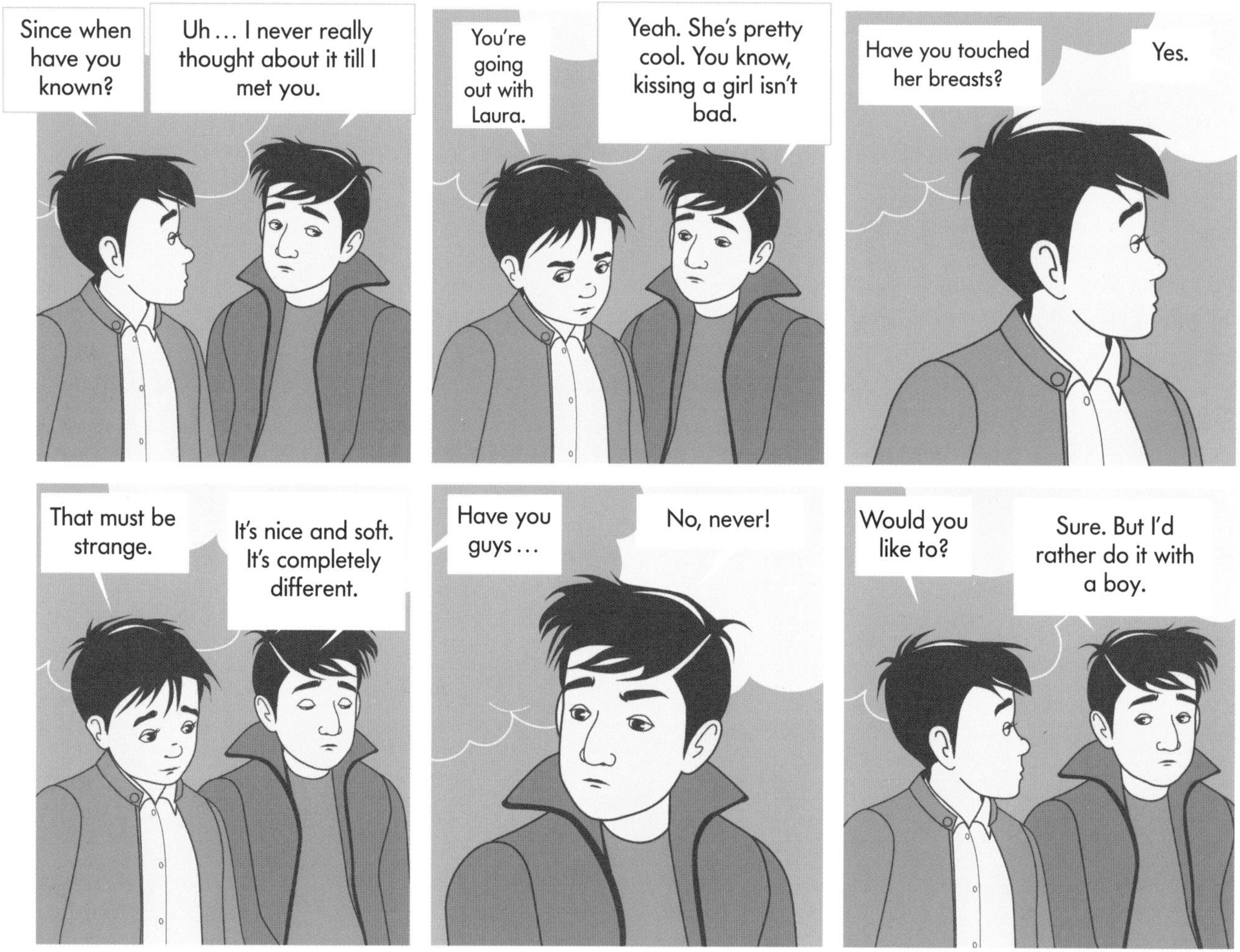
Since when have you known?
Uh … I never really thought about it till I met you.
You're going out with Laura.
Yeah. She's pretty cool. You know, kissing a girl isn't bad.
Have you touched her breasts?
Yes.
That must be strange.
It's nice and soft. It's completely different.
Have you guys …
No, never!
Would you like to?
Sure. But I'd rather do it with a boy.

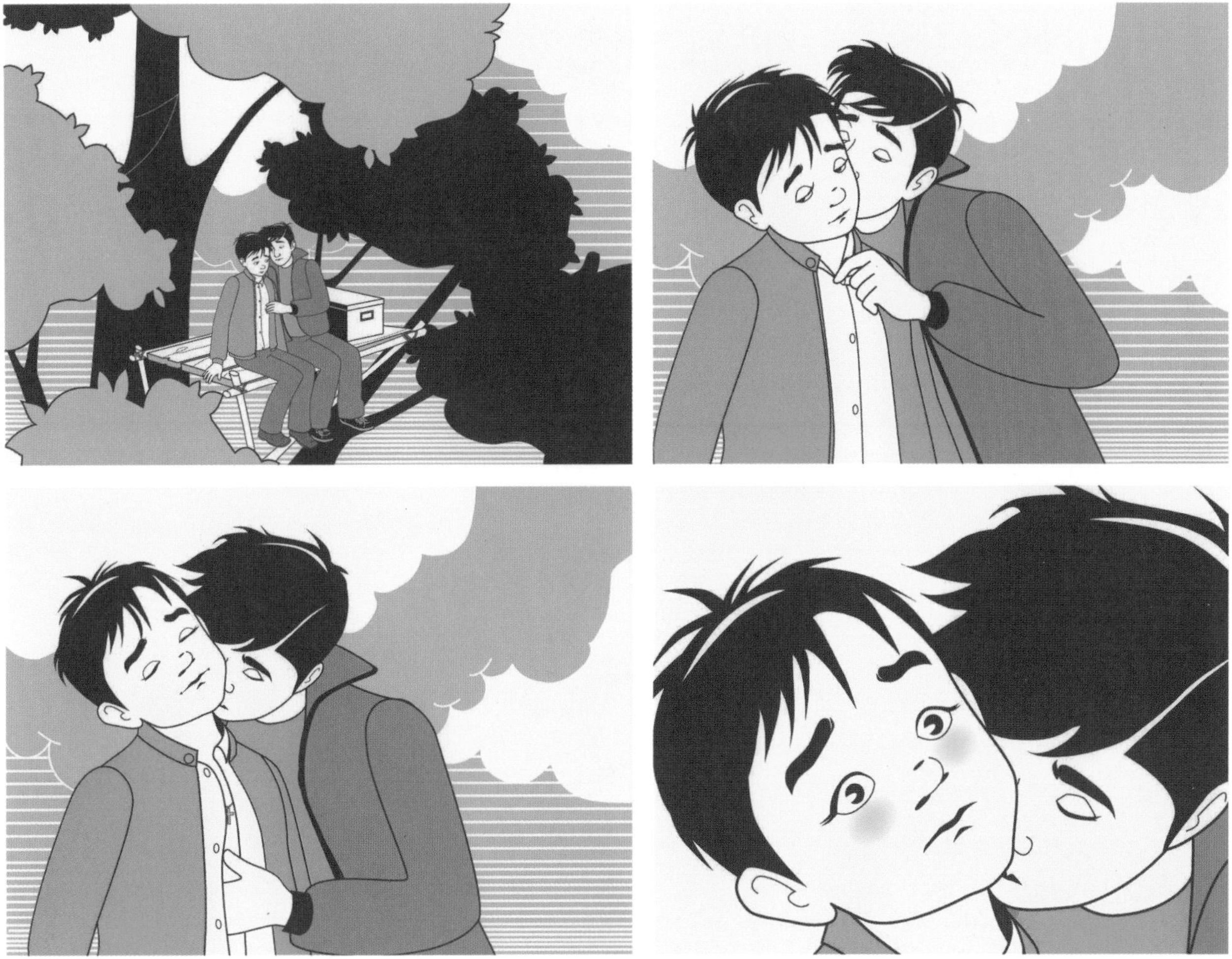

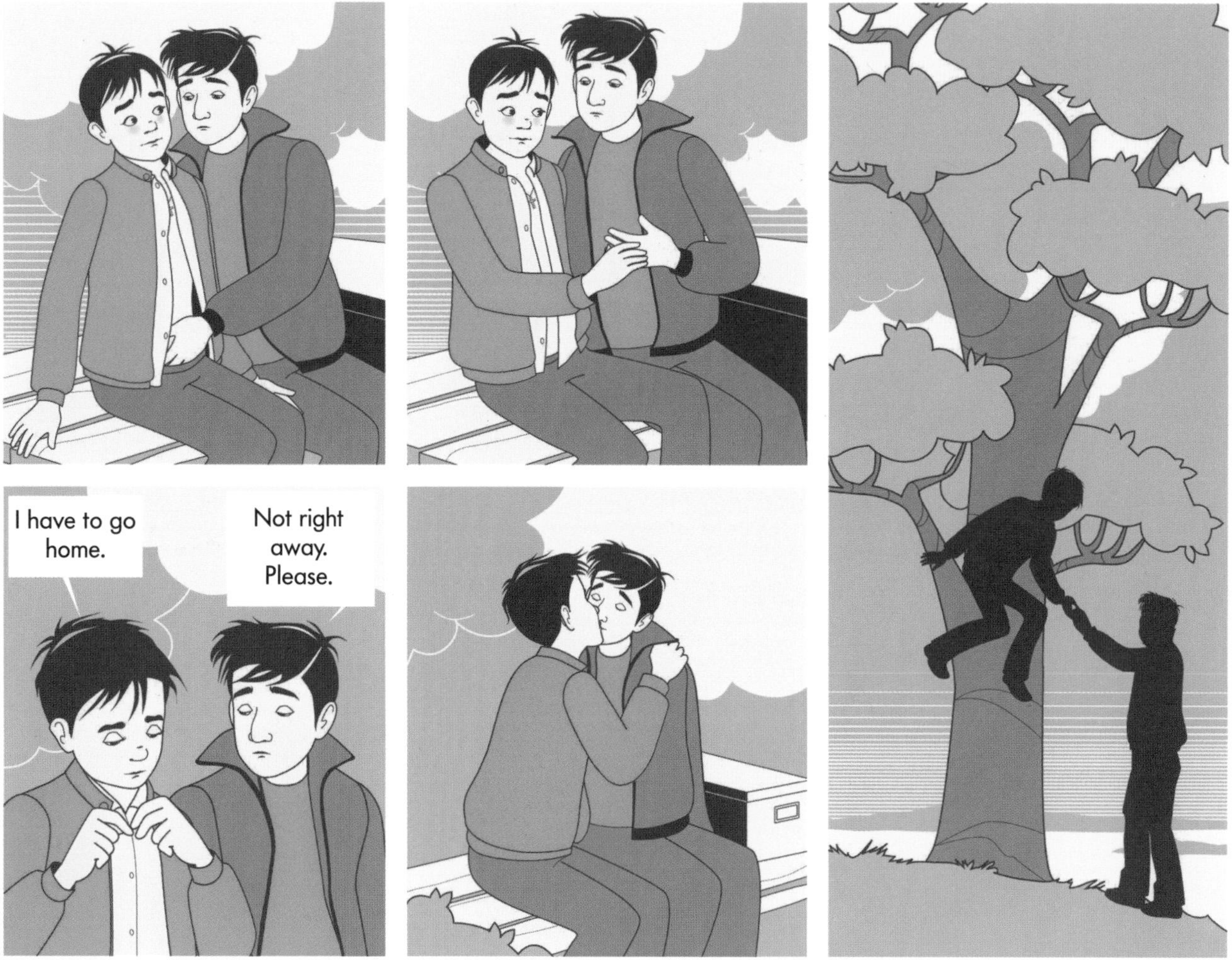
I have to go home.
Not right away. Please.

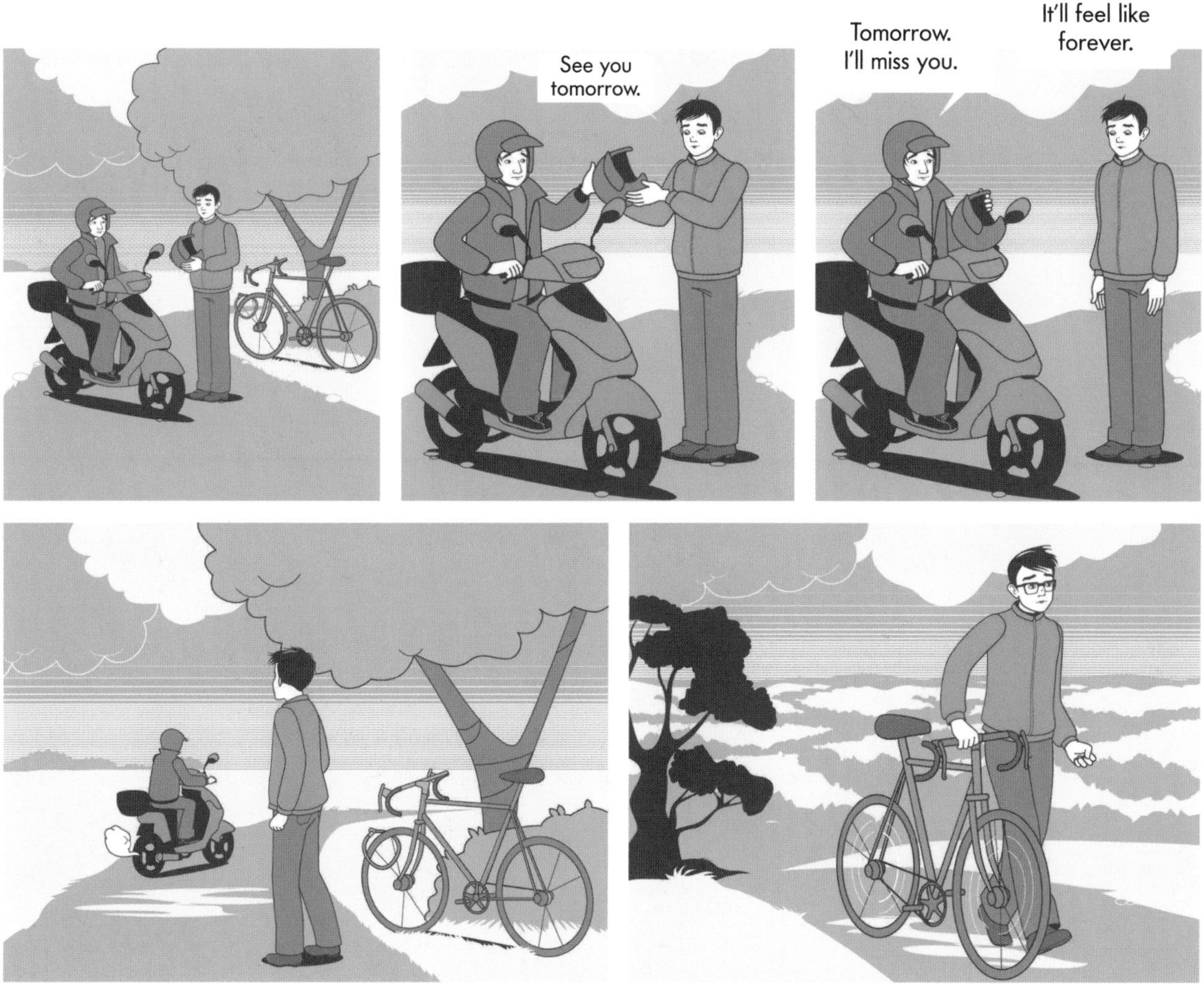
See you tomorrow.
Tomorrow. I'll miss you.
It'll feel like forever.

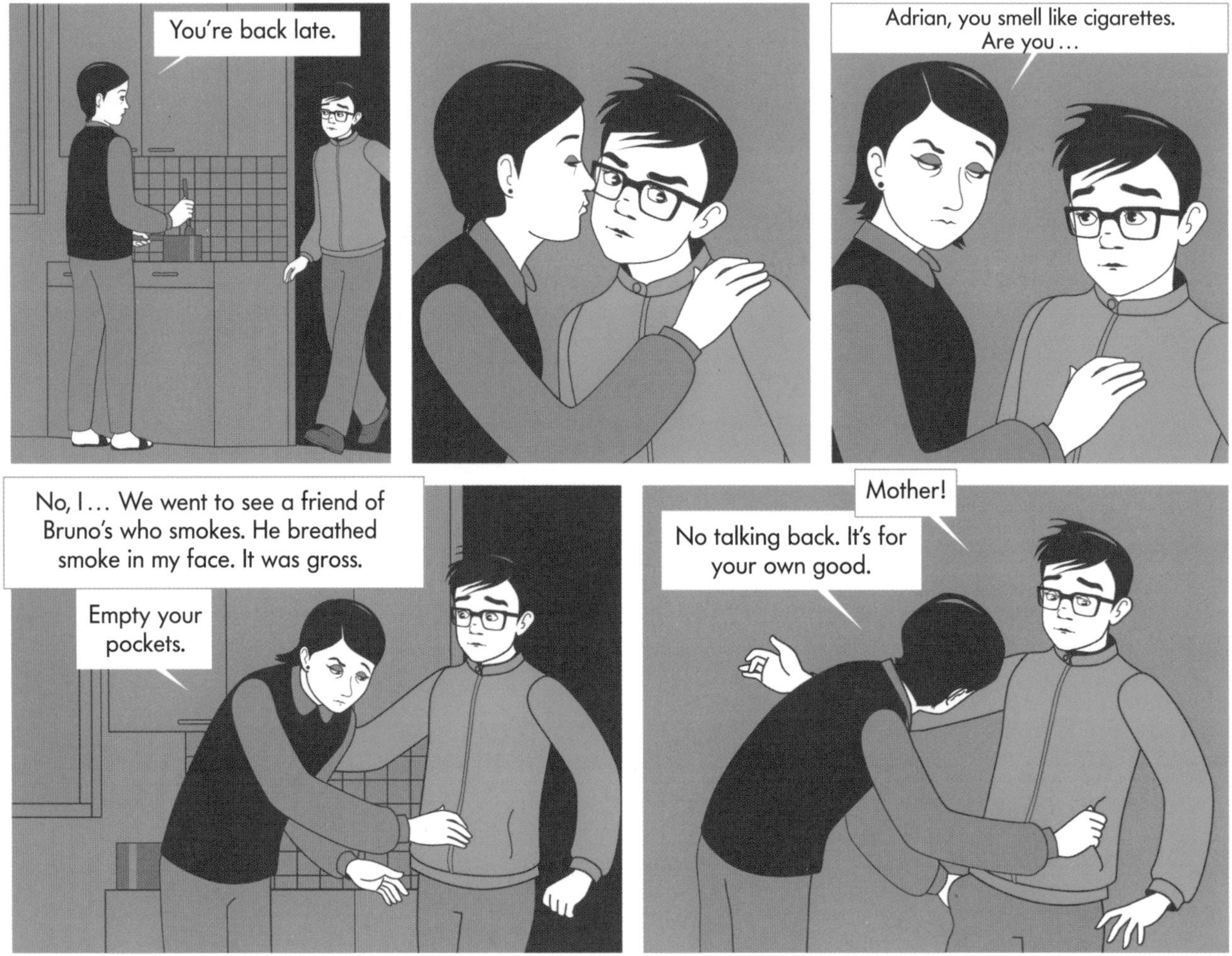
You're back late.
Adrian, you smell like cigarettes. Are you…
No, I… We went to see a friend of Bruno's who smokes. He breathed smoke in my face. It was gross.
Empty your pockets.
Mother!
No talking back. It's for your own good.

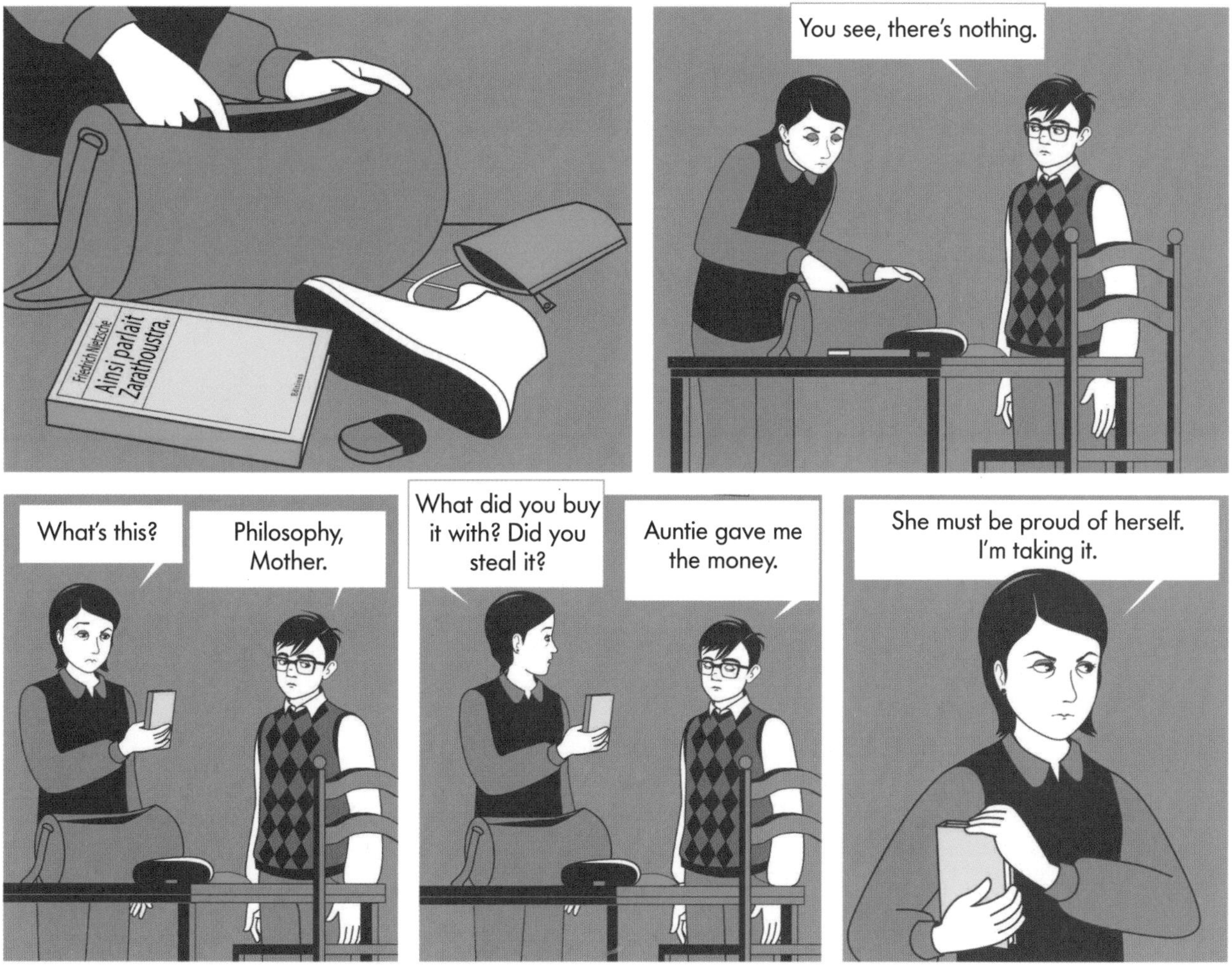
Friedrich Nietzsche
Ainsi parlait Zarathoustra.
You see, there's nothing.
What's this?
Philosophy, Mother.
What did you buy it with? Did you steal it?
Auntie gave me the money.
She must be proud of herself. I'm taking it.

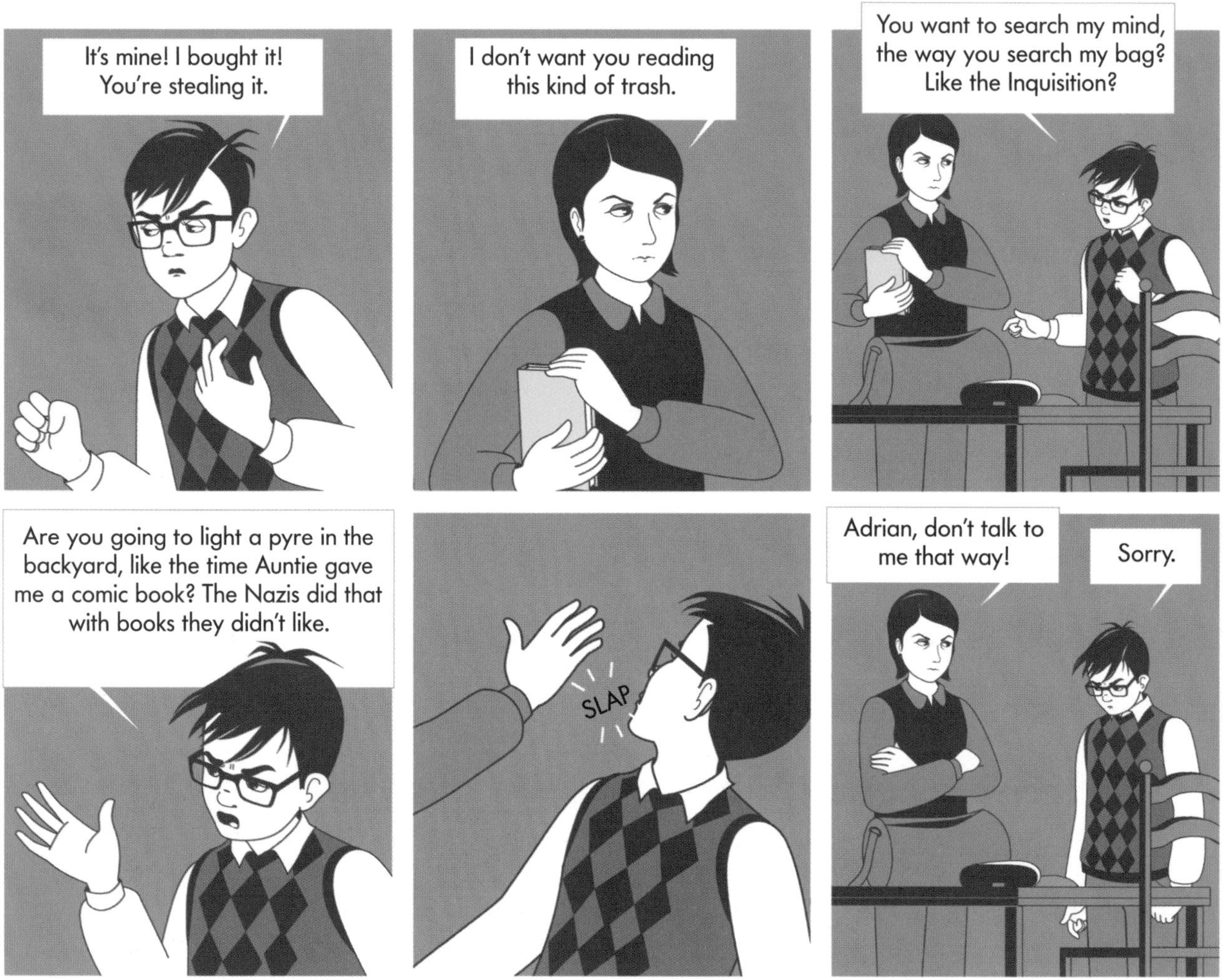
It's mine! I bought it! You're stealing it.
I don't want you reading this kind of trash.
You want to search my mind, the way you search my bag? Like the Inquisition?
Are you going to light a pyre in the backyard, like the time Auntie gave me a comic book? The Nazis did that with books they didn't like.
SLAP
Adrian, don't talk to me that way!
Sorry.

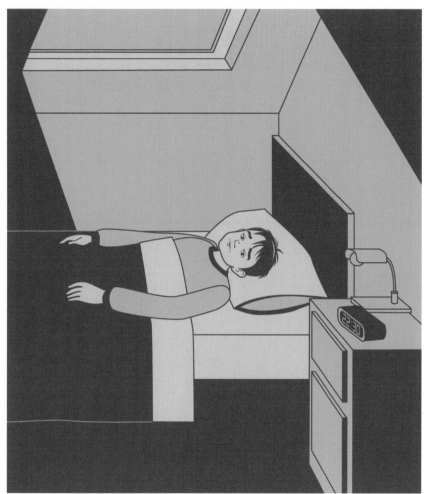

beep
beep

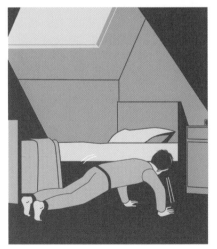

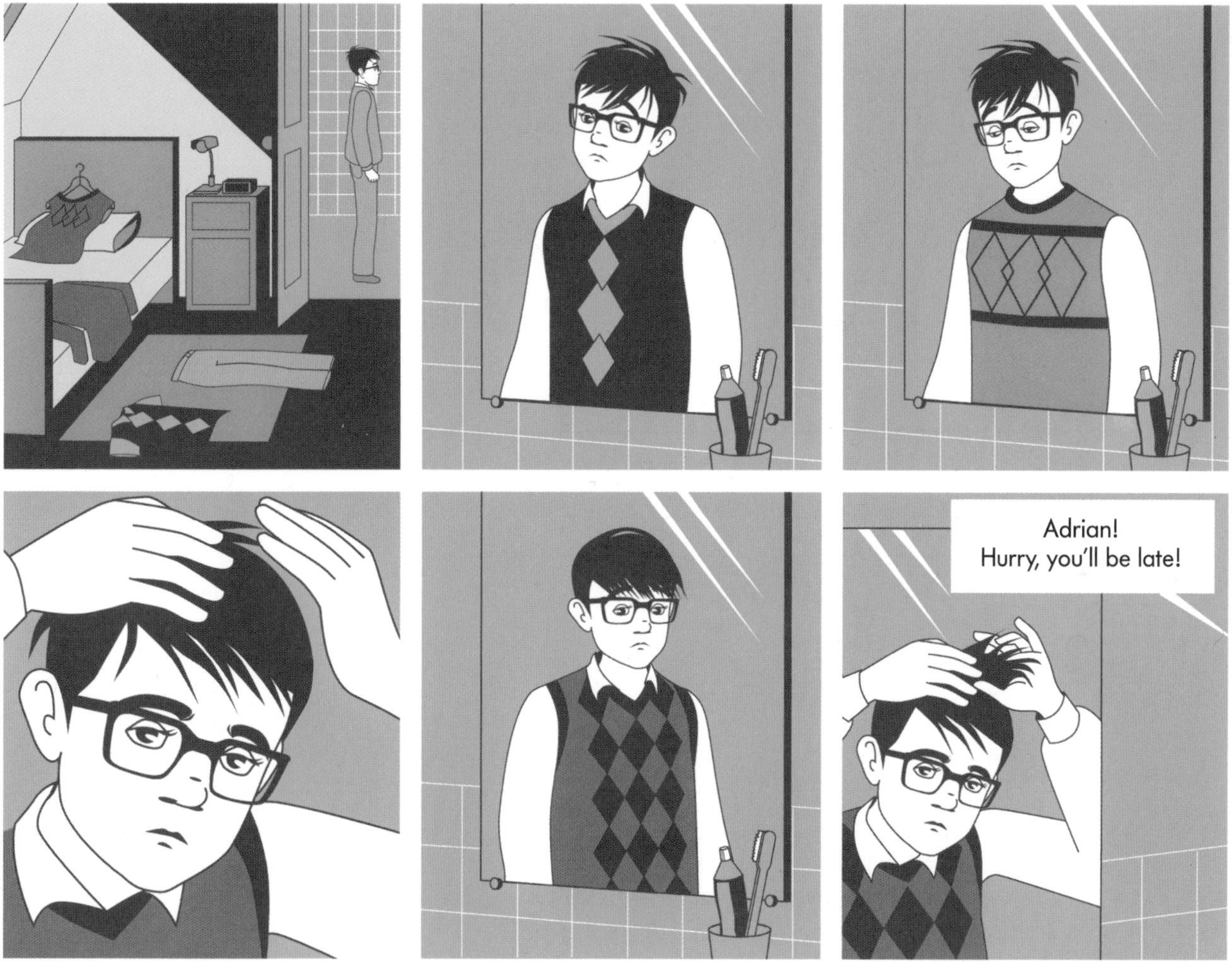
Adrian!
Hurry, you'll be late!

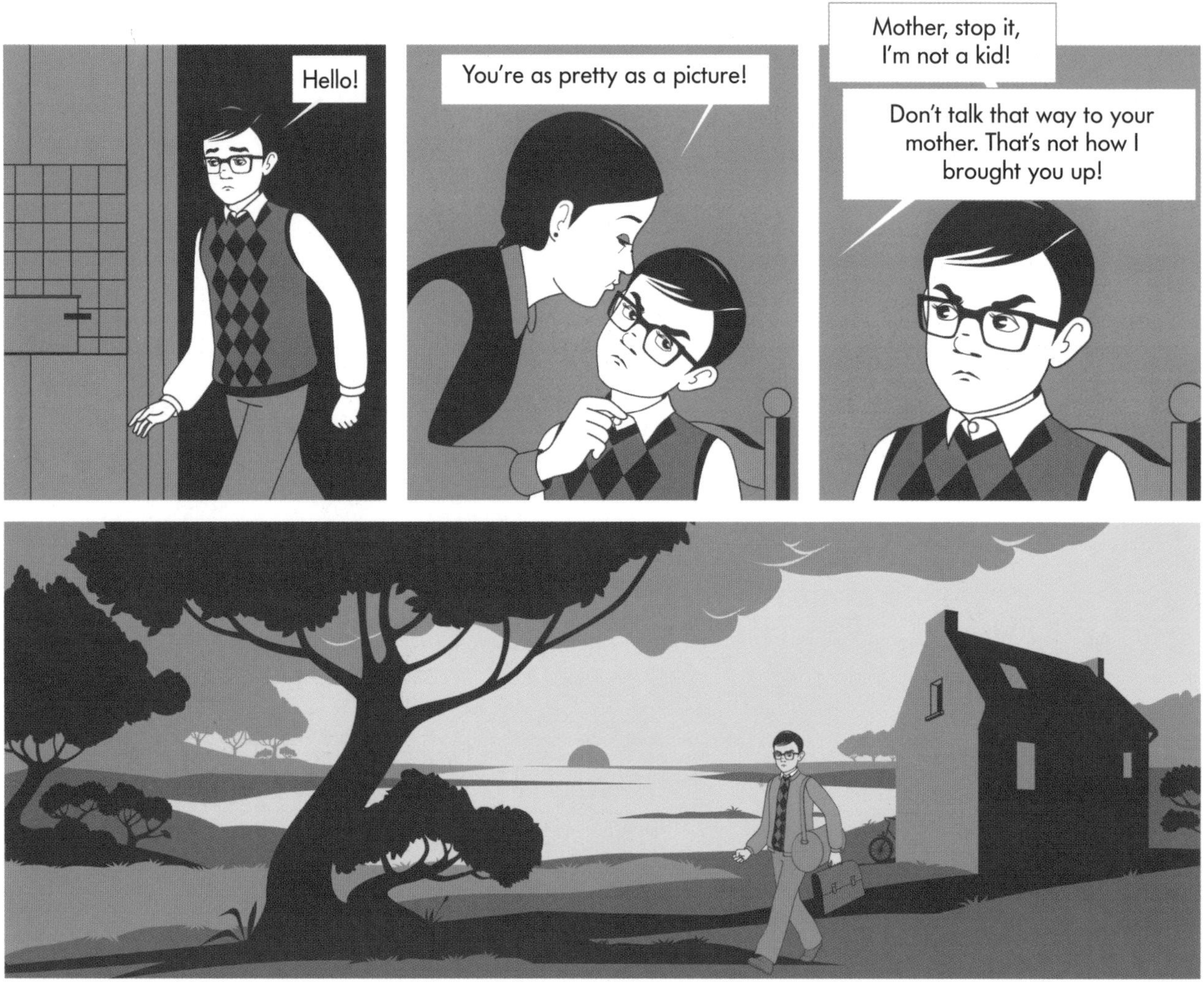
Hello!
You're as pretty as a picture!
Mother, stop it, I'm not a kid!
Don't talk that way to your mother. That's not how I brought you up!

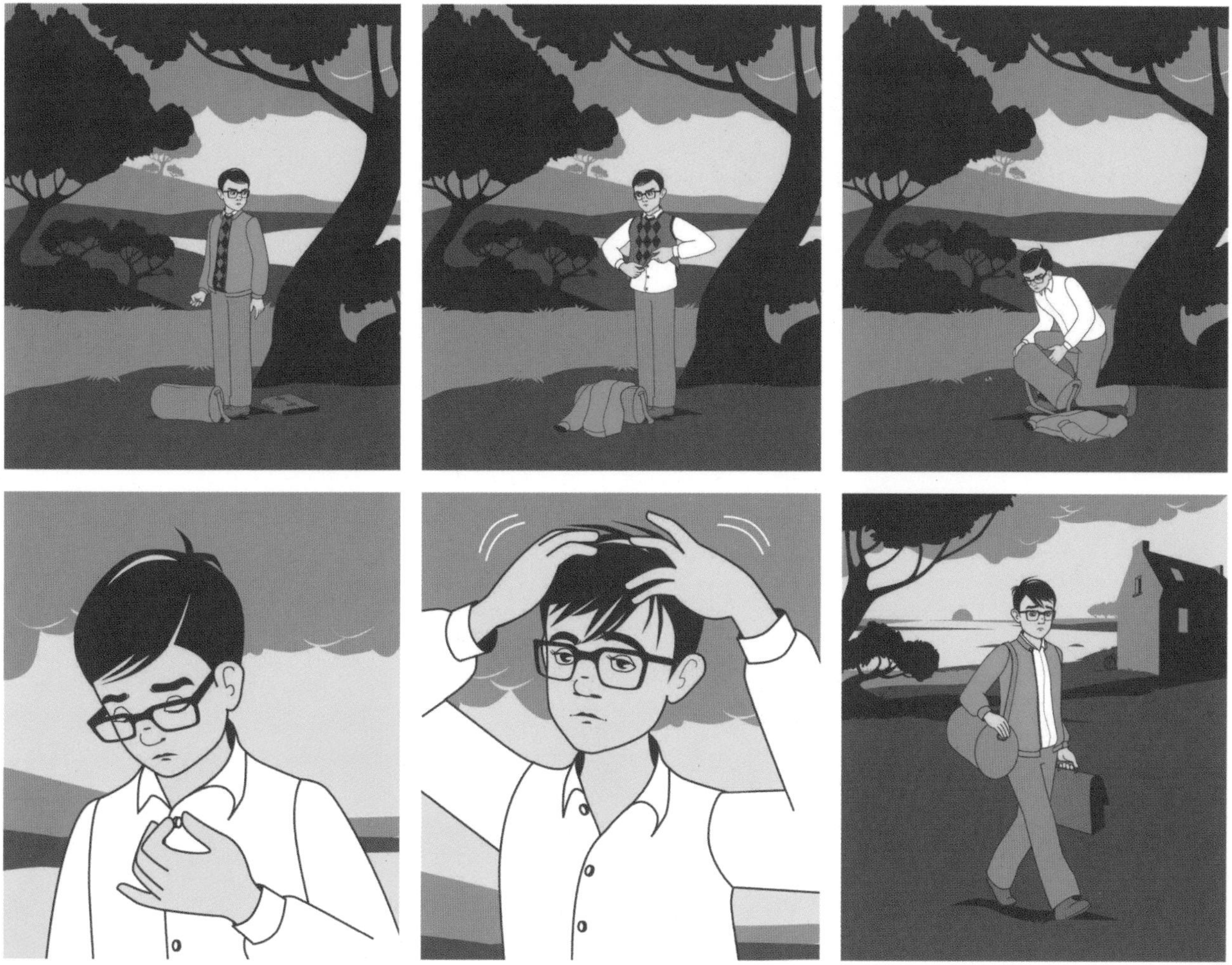

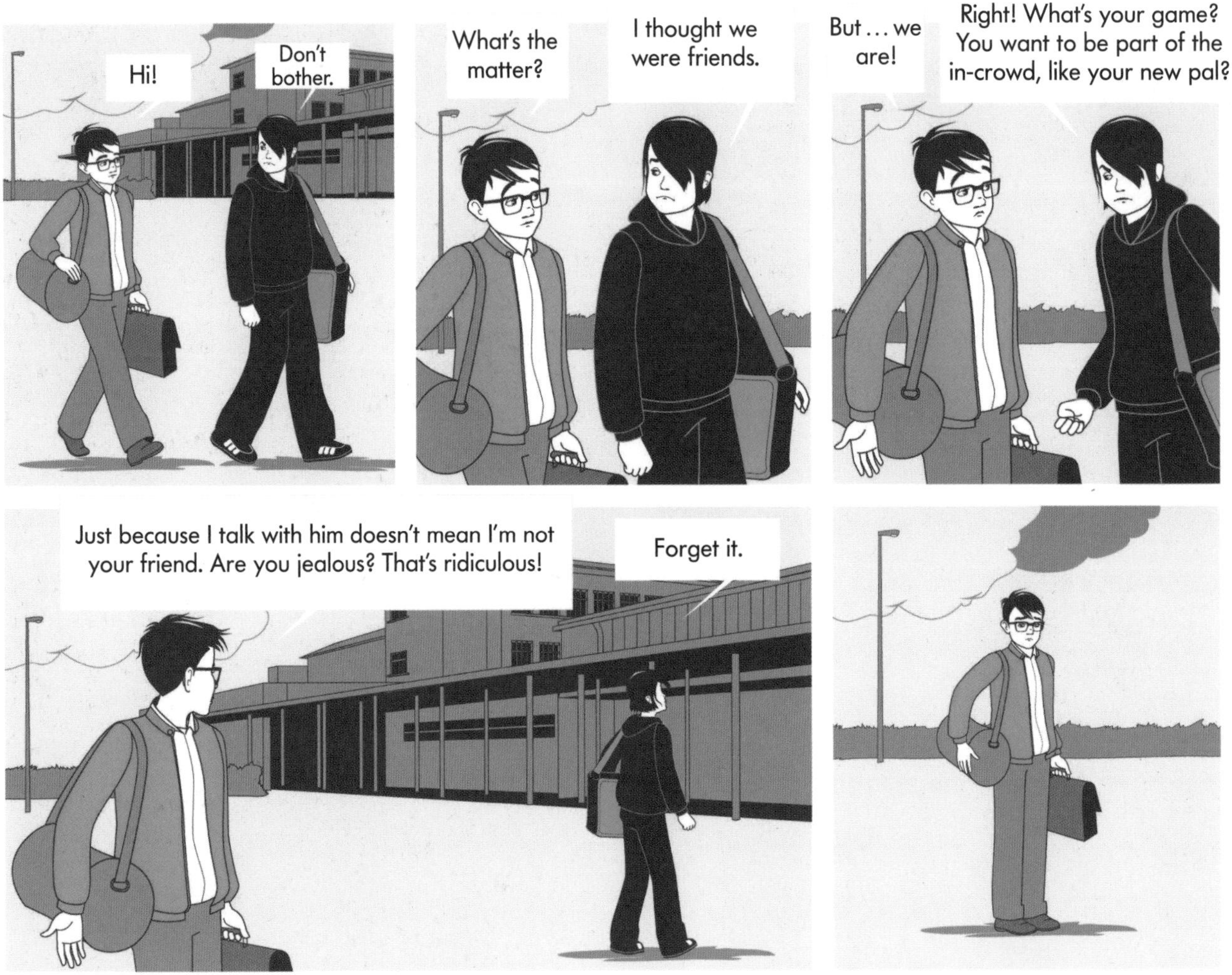
Hi!
Don't bother.
What's the matter?
I thought we were friends.
But... we are!
Right! What's your game? You want to be part of the in-crowd, like your new pal?
Just because I talk with him doesn't mean I'm not your friend. Are you jealous? That's ridiculous!
Forget it.

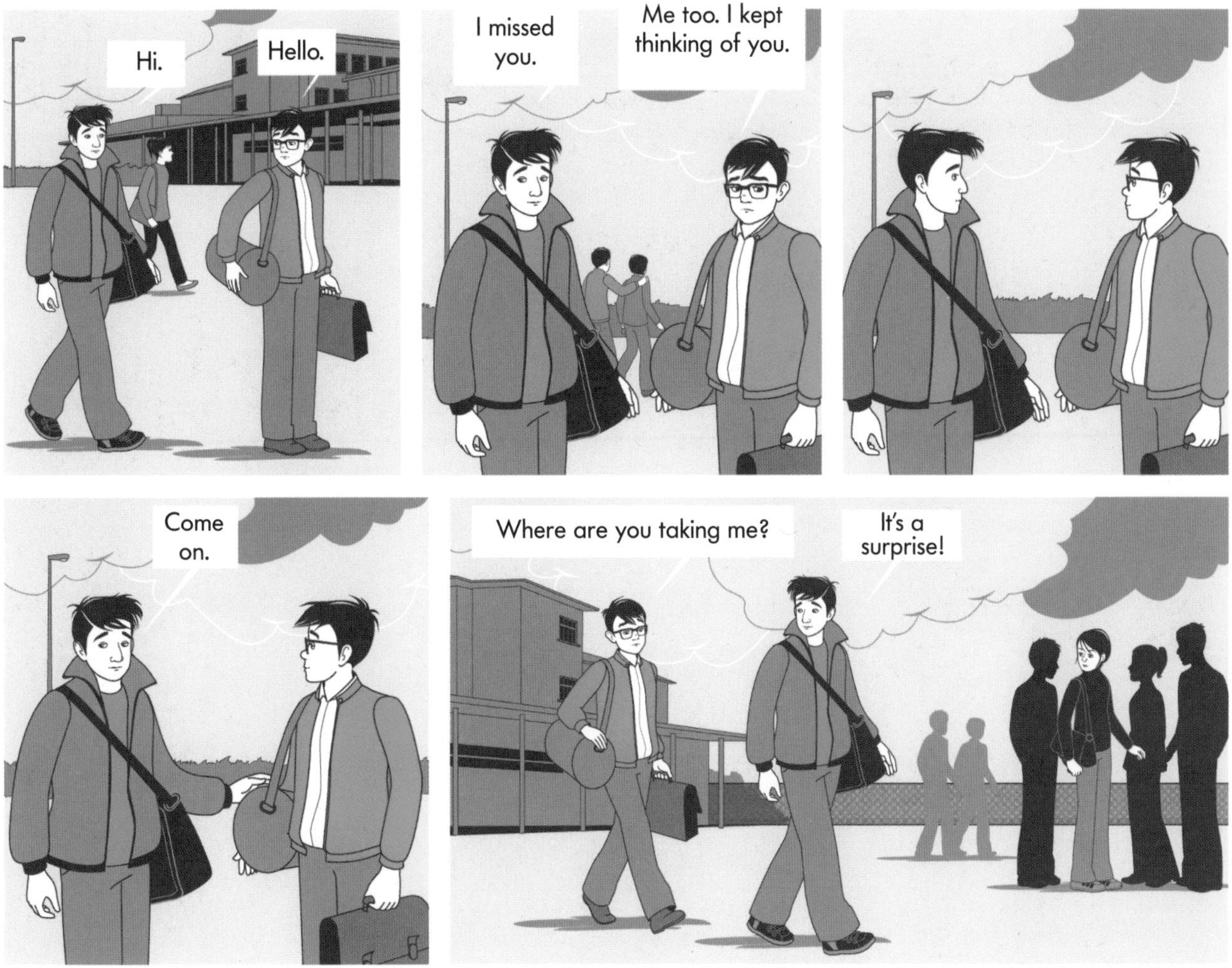
Hi.
Hello.
I missed you.
Me too. I kept thinking of you.
Come on.
Where are you taking me?
It's a surprise!

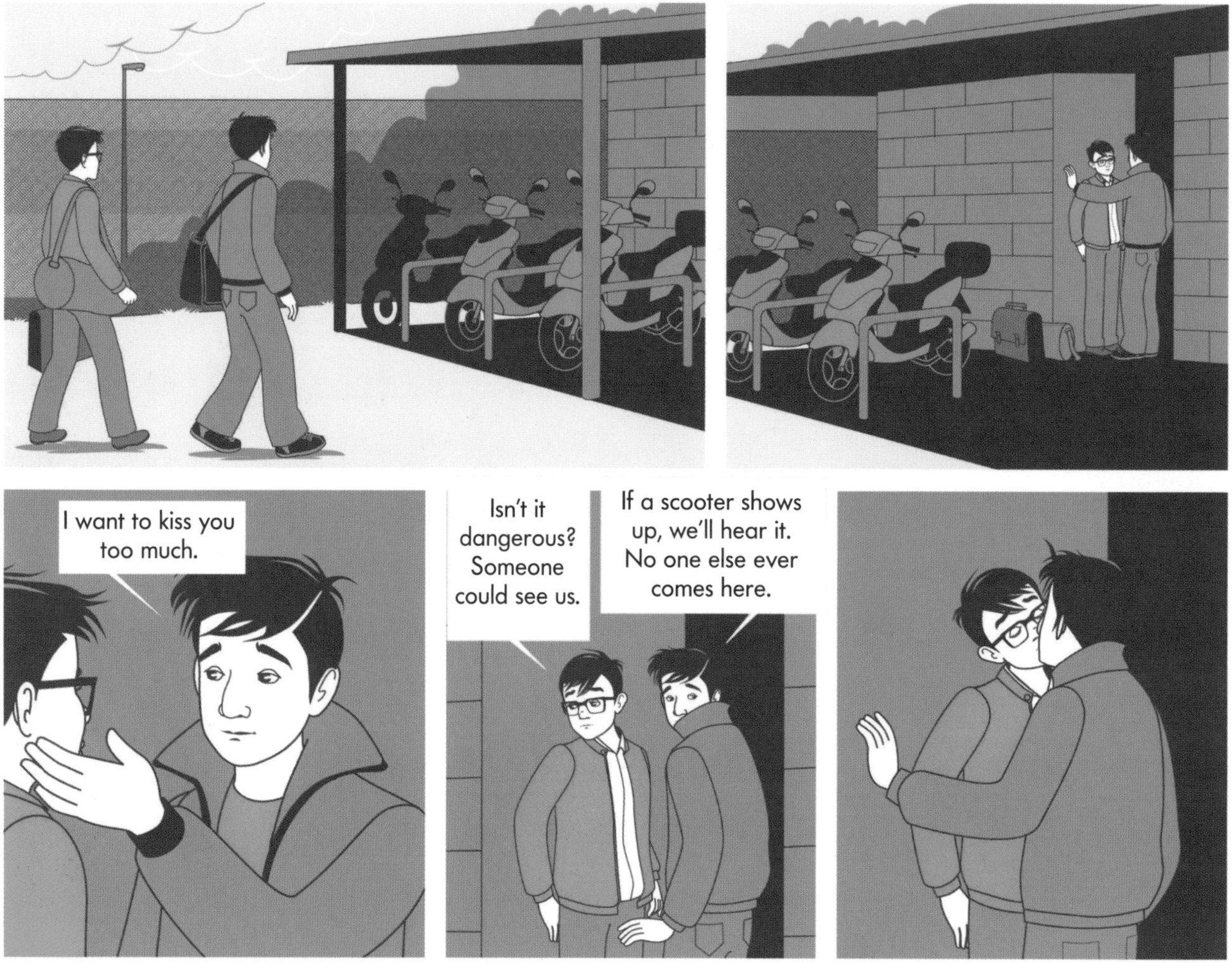
I want to kiss you too much.
Isn't it dangerous? Someone could see us.
If a scooter shows up, we'll hear it. No one else ever comes here.

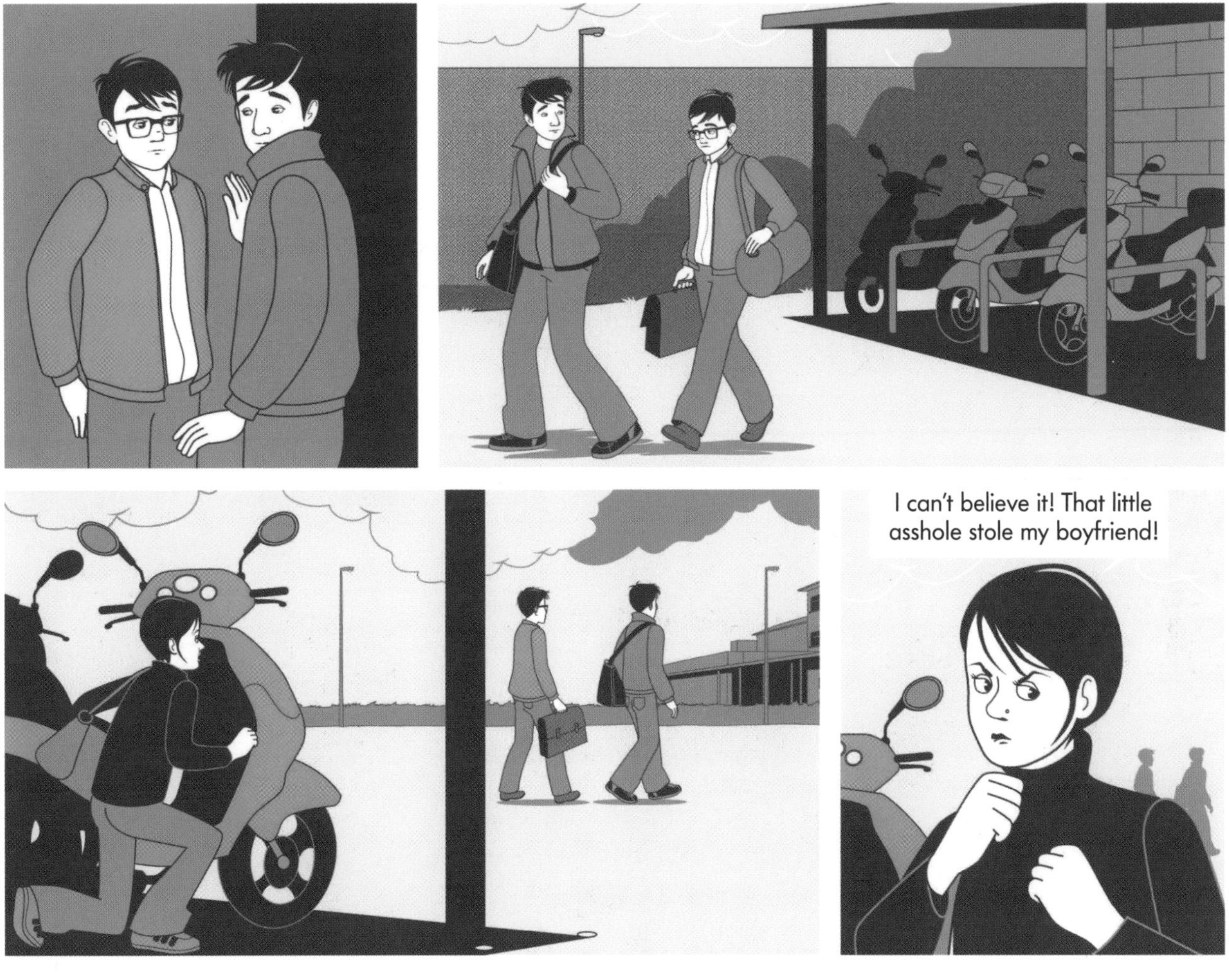
I can't believe it! That little asshole stole my boyfriend!

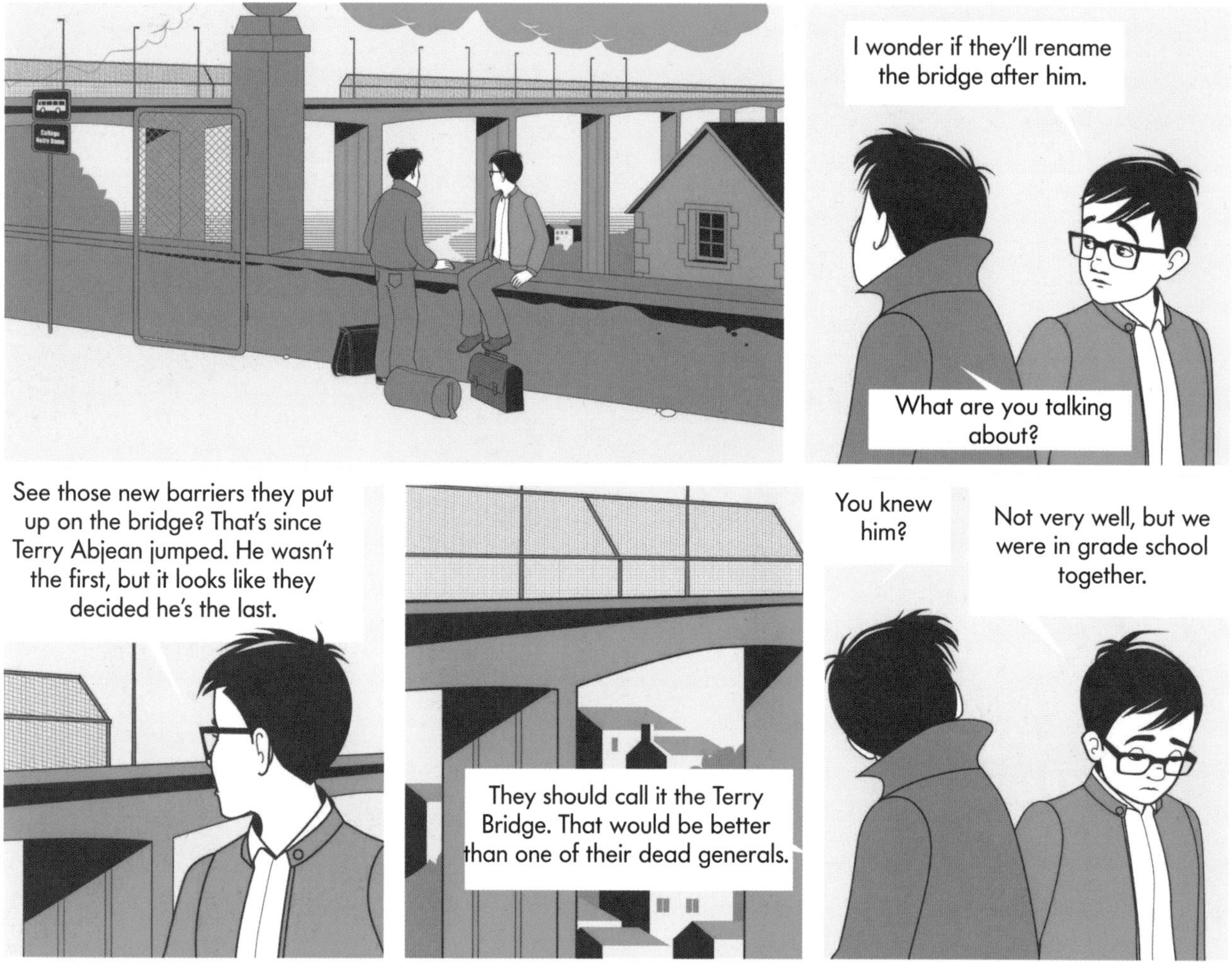
I wonder if they'll rename the bridge after him.
What are you talking about?
See those new barriers they put up on the bridge? That's since Terry Abjean jumped. He wasn't the first, but it looks like they decided he's the last.
They should call it the Terry Bridge. That would be better than one of their dead generals.
You knew him?
Not very well, but we were in grade school together.

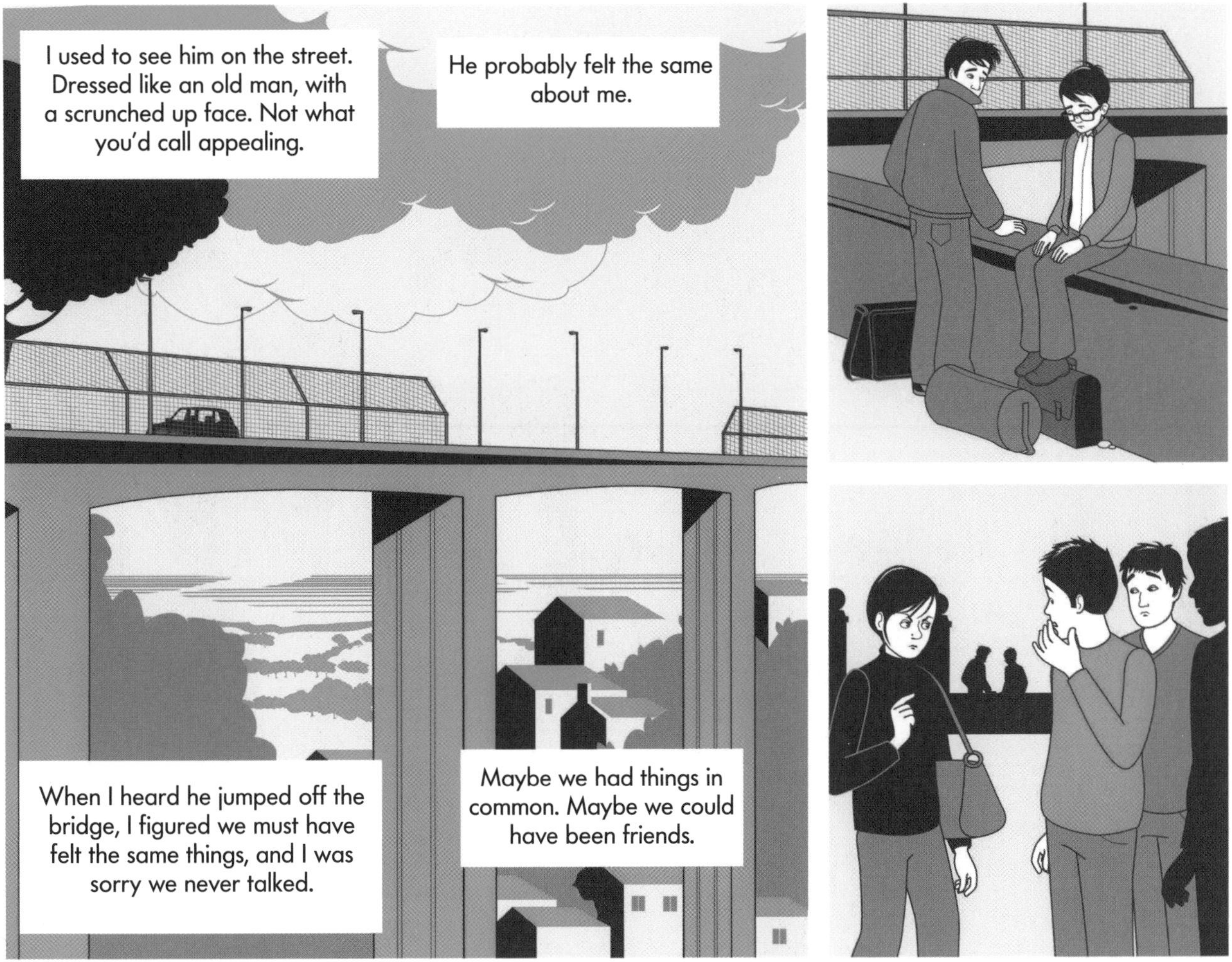
I used to see him on the street. Dressed like an old man, with a scrunched up face. Not what you'd call appealing.
He probably felt the same about me.
When I heard he jumped off the bridge, I figured we must have felt the same things, and I was sorry we never talked.
Maybe we had things in common. Maybe we could have been friends.

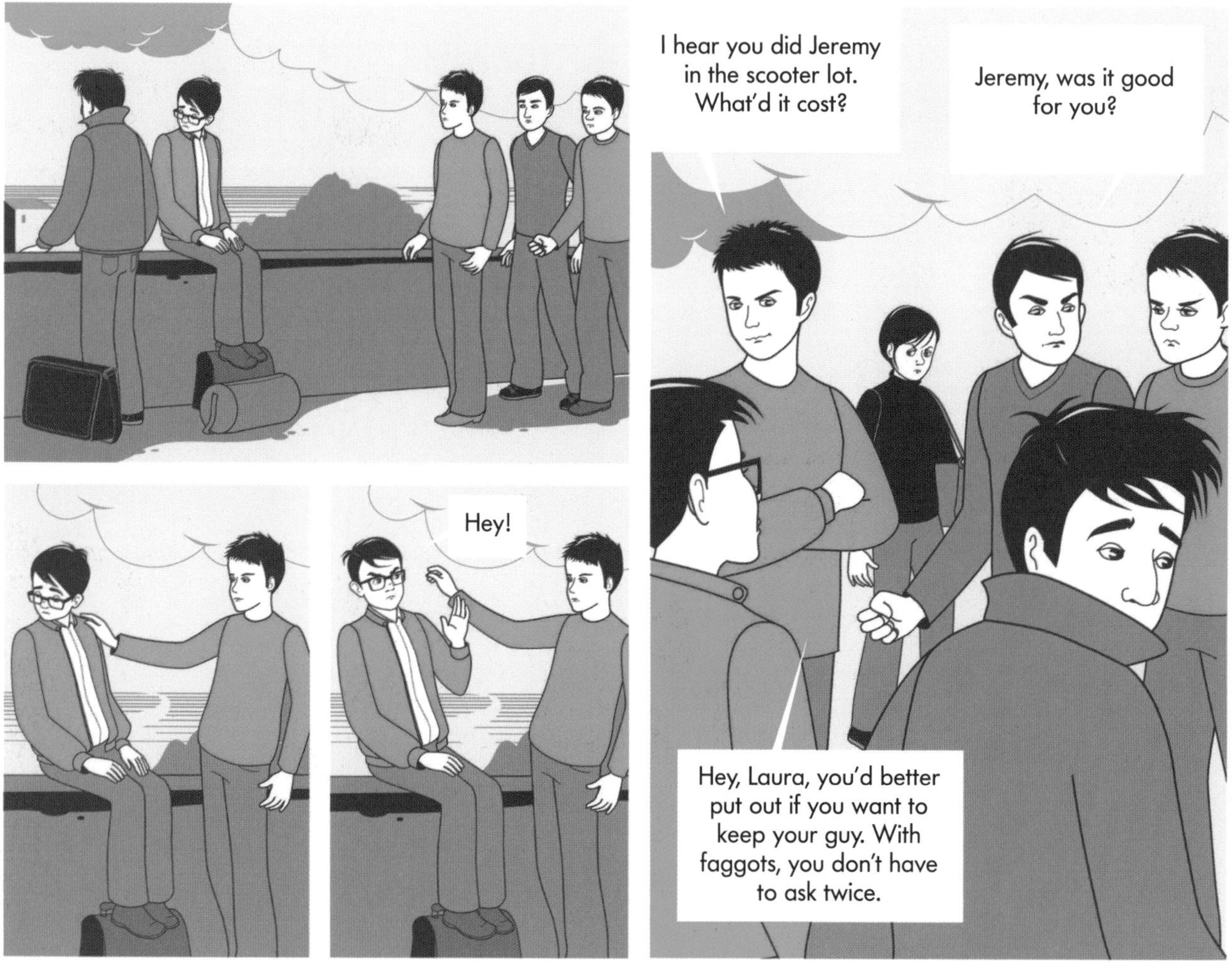
Hey!
I hear you did Jeremy in the scooter lot. What'd it cost?
Jeremy, was it good for you?
Hey, Laura, you'd better put out if you want to keep your guy. With faggots, you don't have to ask twice.

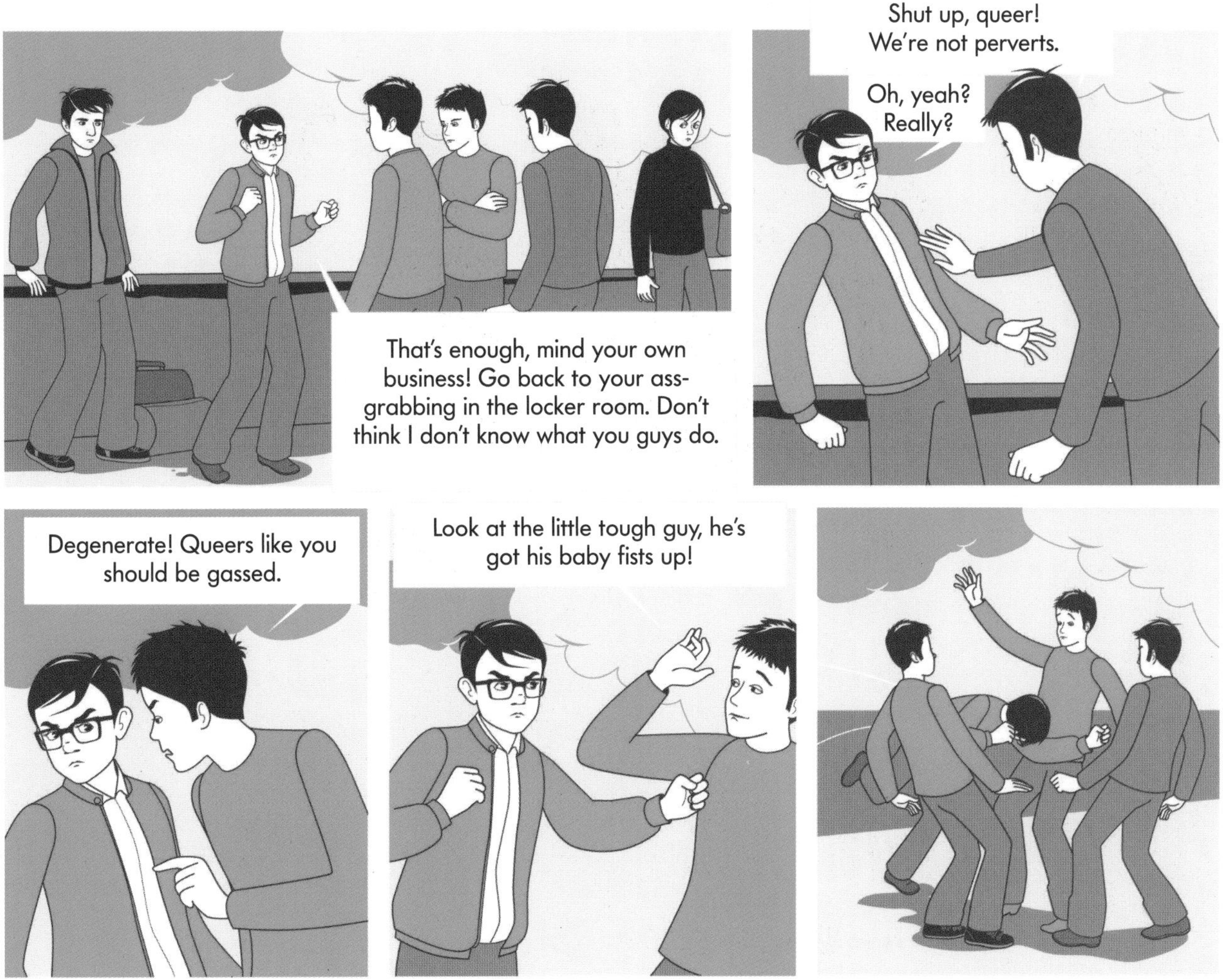
That's enough, mind your own business! Go back to your ass-grabbing in the locker room. Don't think I don't know what you guys do.
Shut up, queer! We're not perverts.
Oh, yeah? Really?
Degenerate! Queers like you should be gassed.
Look at the little tough guy, he's got his baby fists up!

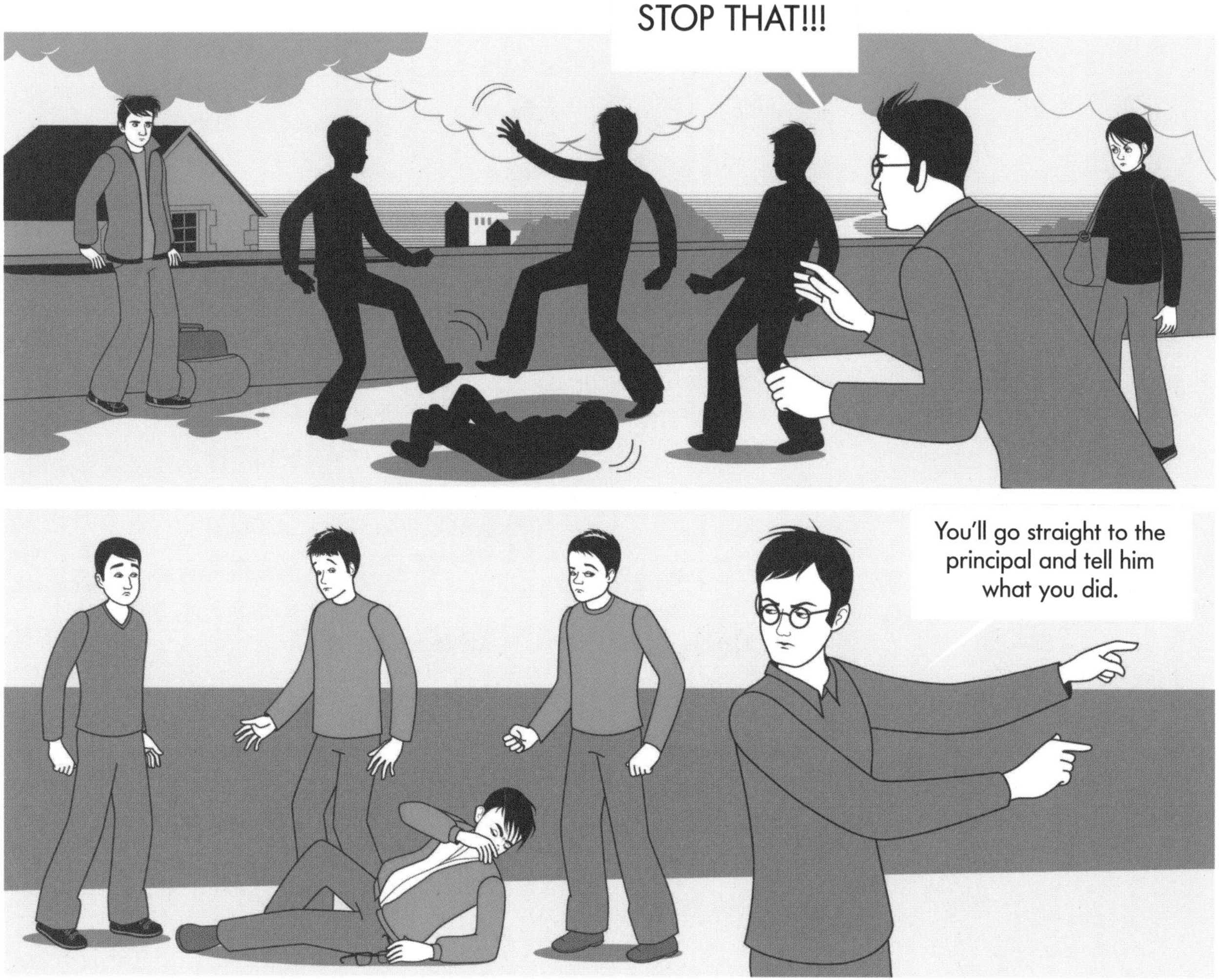
STOP THAT!!!
You'll go straight to the principal and tell him what you did.

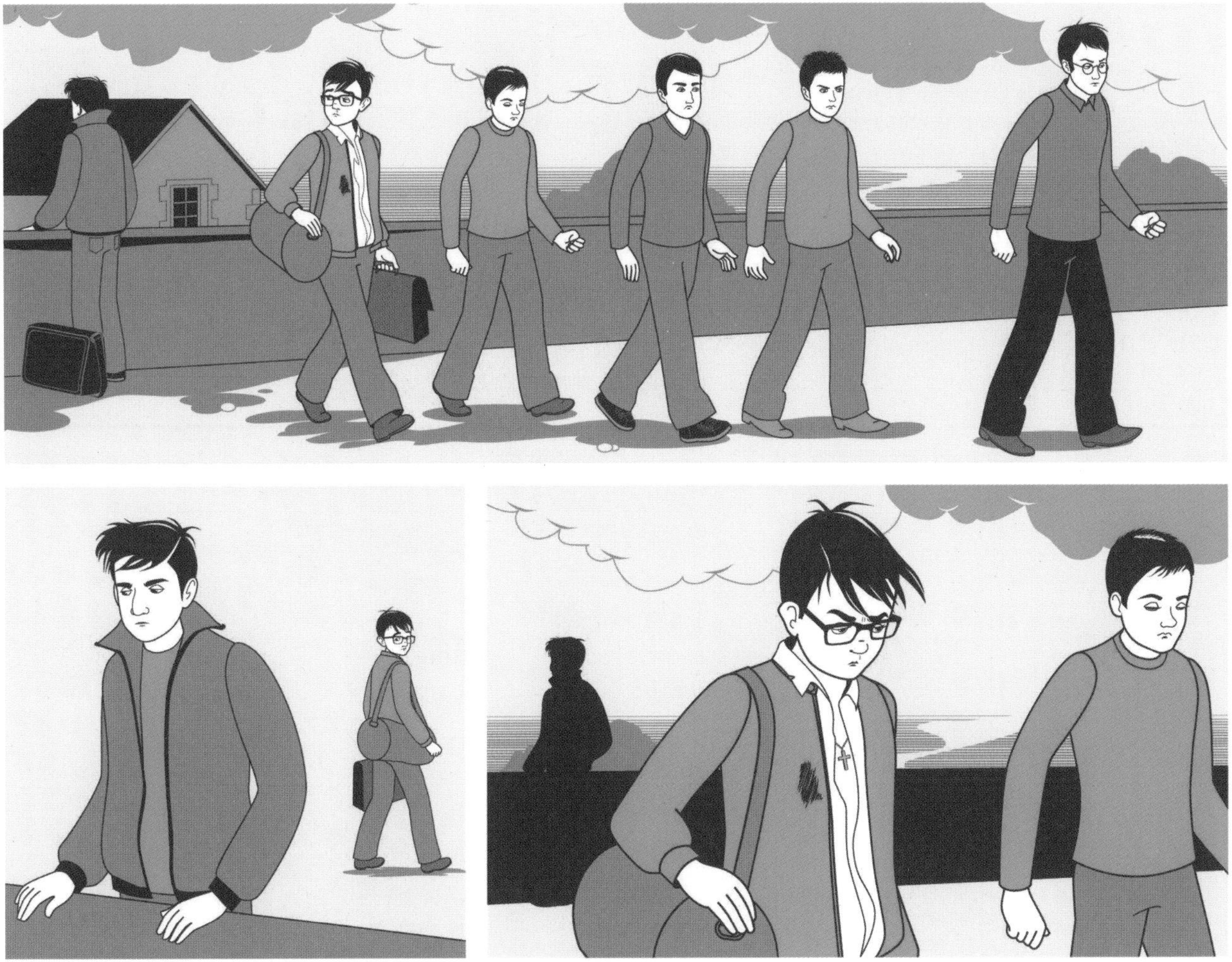

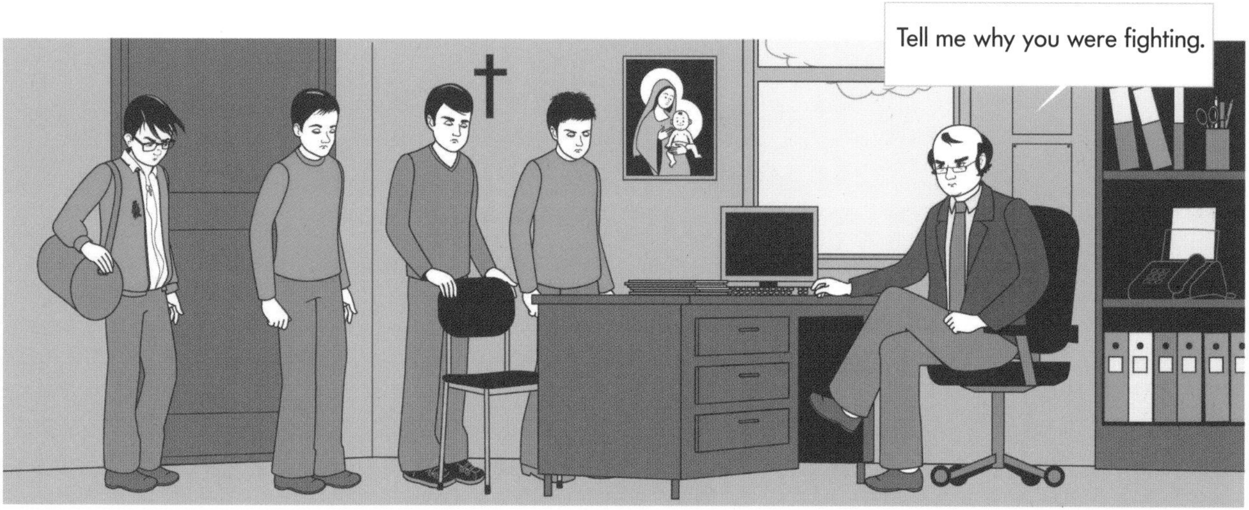
Tell me why you were fighting.

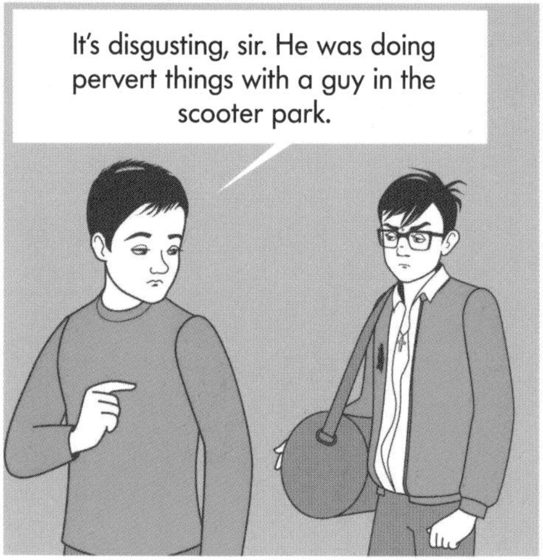
It's disgusting, sir. He was doing pervert things with a guy in the scooter park.

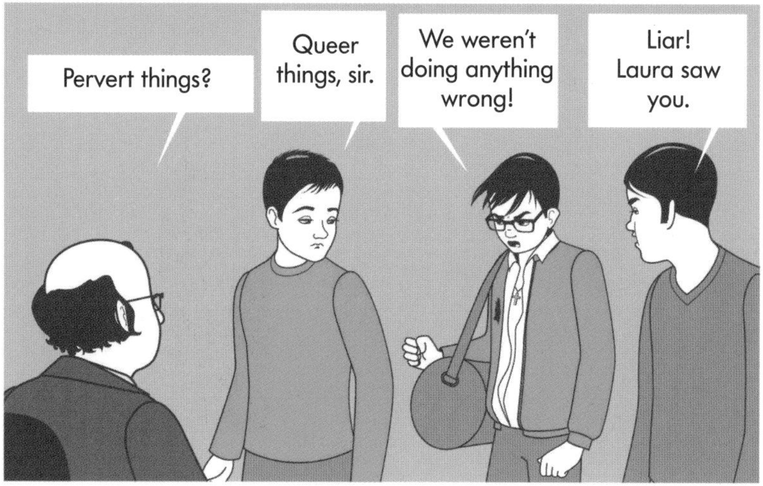
Pervert things?
Queer things, sir.
We weren't doing anything wrong!
Liar! Laura saw you.

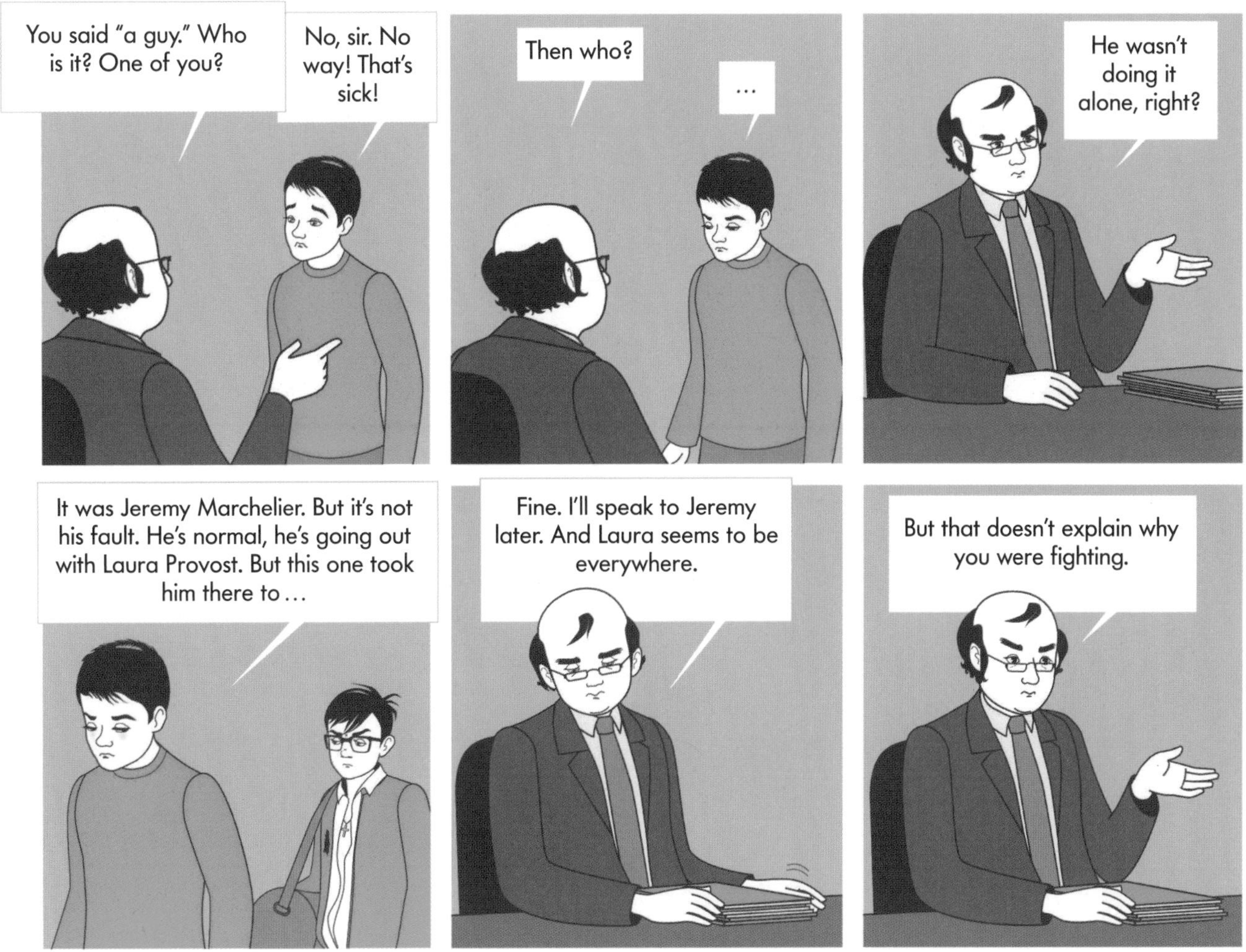
You said "a guy." Who is it? One of you?
No, sir. No way! That's sick!
Then who?
...
He wasn't doing it alone, right?
It was Jeremy Marchelier. But it's not his fault. He's normal, he's going out with Laura Provost. But this one took him there to ...
Fine. I'll speak to Jeremy later. And Laura seems to be everywhere.
But that doesn't explain why you were fighting.

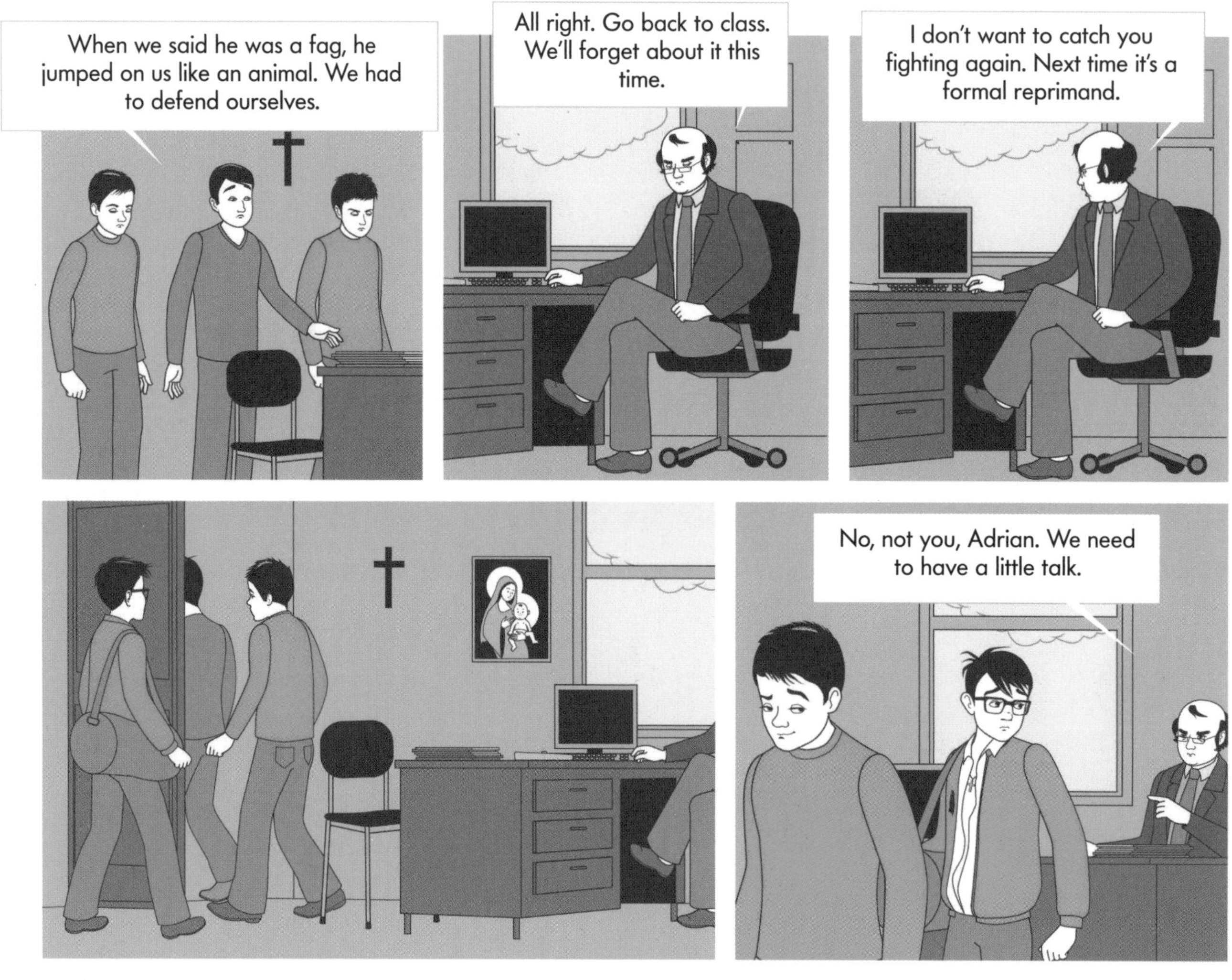
When we said he was a fag, he jumped on us like an animal. We had to defend ourselves.
All right. Go back to class. We'll forget about it this time.
I don't want to catch you fighting again. Next time it's a formal reprimand.
No, not you, Adrian. We need to have a little talk.

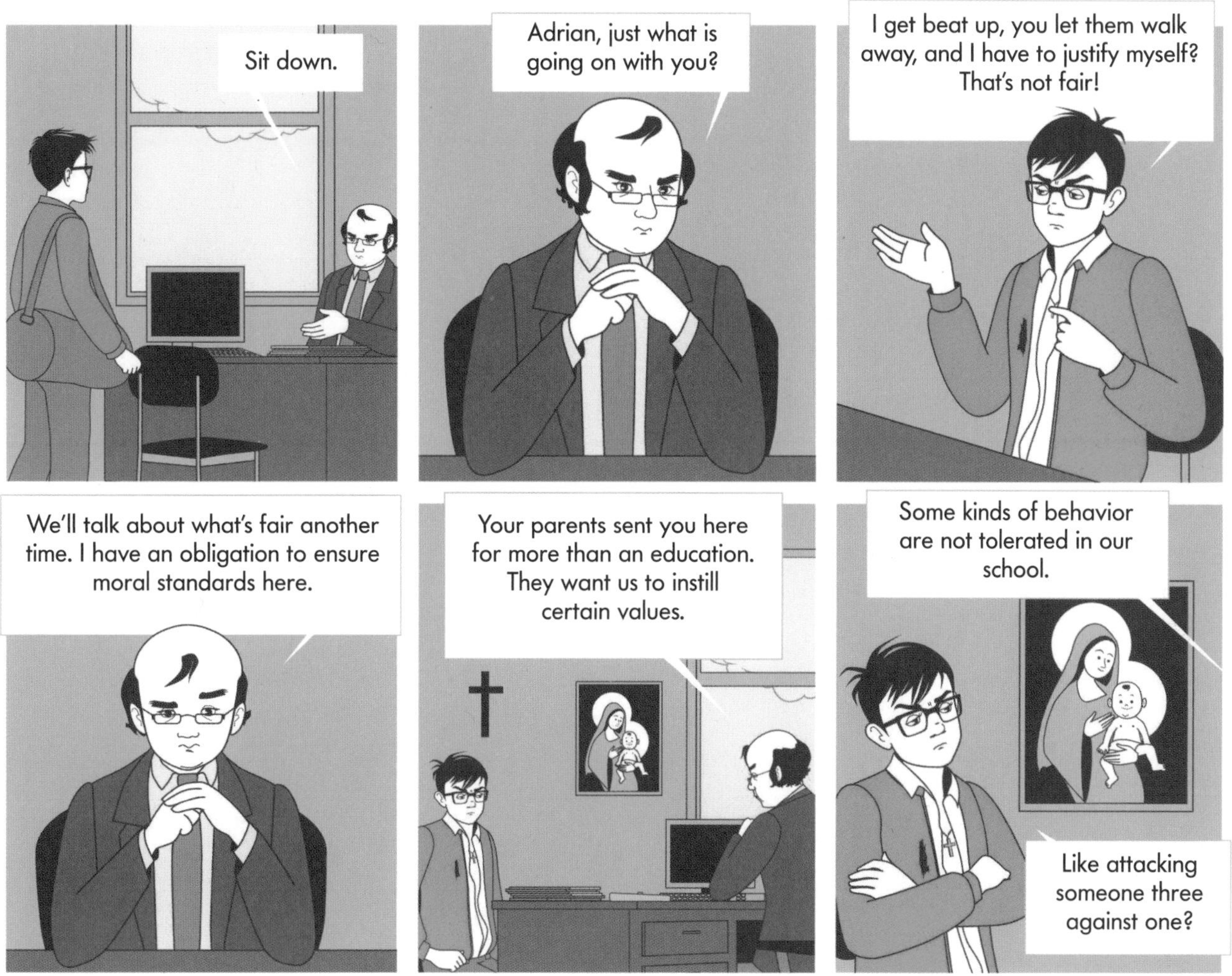
Sit down.
Adrian, just what is going on with you?
I get beat up, you let them walk away, and I have to justify myself? That's not fair!
We'll talk about what's fair another time. I have an obligation to ensure moral standards here.
Your parents sent you here for more than an education. They want us to instill certain values.
Some kinds of behavior are not tolerated in our school.
Like attacking someone three against one?

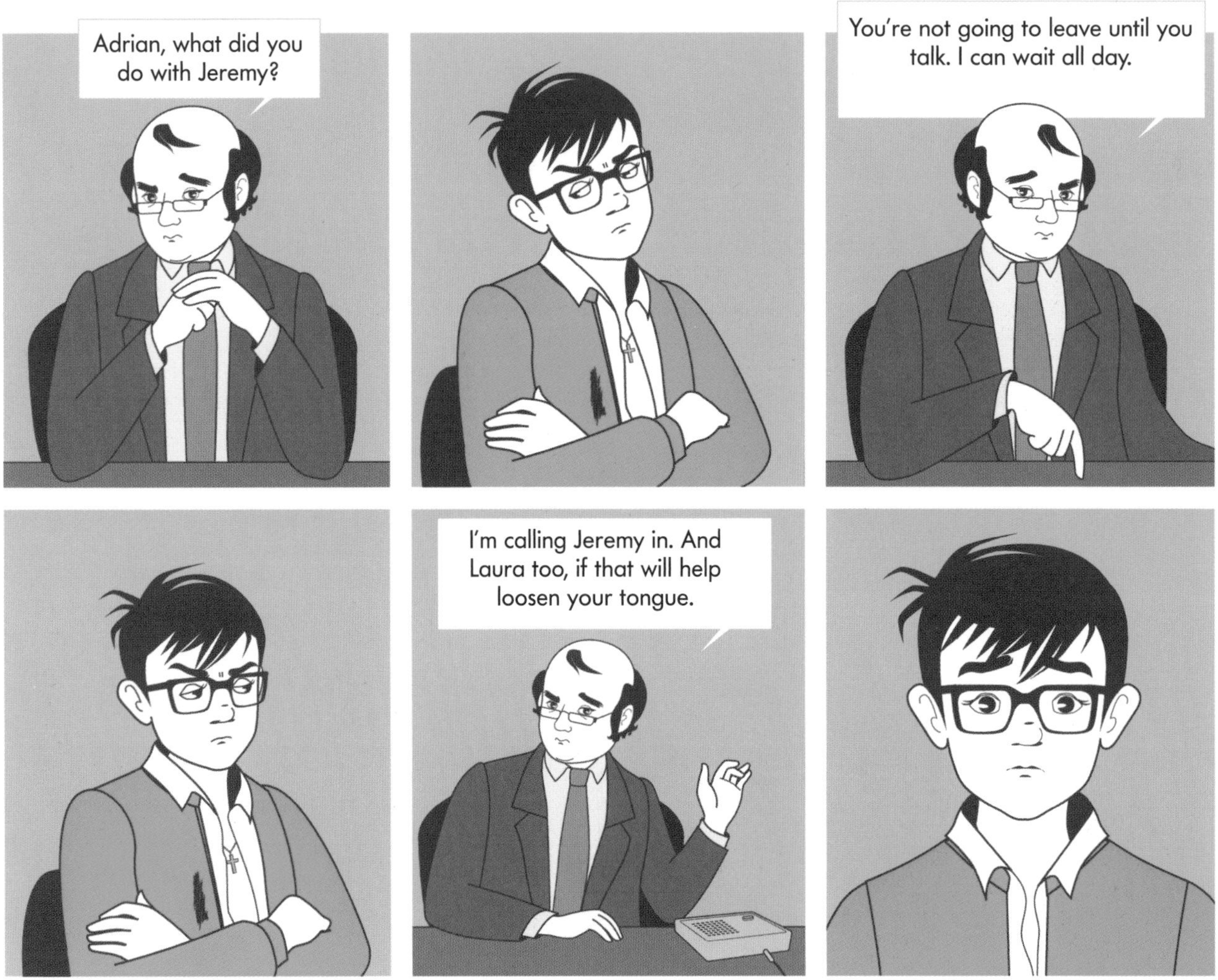
Adrian, what did you do with Jeremy?
You're not going to leave until you talk. I can wait all day.
I'm calling Jeremy in. And Laura too, if that will help loosen your tongue.

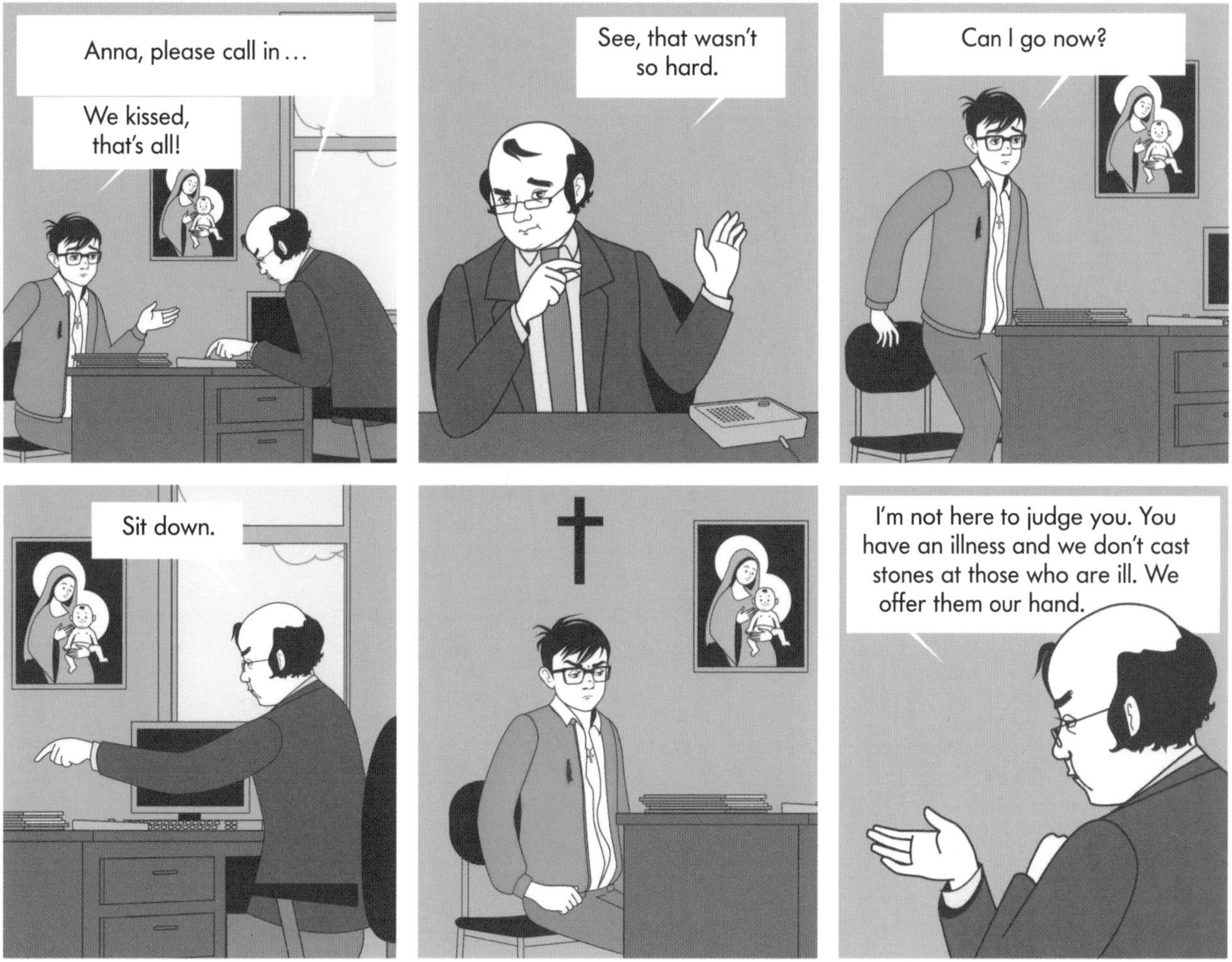
Anna, please call in . . .
We kissed, that's all!
See, that wasn't so hard.
Can I go now?
Sit down.
I'm not here to judge you. You have an illness and we don't cast stones at those who are ill. We offer them our hand.

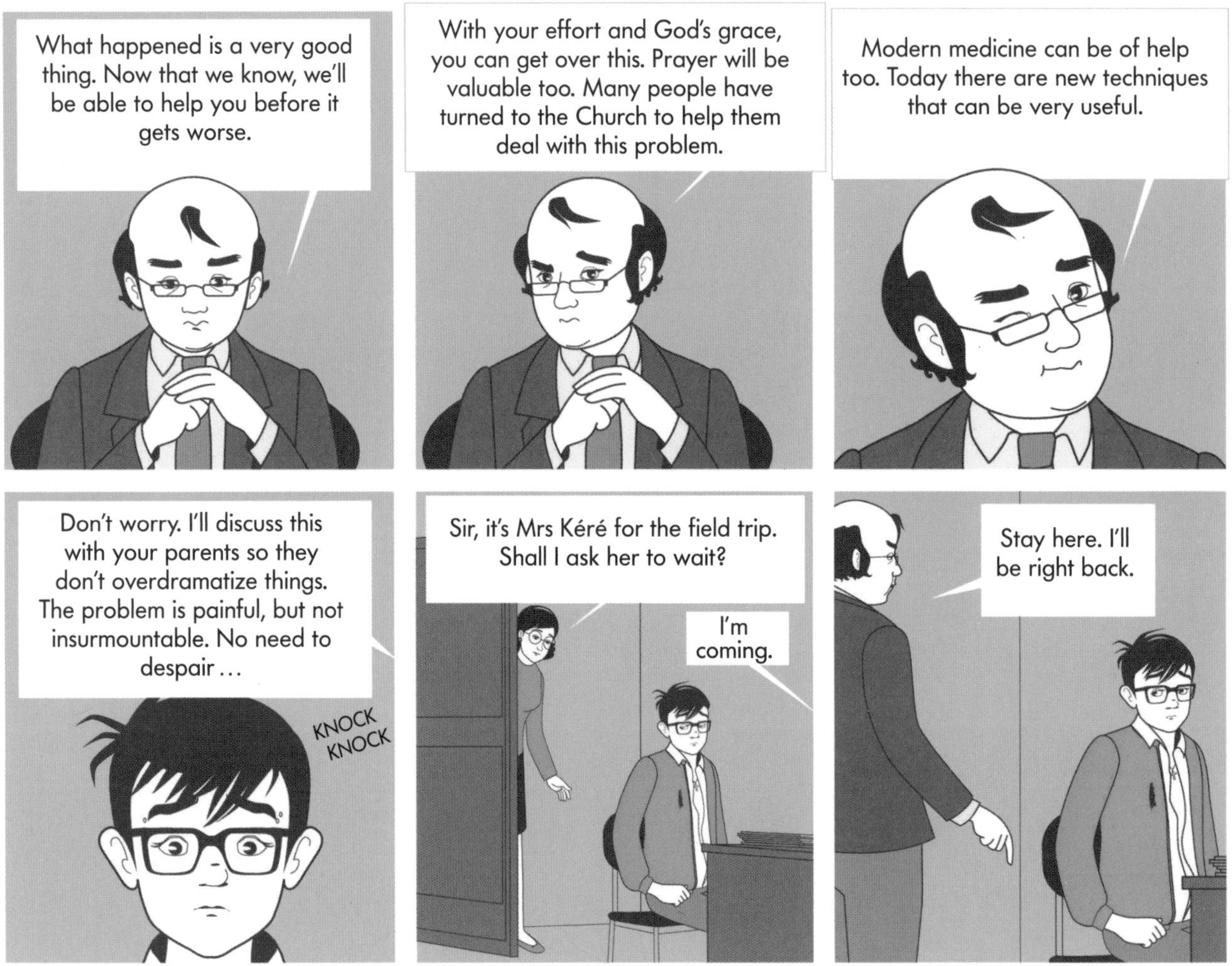
What happened is a very good thing. Now that we know, we'll be able to help you before it gets worse.
With your effort and God's grace, you can get over this. Prayer will be valuable too. Many people have turned to the Church to help them deal with this problem.
Modern medicine can be of help too. Today there are new techniques that can be very useful.
Don't worry. I'll discuss this with your parents so they don't overdramatize things. The problem is painful, but not insurmountable. No need to despair …
KNOCK KNOCK
Sir, it's Mrs Kéré for the field trip. Shall I ask her to wait?
I'm coming.
Stay here. I'll be right back.

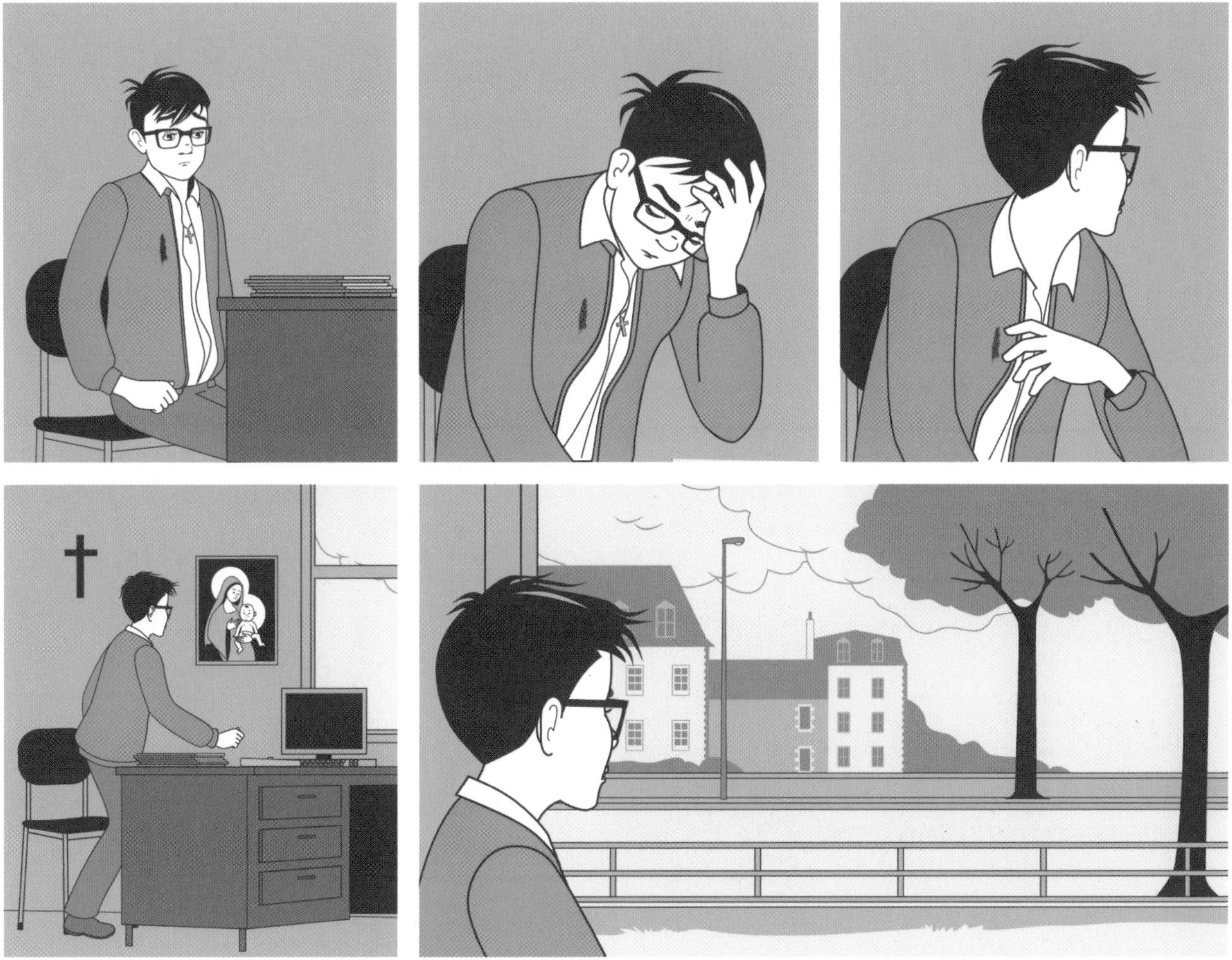

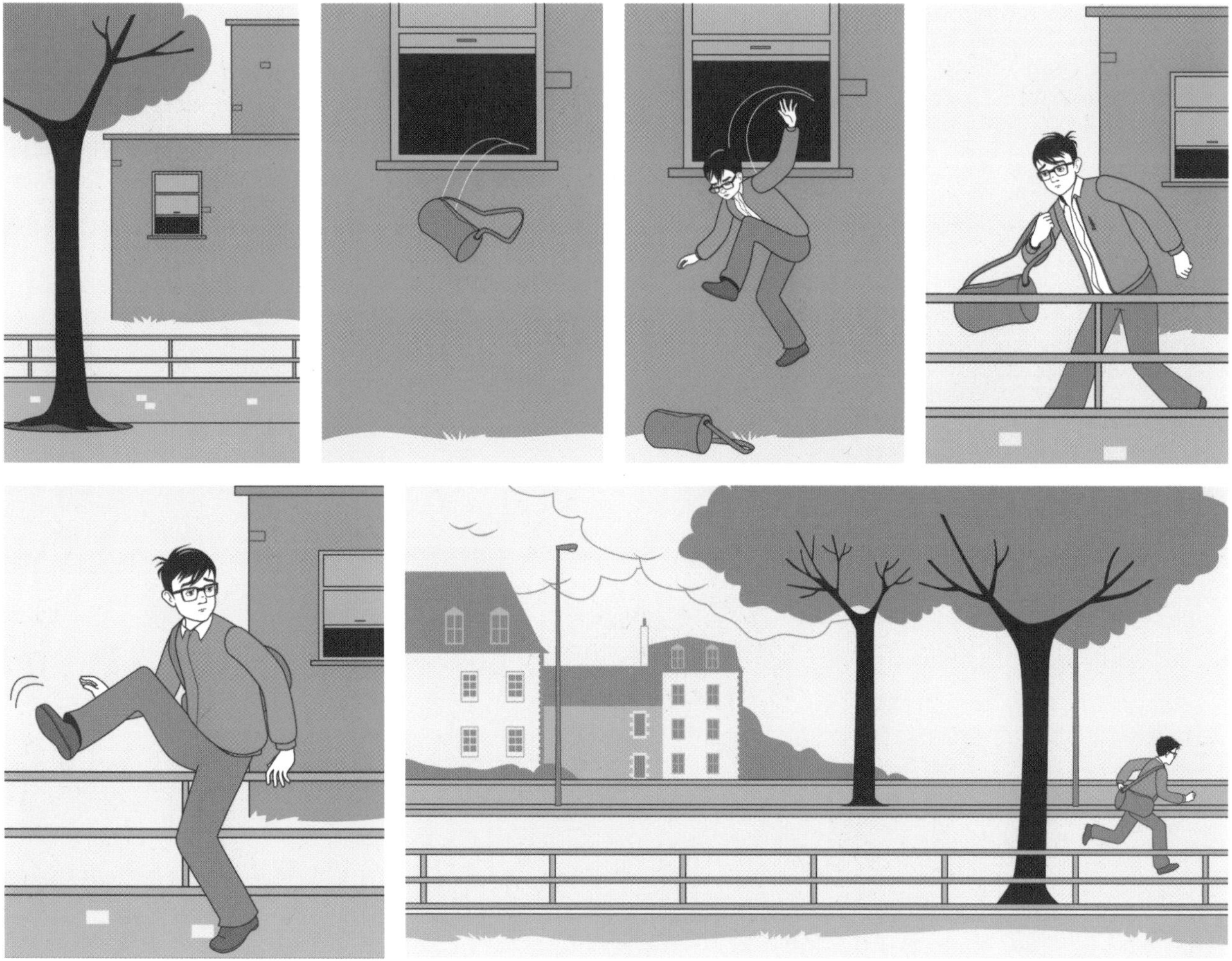

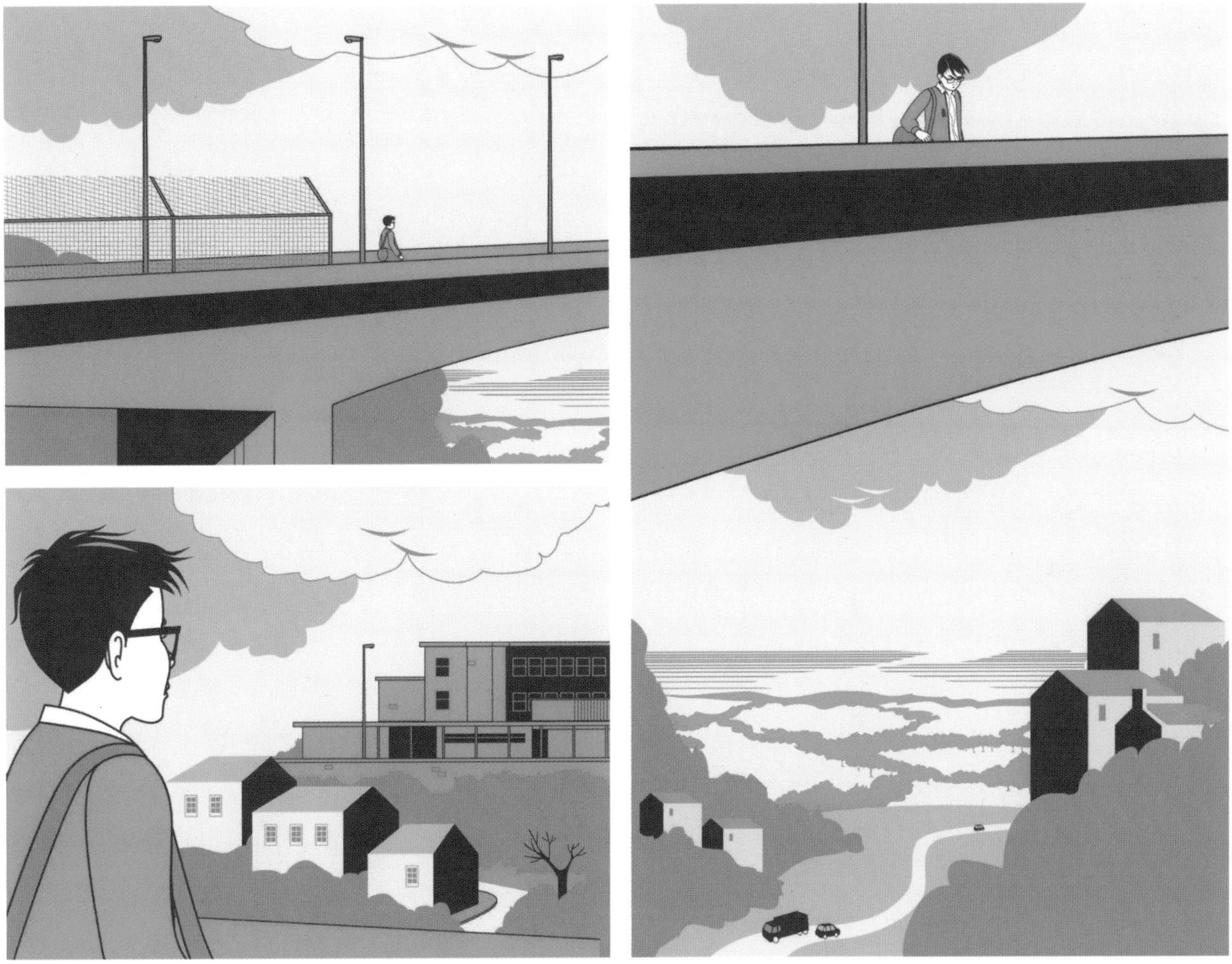

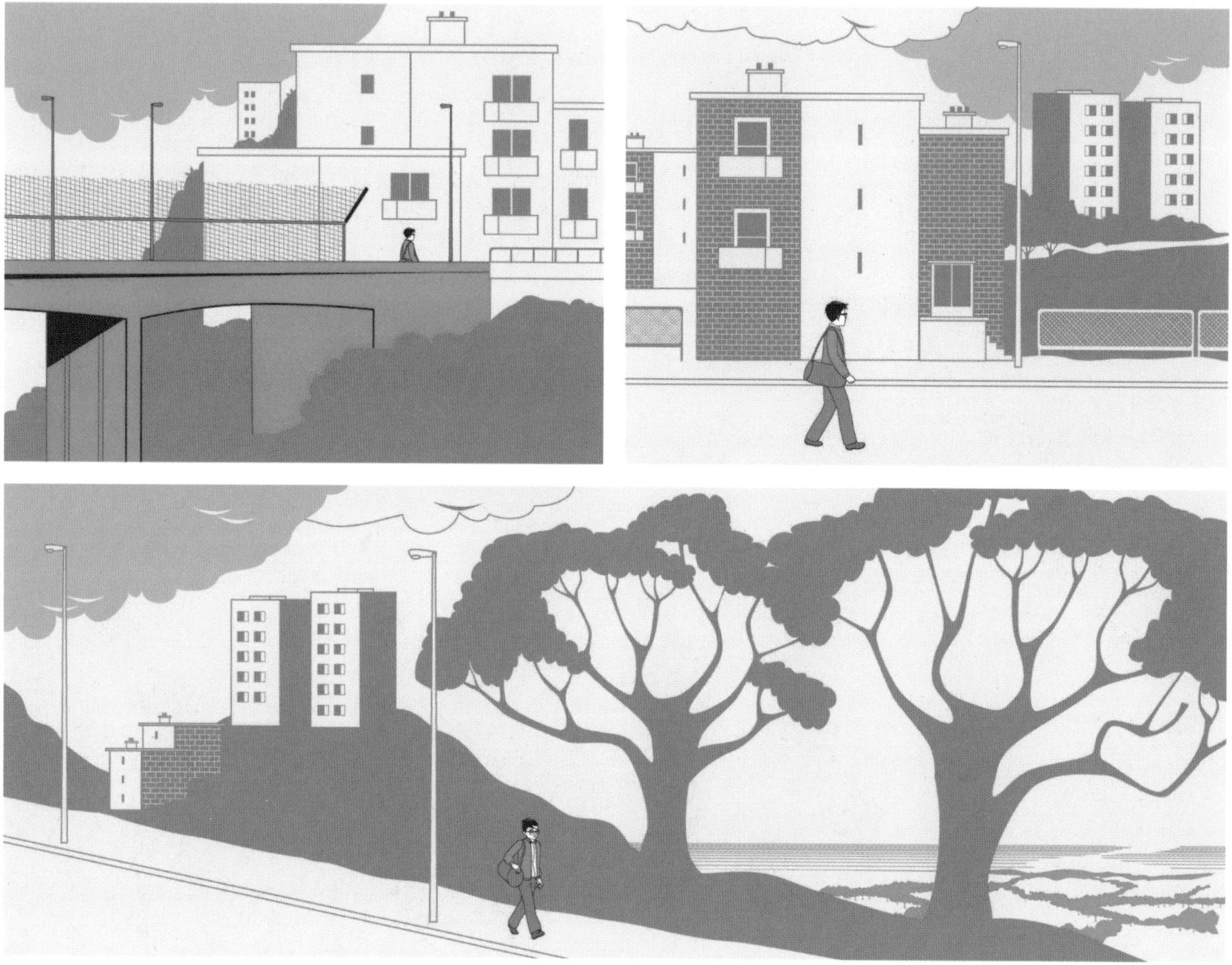

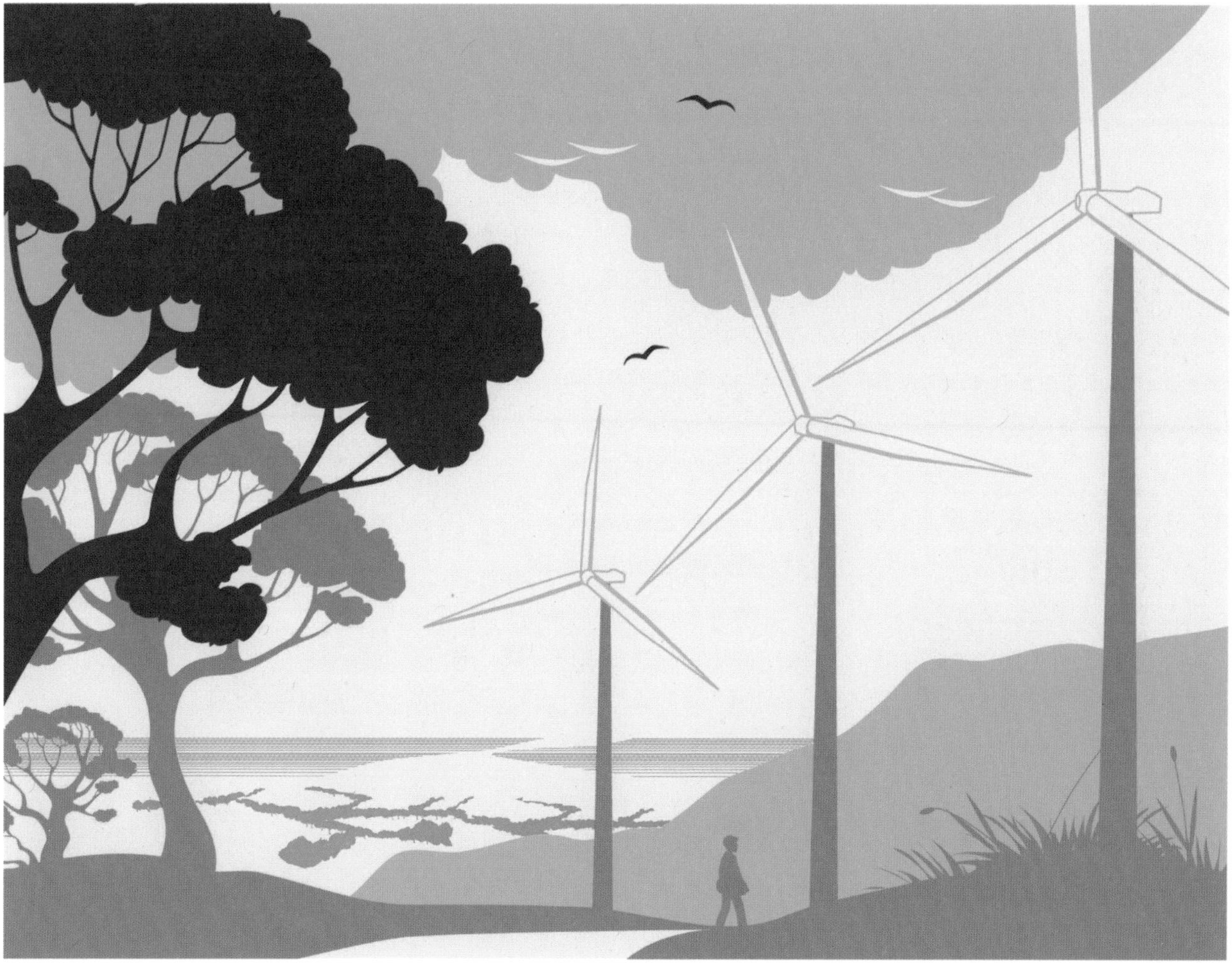

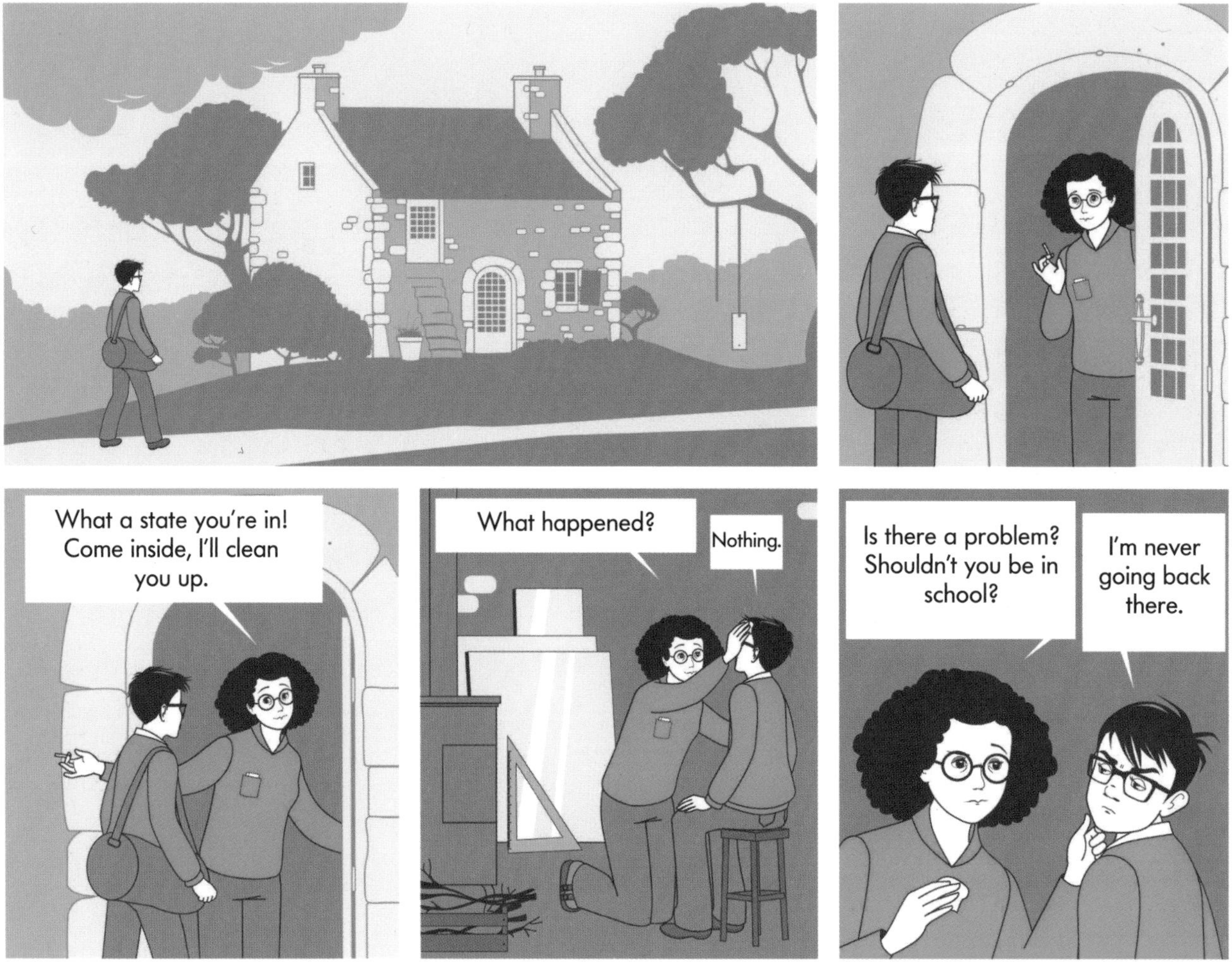
What a state you're in! Come inside, I'll clean you up.
What happened?
Nothing.
Is there a problem? Shouldn't you be in school?
I'm never going back there.

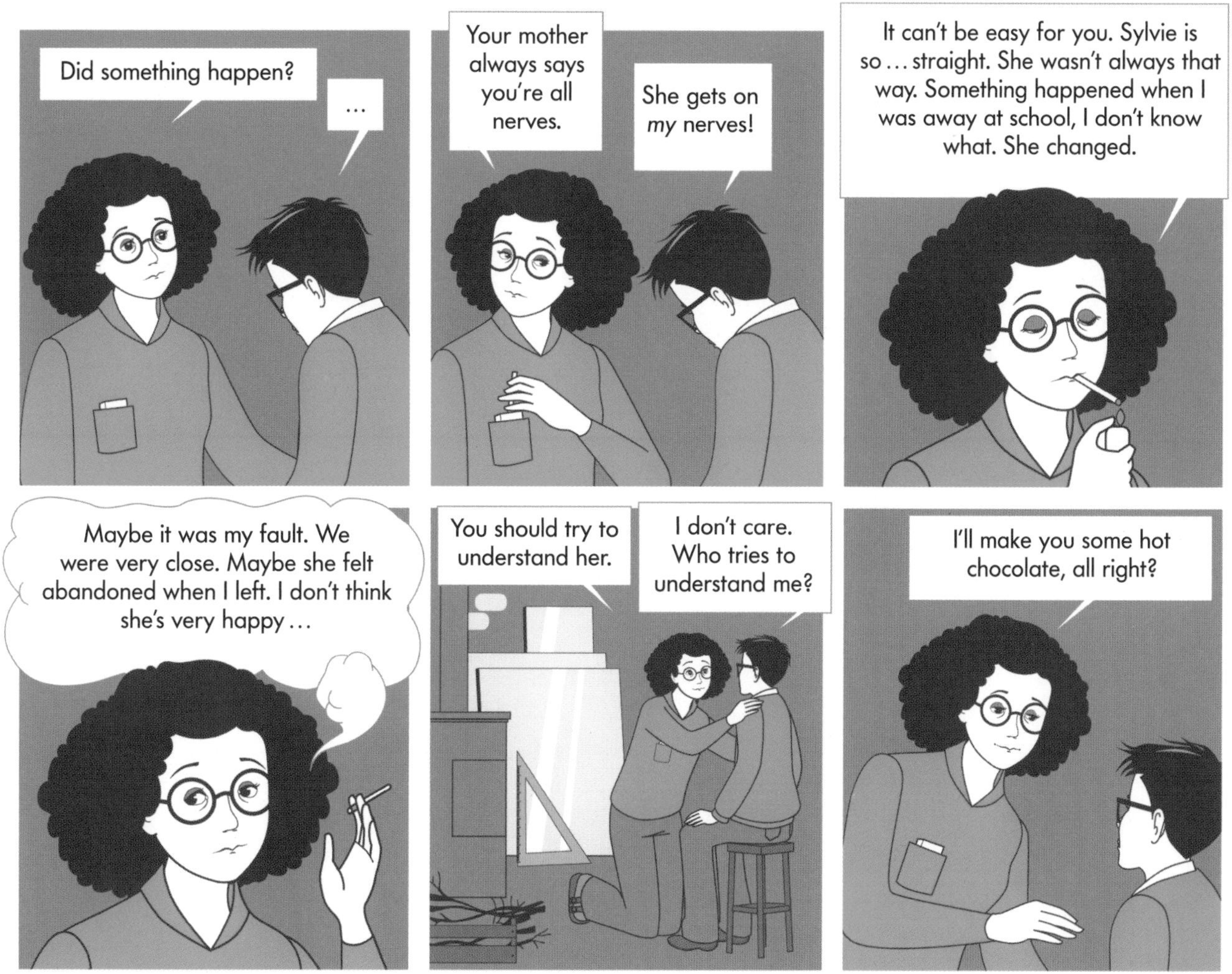
Did something happen?
...
Your mother always says you're all nerves.
She gets on *my* nerves!
It can't be easy for you. Sylvie is so ... straight. She wasn't always that way. Something happened when I was away at school, I don't know what. She changed.
Maybe it was my fault. We were very close. Maybe she felt abandoned when I left. I don't think she's very happy ...
You should try to understand her.
I don't care. Who tries to understand me?
I'll make you some hot chocolate, all right?

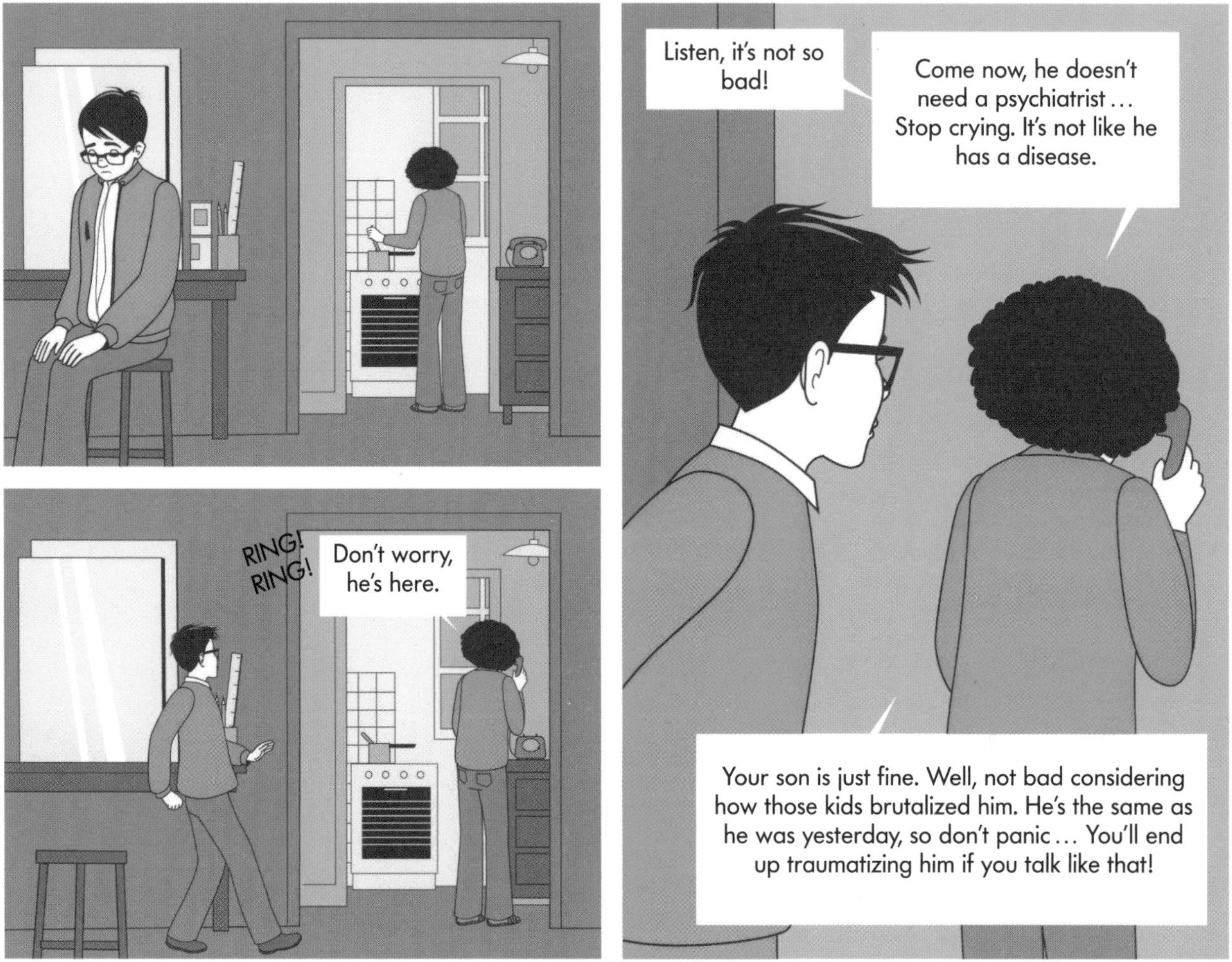

RING! RING!
Don't worry, he's here.
Listen, it's not so bad!
Come now, he doesn't need a psychiatrist... Stop crying. It's not like he has a disease.
Your son is just fine. Well, not bad considering how those kids brutalized him. He's the same as he was yesterday, so don't panic... You'll end up traumatizing him if you talk like that!

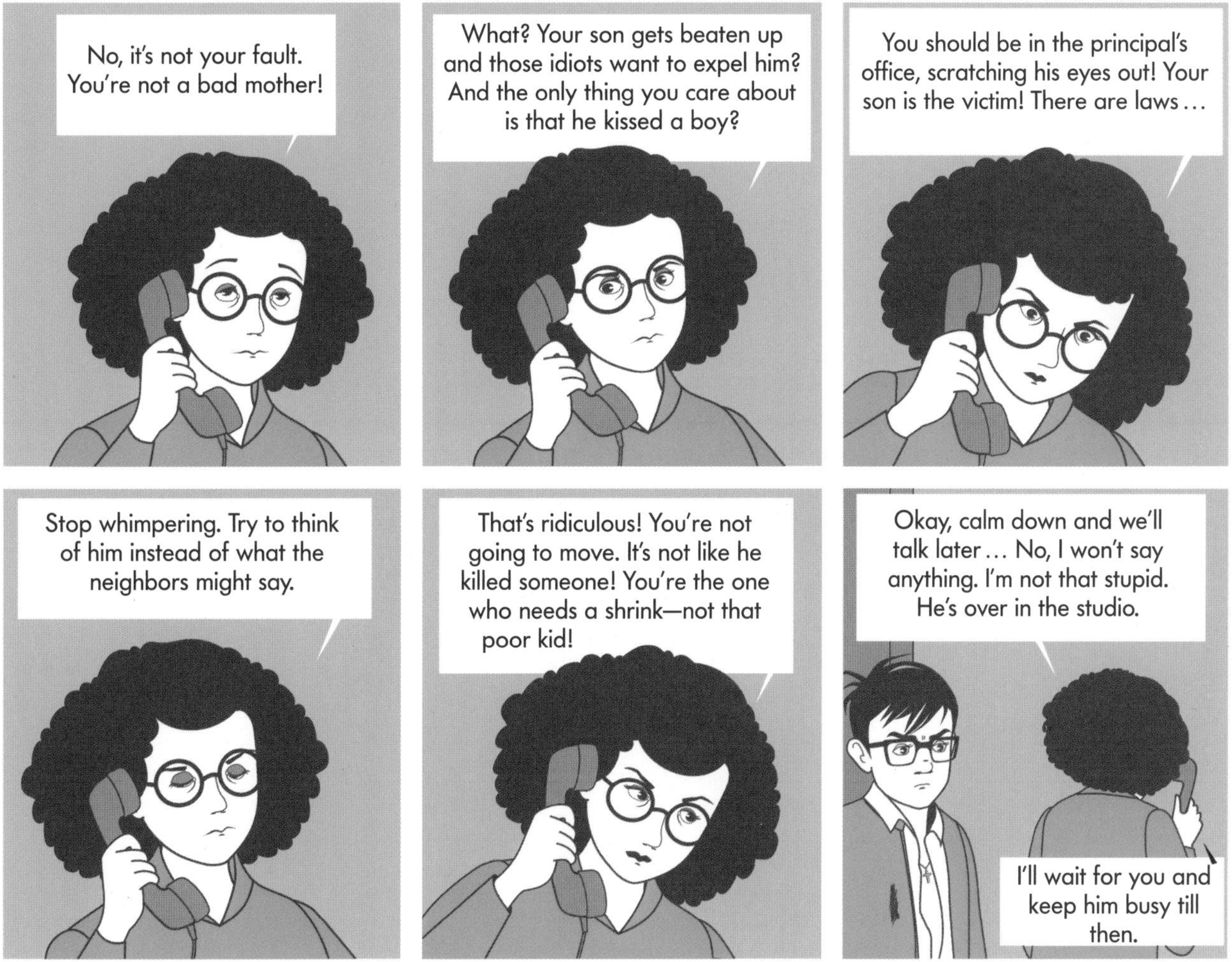
No, it's not your fault. You're not a bad mother!
What? Your son gets beaten up and those idiots want to expel him? And the only thing you care about is that he kissed a boy?
You should be in the principal's office, scratching his eyes out! Your son is the victim! There are laws…
Stop whimpering. Try to think of him instead of what the neighbors might say.
That's ridiculous! You're not going to move. It's not like he killed someone! You're the one who needs a shrink—not that poor kid!
Okay, calm down and we'll talk later… No, I won't say anything. I'm not that stupid. He's over in the studio.
I'll wait for you and keep him busy till then.

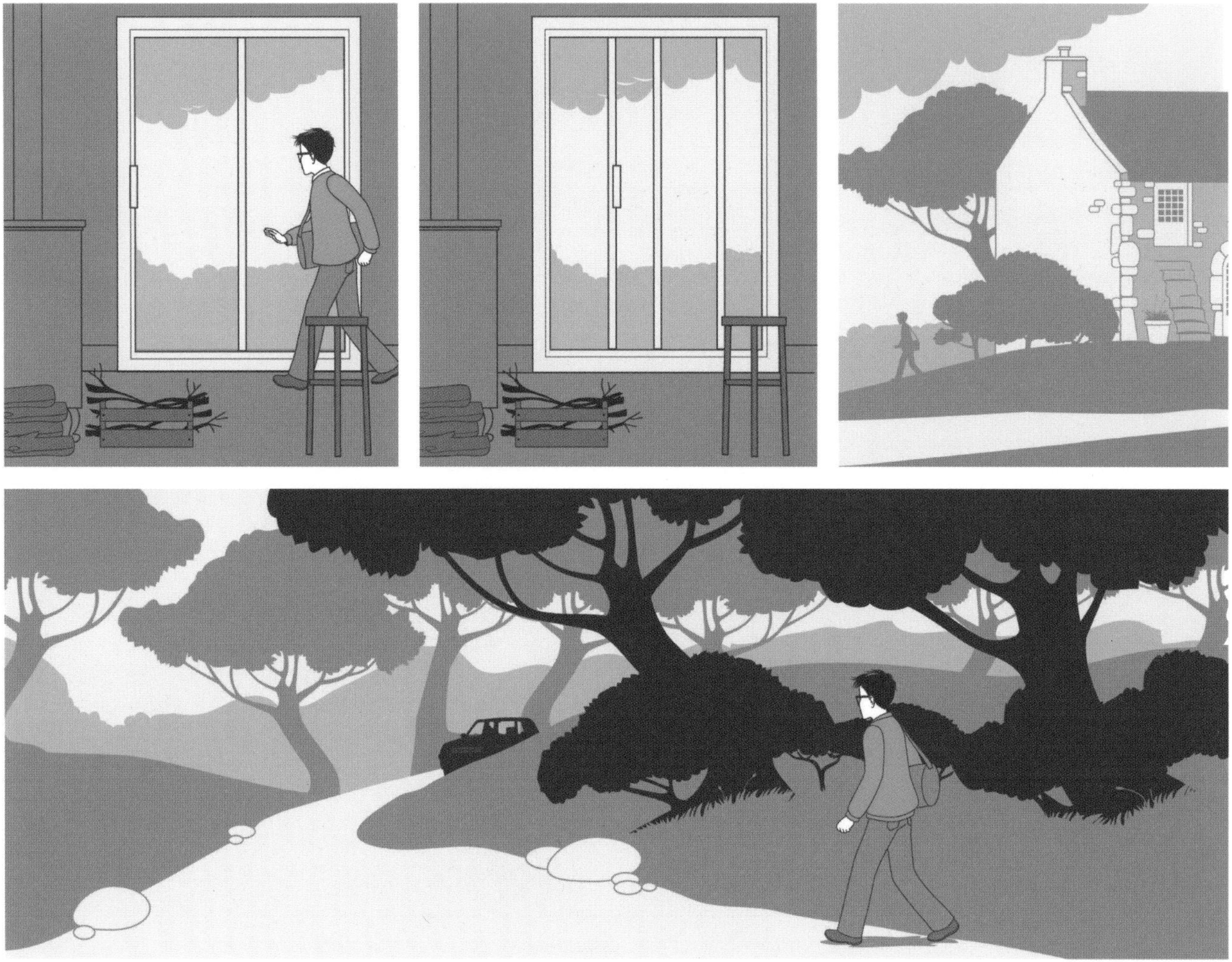

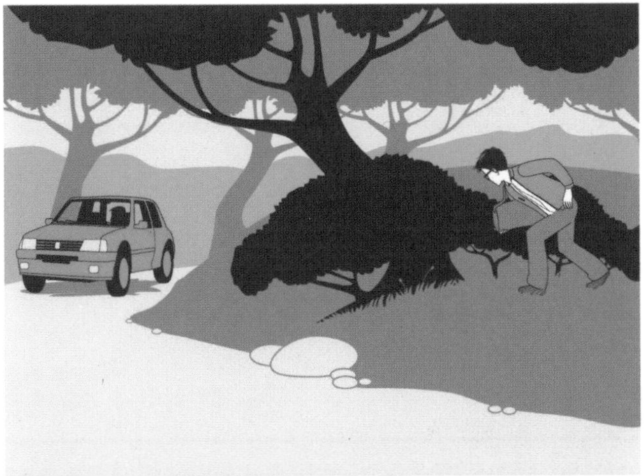

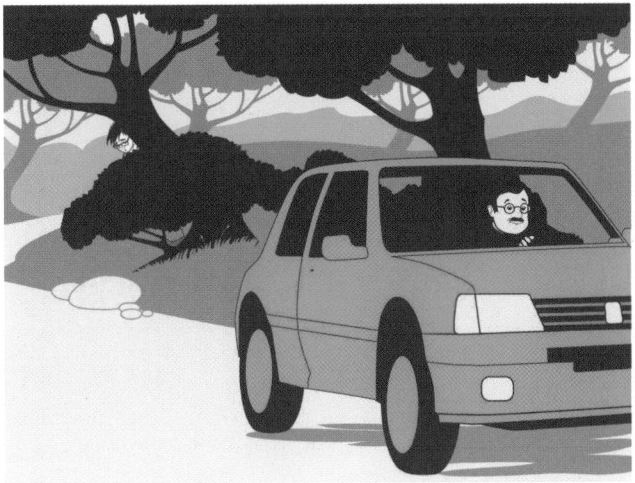

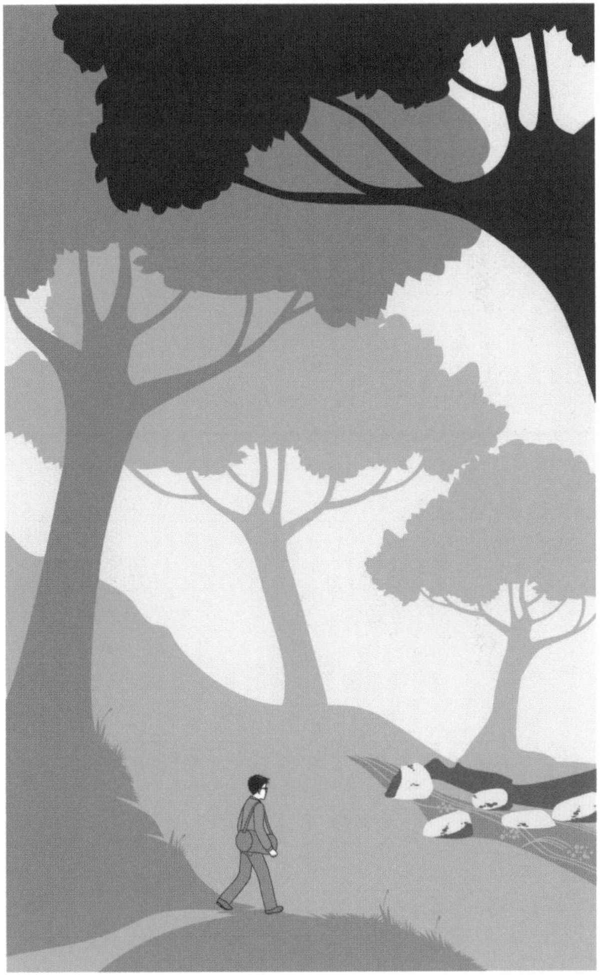

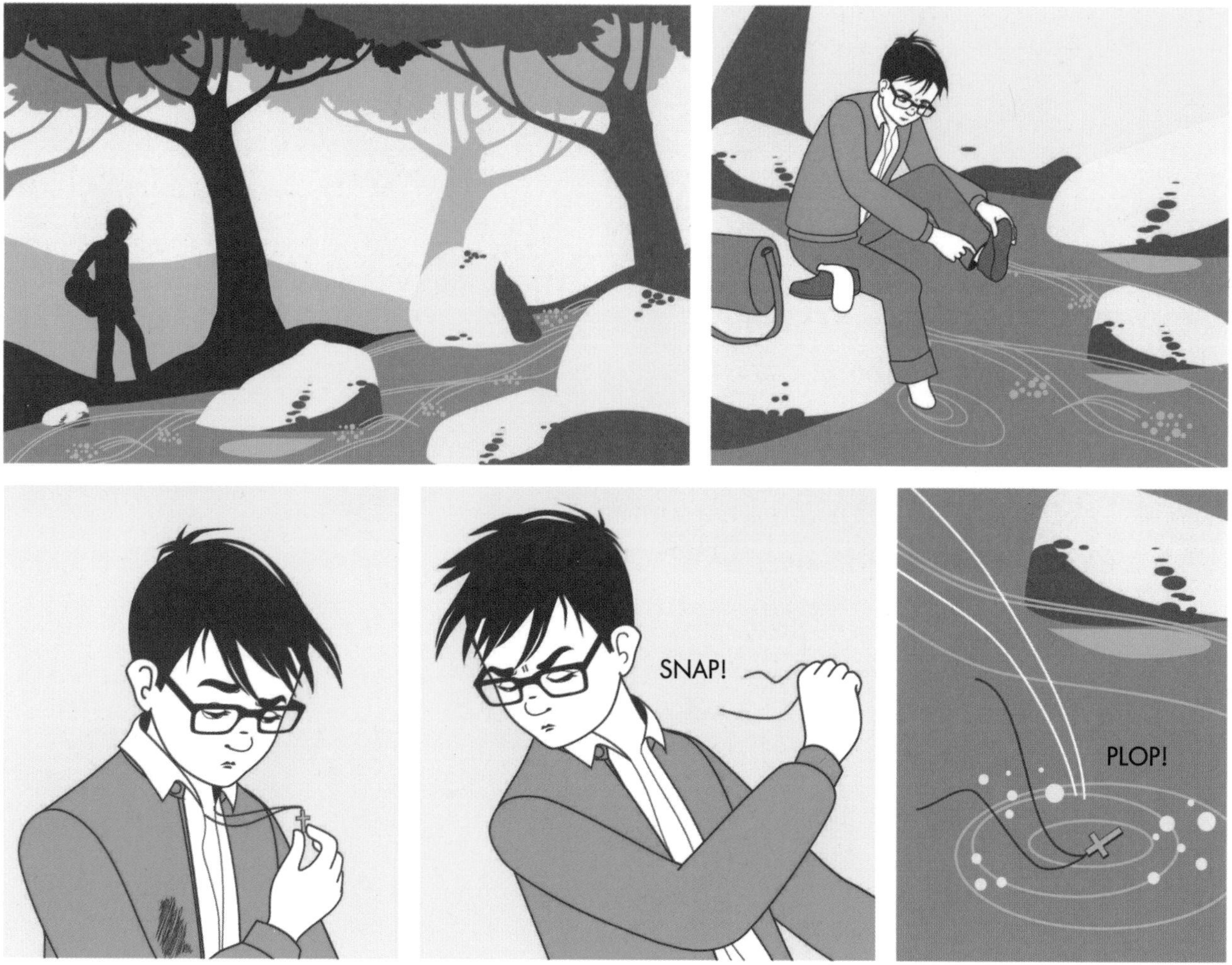
SNAP!
PLOP!

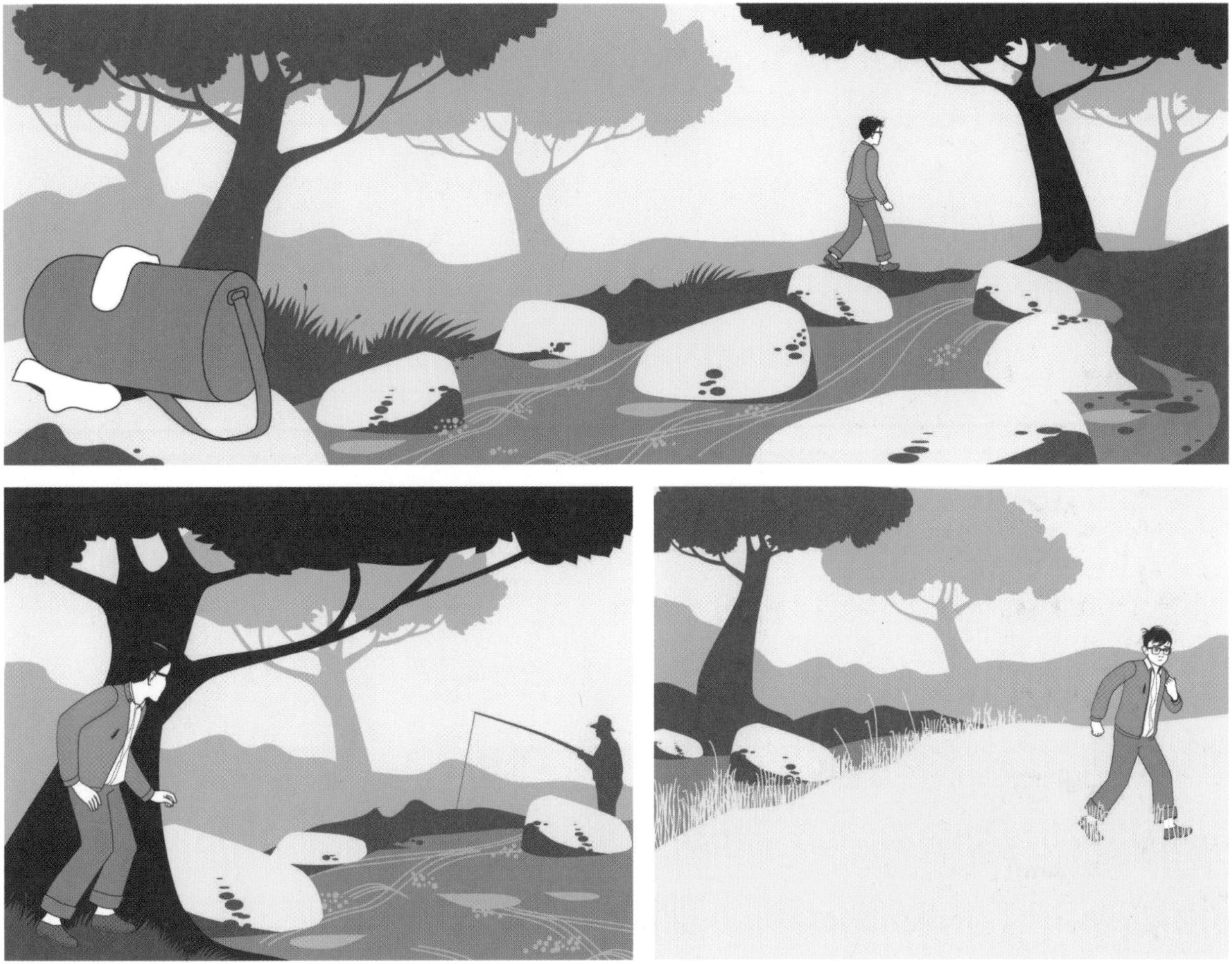

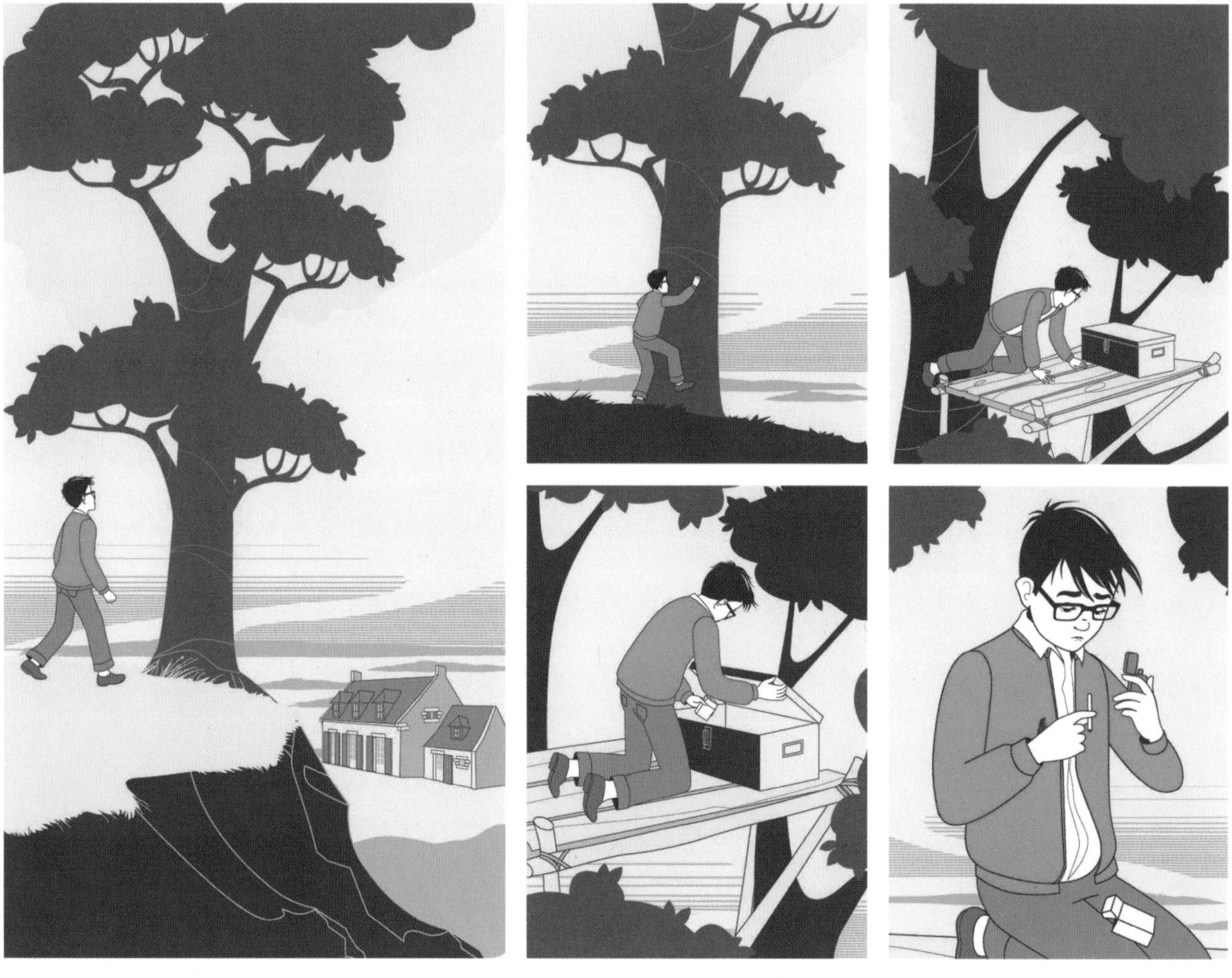

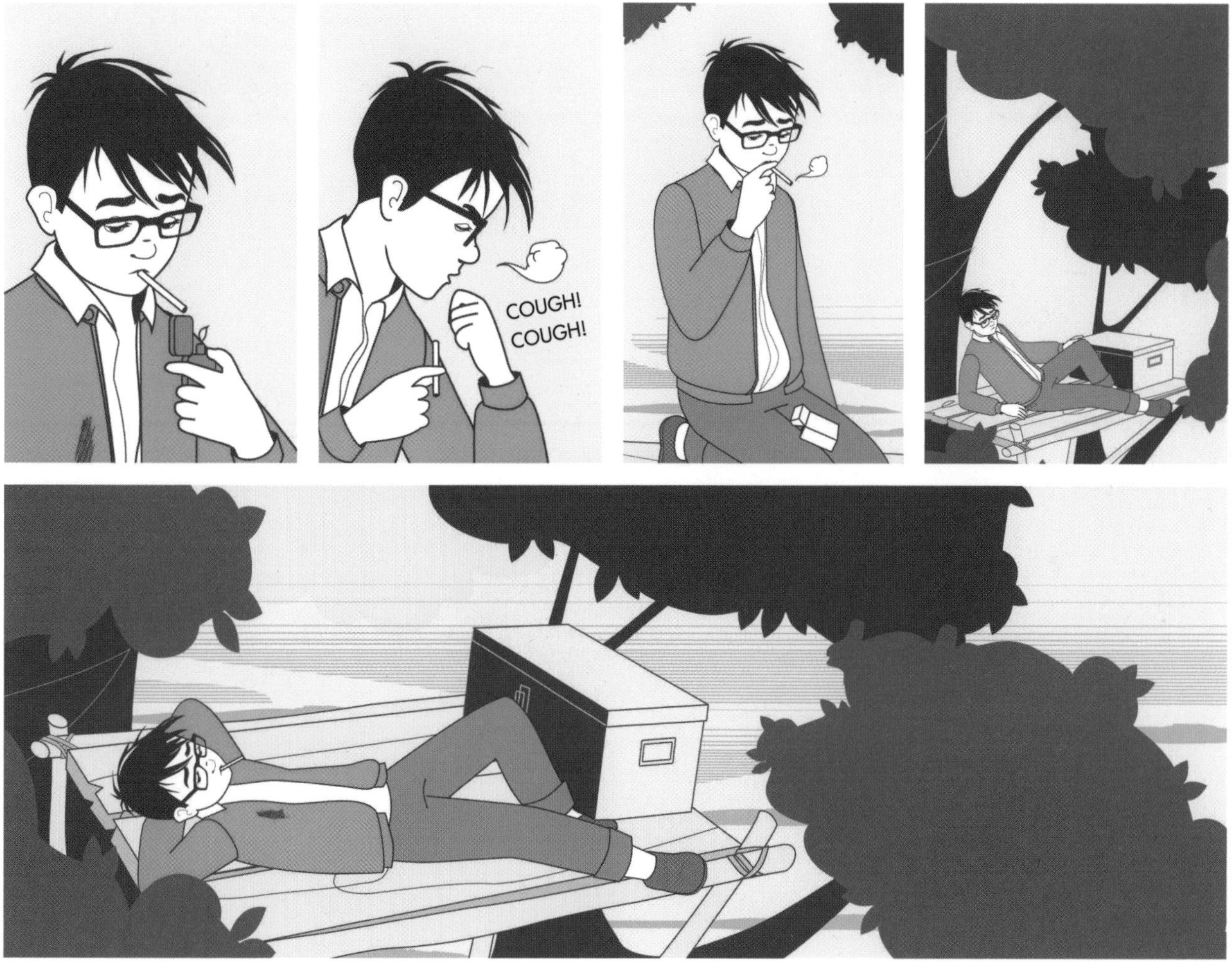
COUGH!
COUGH!

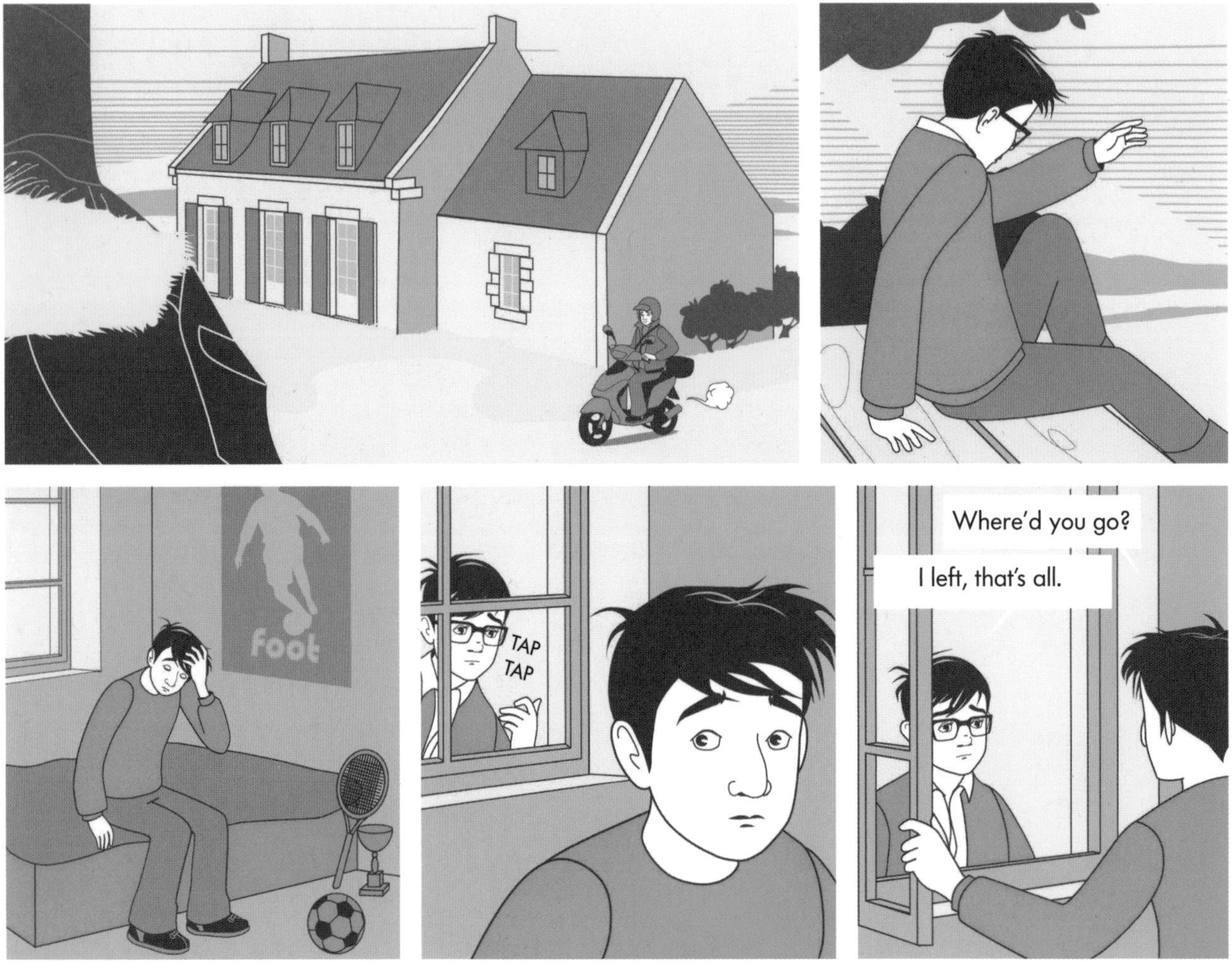
foot
TAP
TAP
Where'd you go?
I left, that's all.

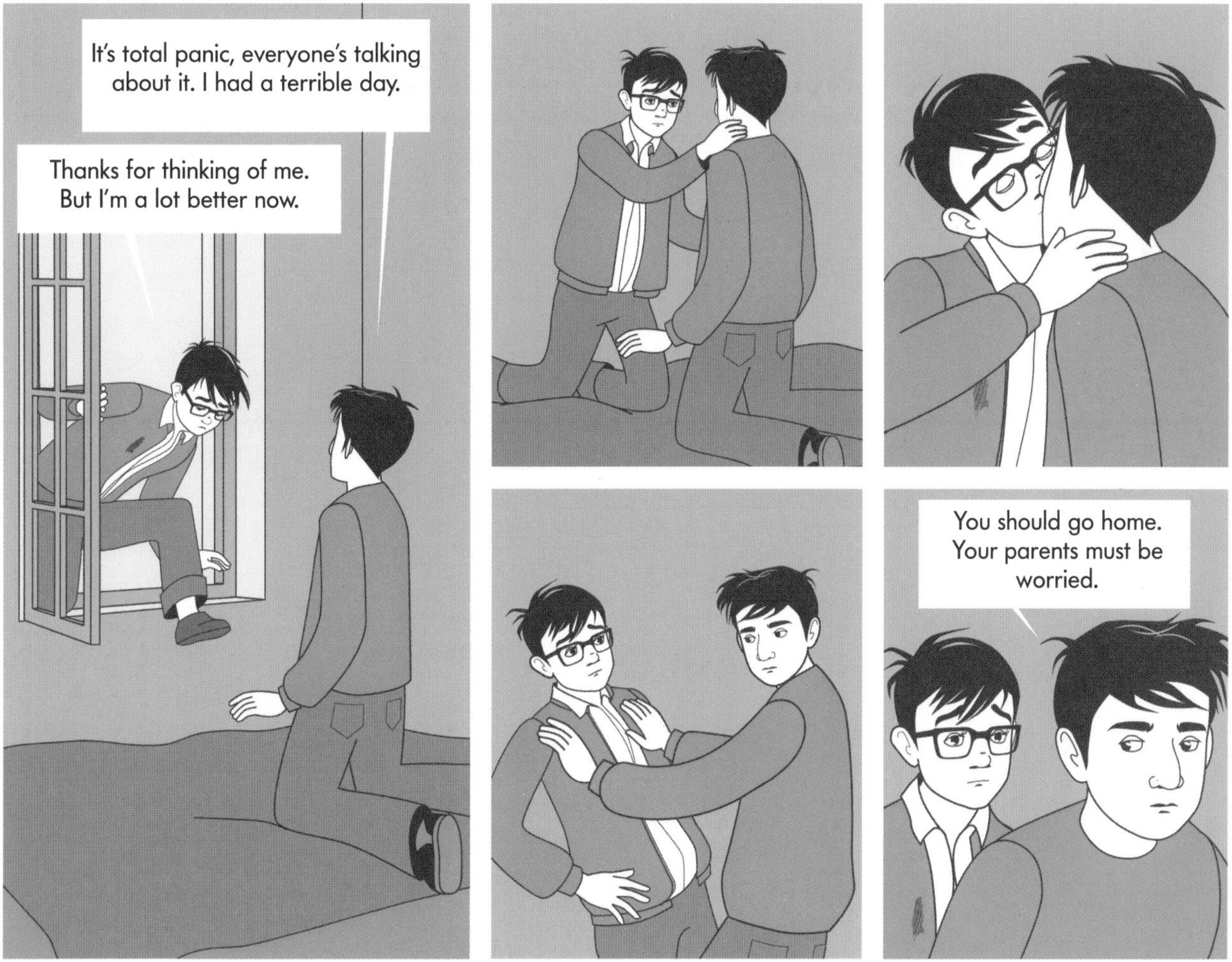
It's total panic, everyone's talking about it. I had a terrible day.
Thanks for thinking of me. But I'm a lot better now.
You should go home. Your parents must be worried.

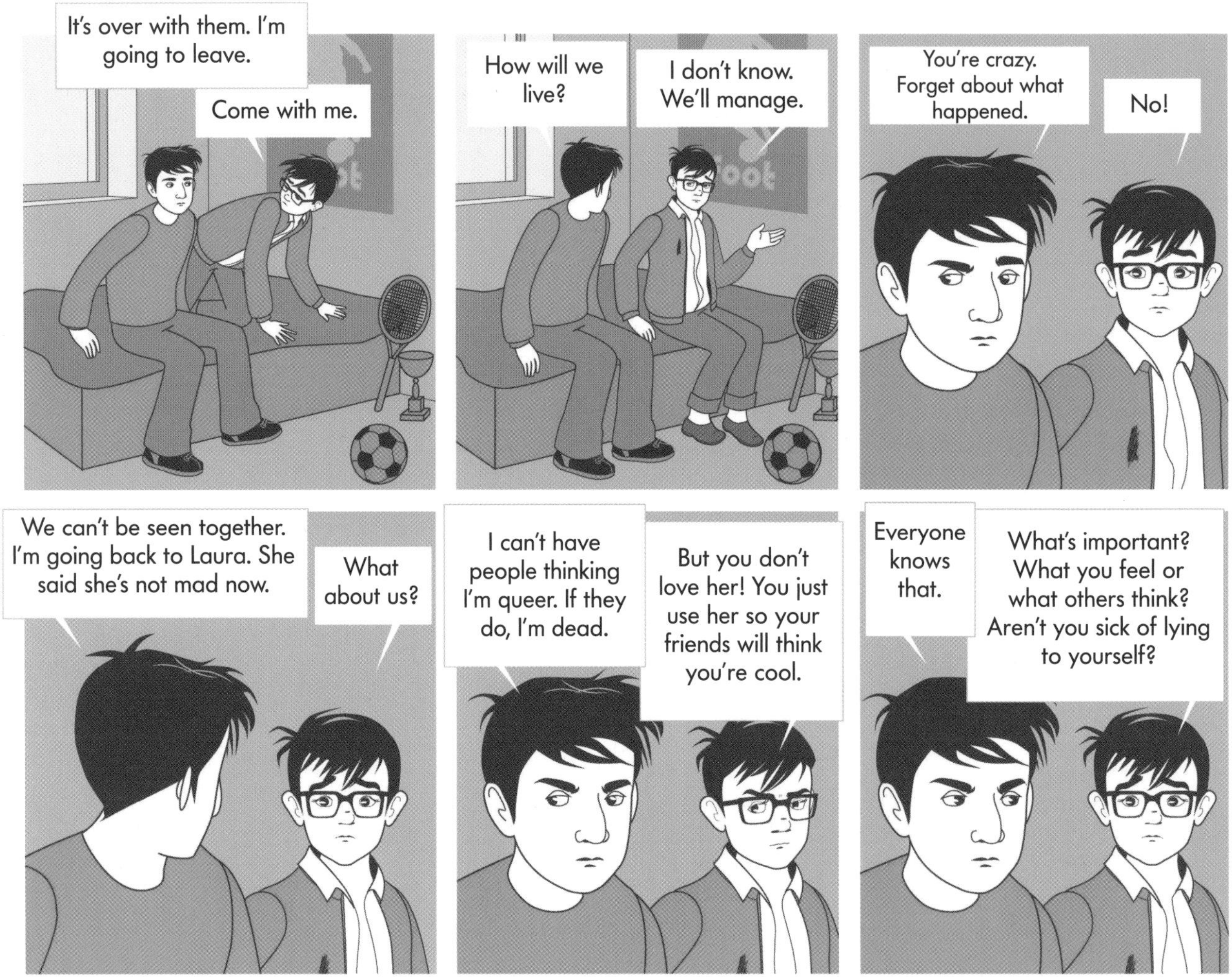
It's over with them. I'm going to leave.
Come with me.
How will we live?
I don't know. We'll manage.
You're crazy. Forget about what happened.
No!
We can't be seen together. I'm going back to Laura. She said she's not mad now.
What about us?
I can't have people thinking I'm queer. If they do, I'm dead.
But you don't love her! You just use her so your friends will think you're cool.
Everyone knows that.
What's important? What you feel or what others think? Aren't you sick of lying to yourself?

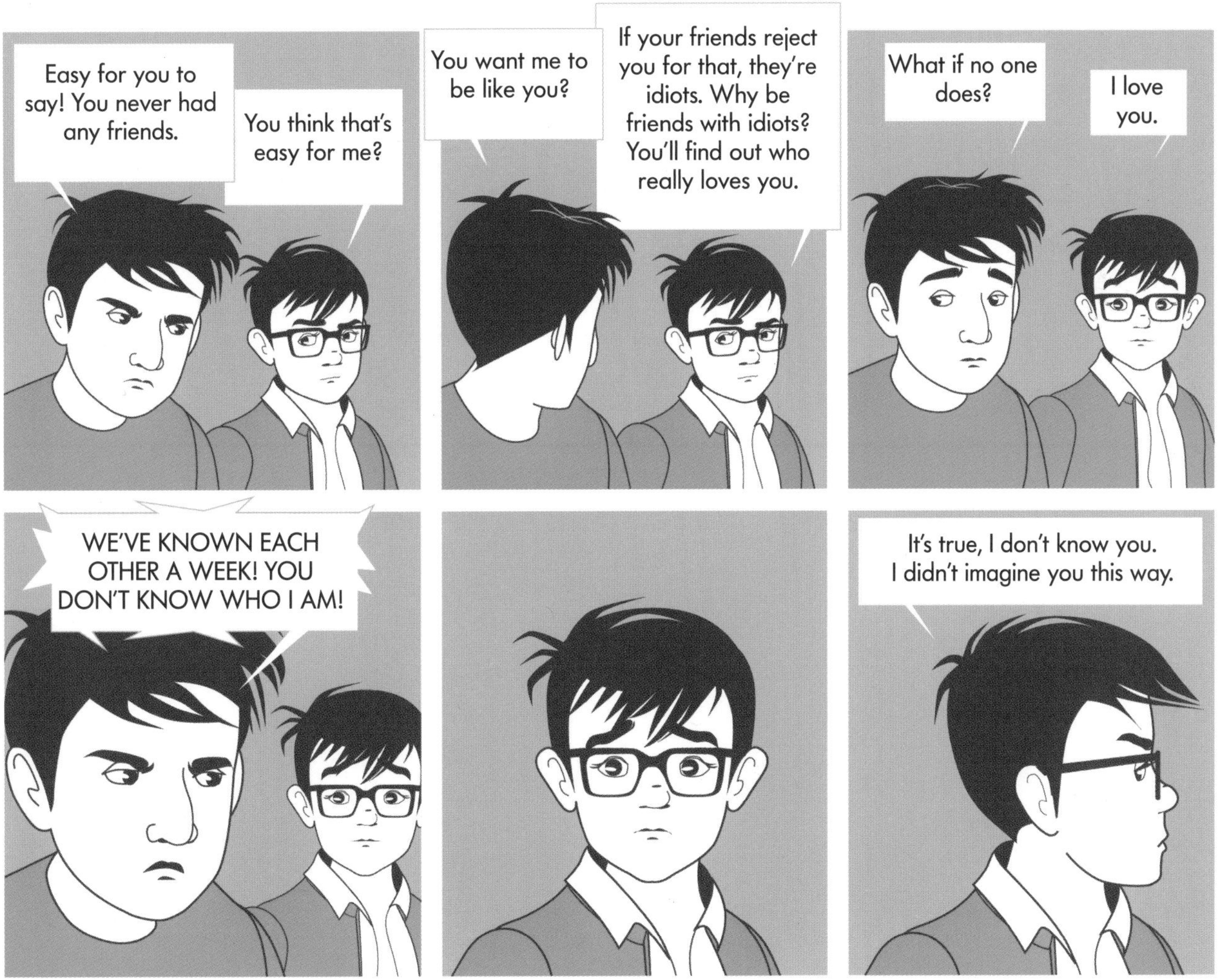
Easy for you to say! You never had any friends.
You think that's easy for me?
You want me to be like you?
If your friends reject you for that, they're idiots. Why be friends with idiots? You'll find out who really loves you.
What if no one does?
I love you.
WE'VE KNOWN EACH OTHER A WEEK! YOU DON'T KNOW WHO I AM!
It's true, I don't know you. I didn't imagine you this way.

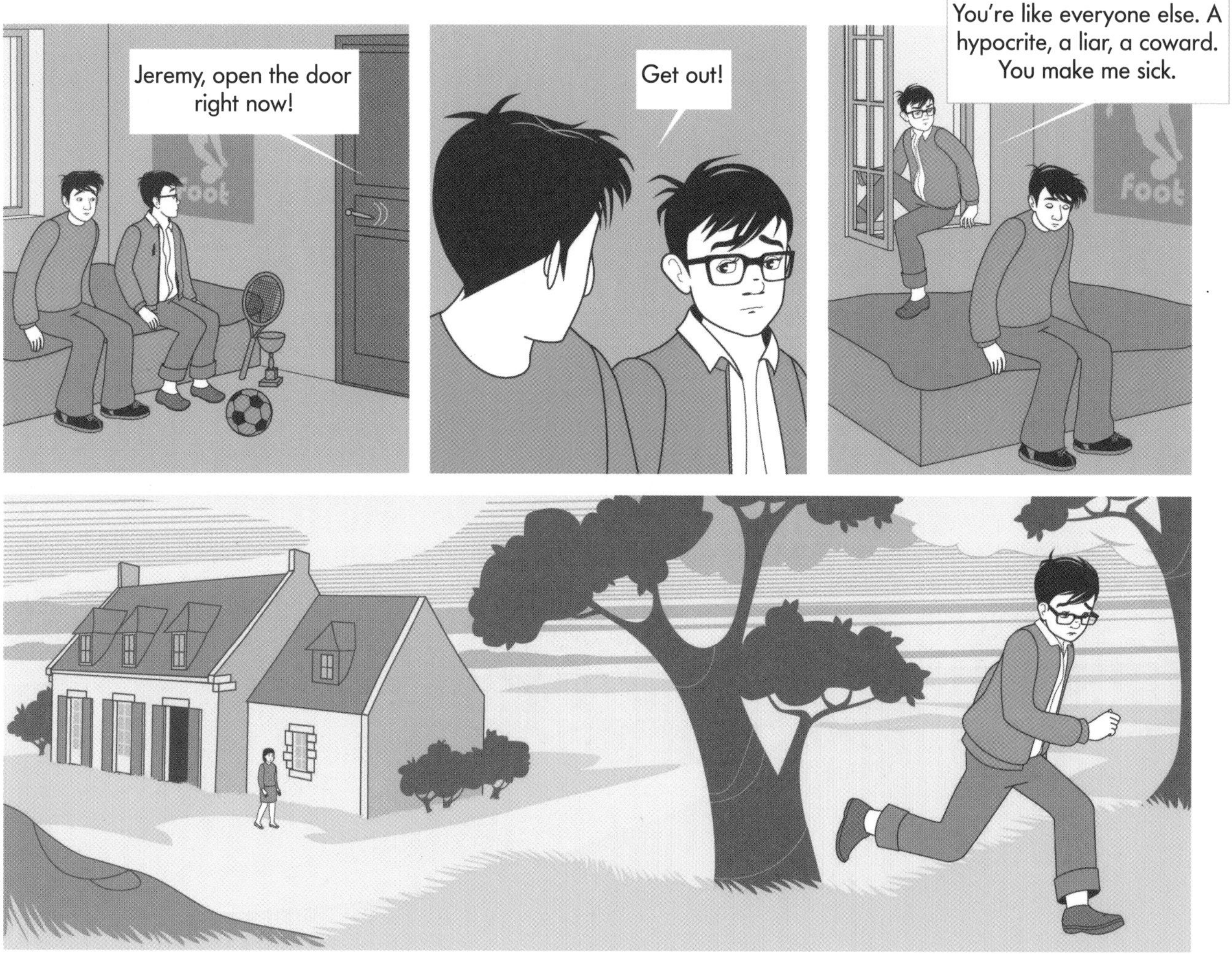
Jeremy, open the door right now!
Get out!
You're like everyone else. A hypocrite, a liar, a coward. You make me sick.
foot

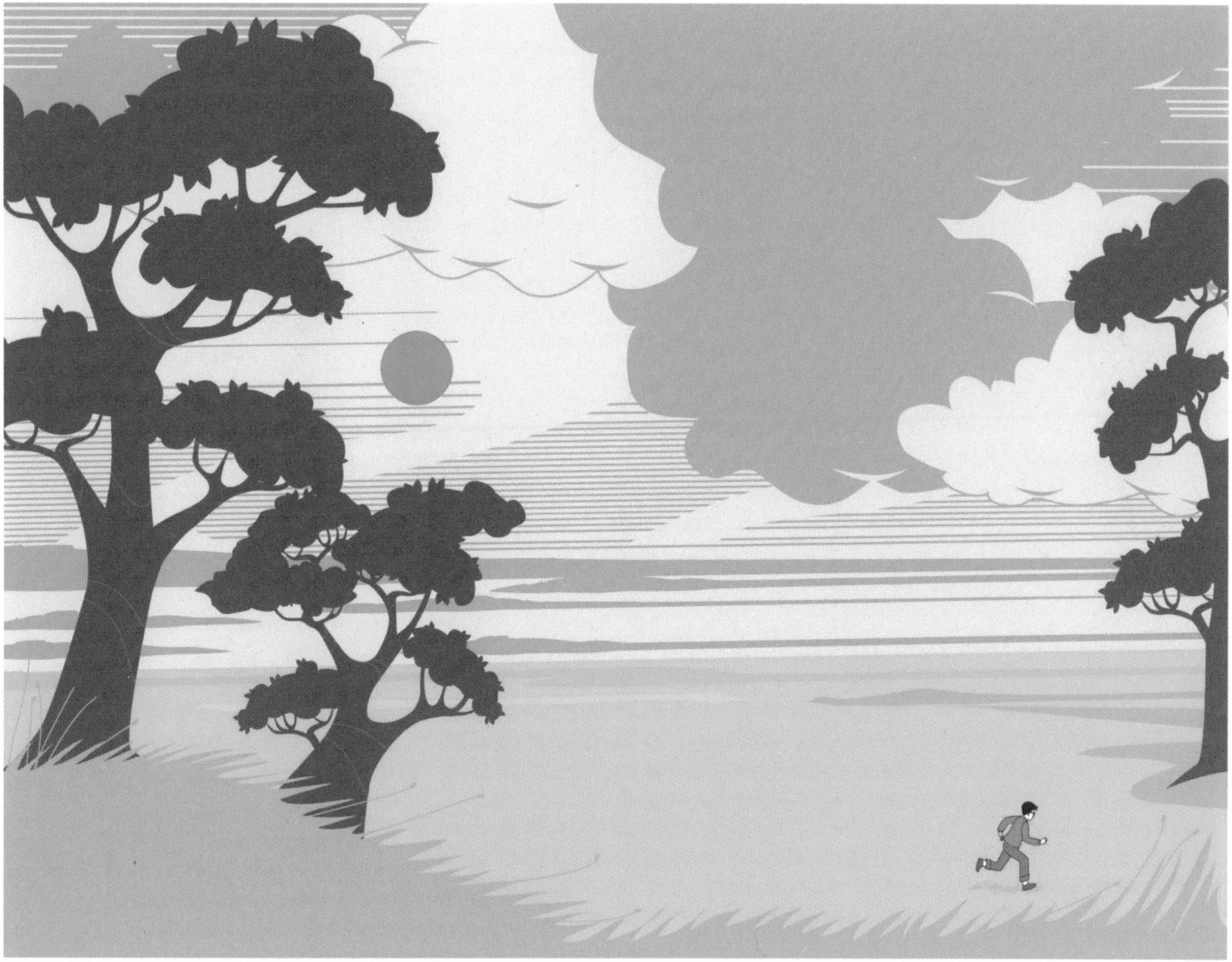

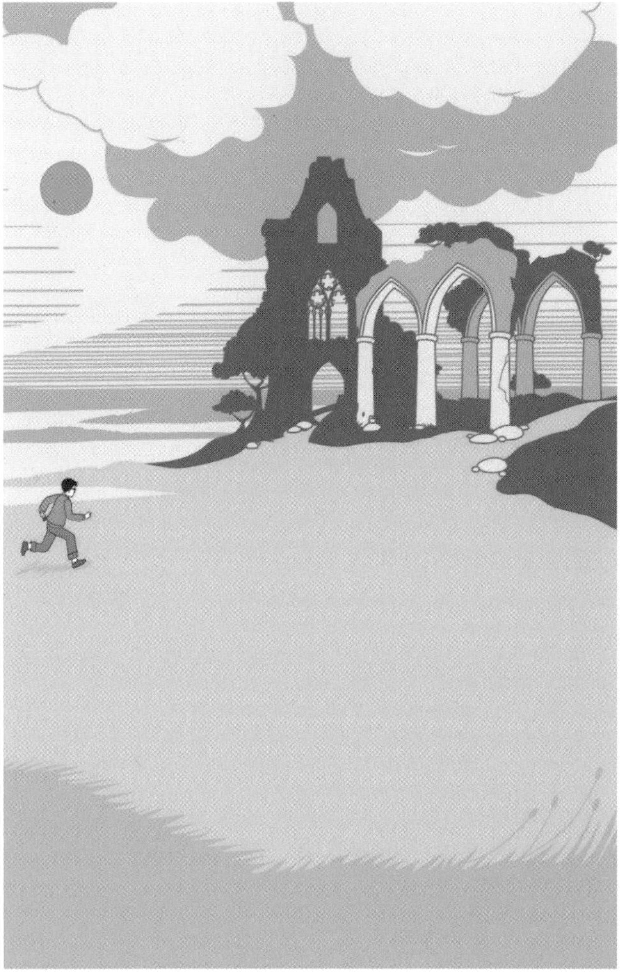

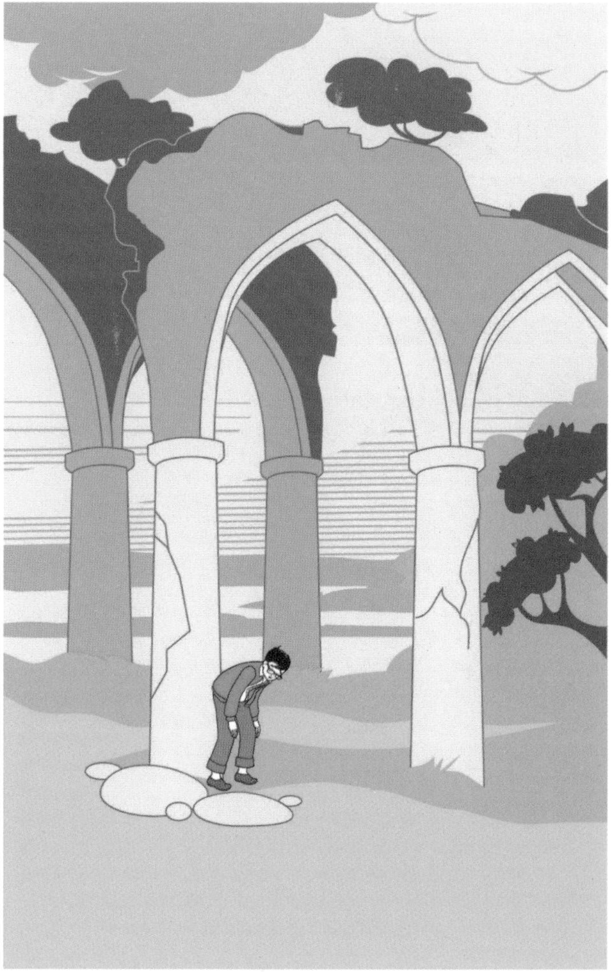

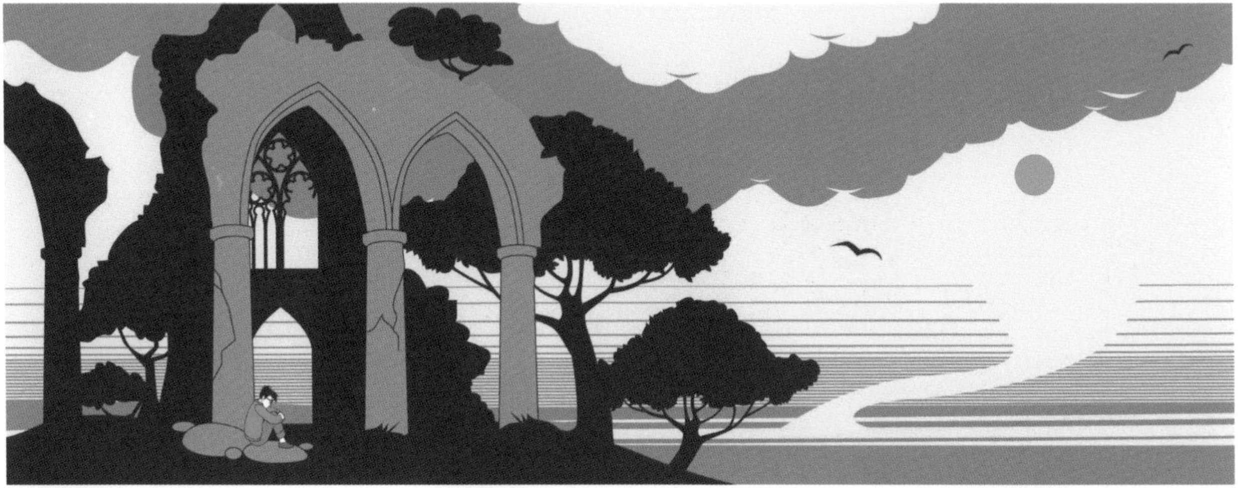

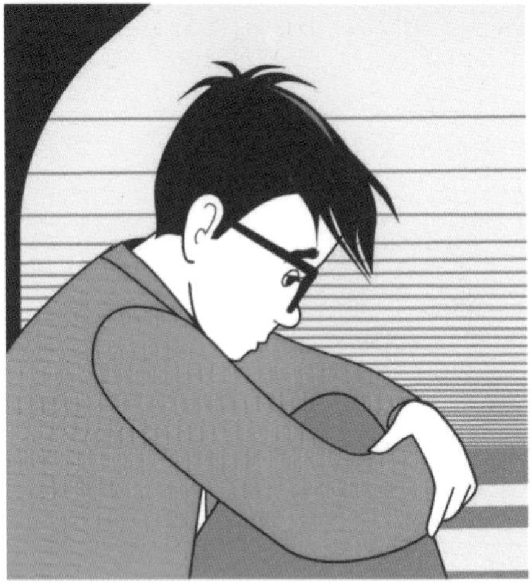

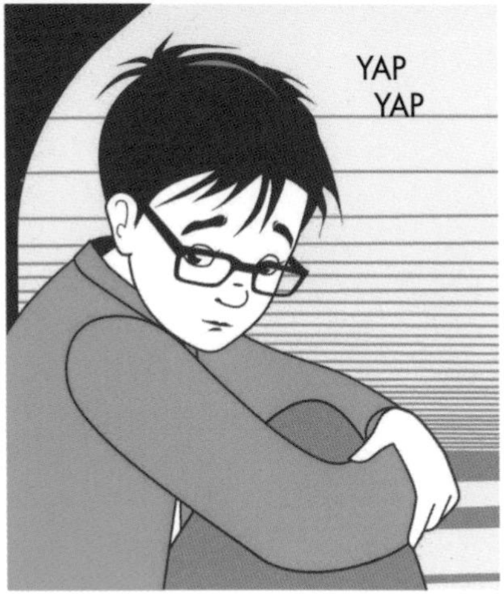
YAP
YAP

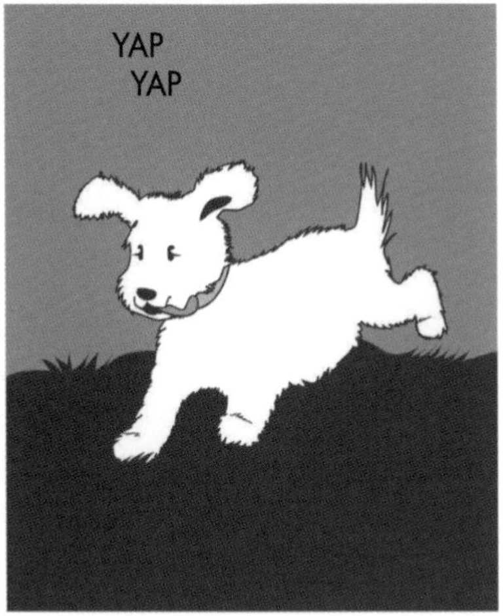
YAP
YAP

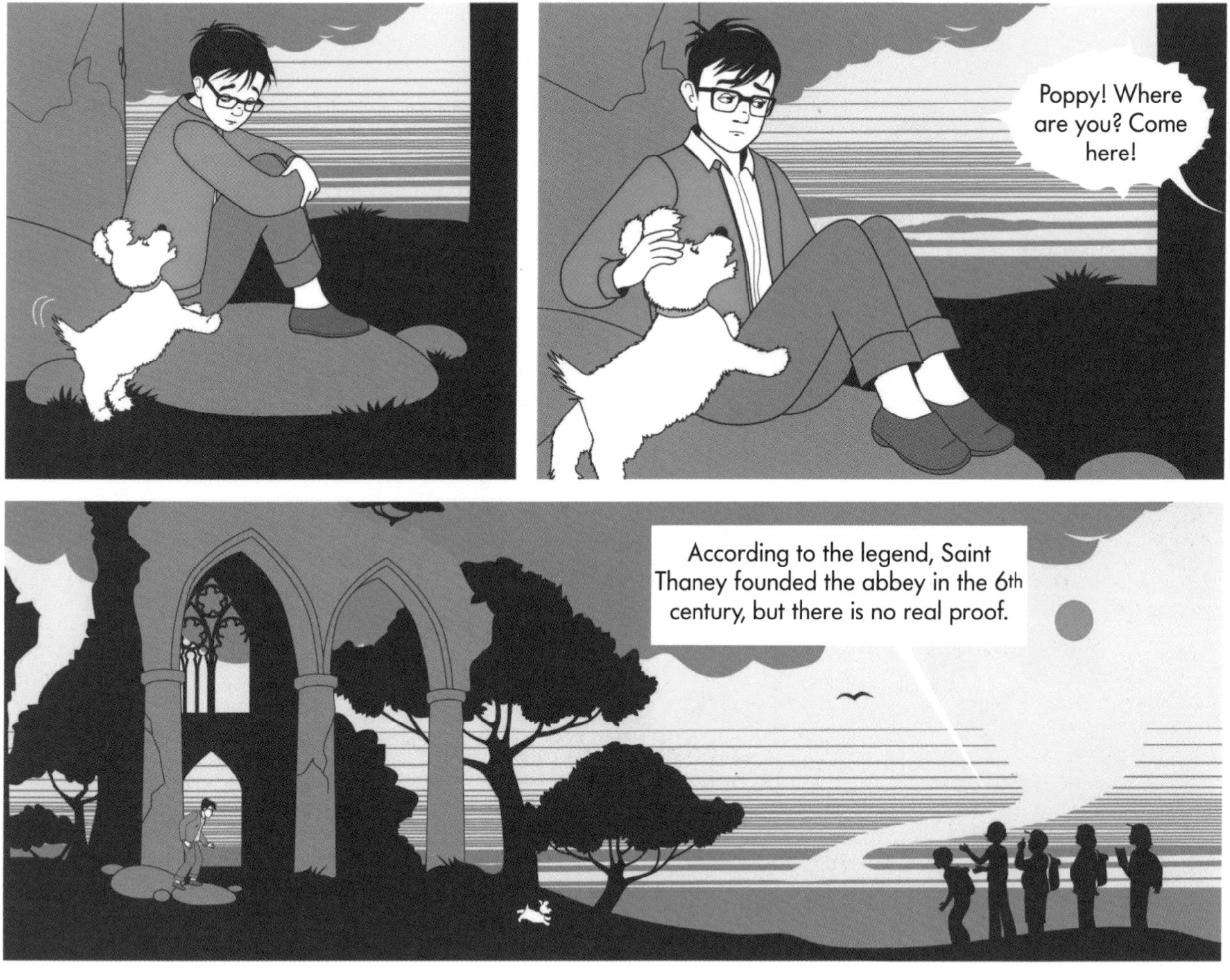
Poppy! Where are you? Come here!
According to the legend, Saint Thaney founded the abbey in the 6th century, but there is no real proof.

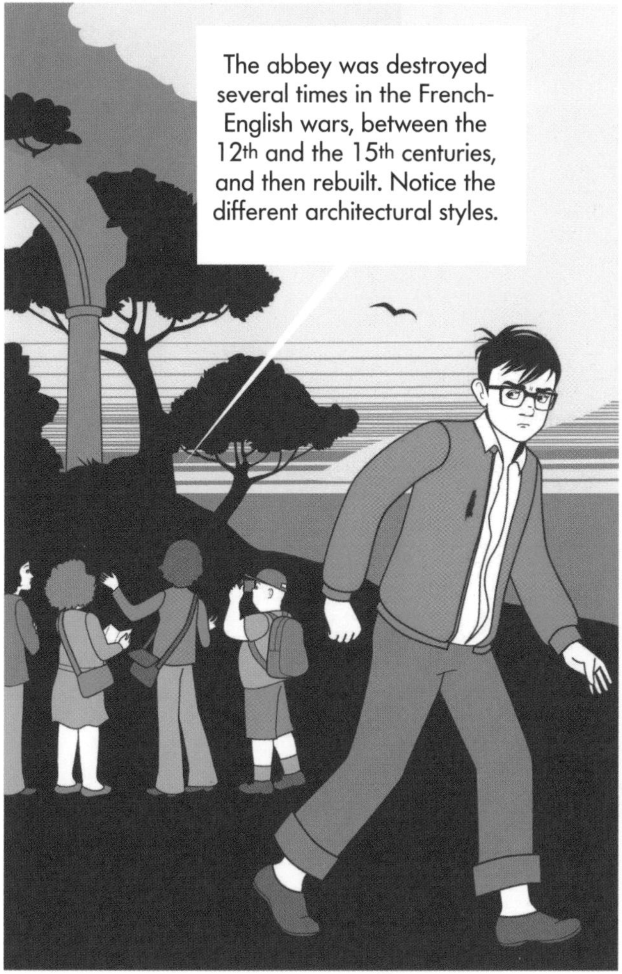
The abbey was destroyed several times in the French-English wars, between the 12th and the 15th centuries, and then rebuilt. Notice the different architectural styles.
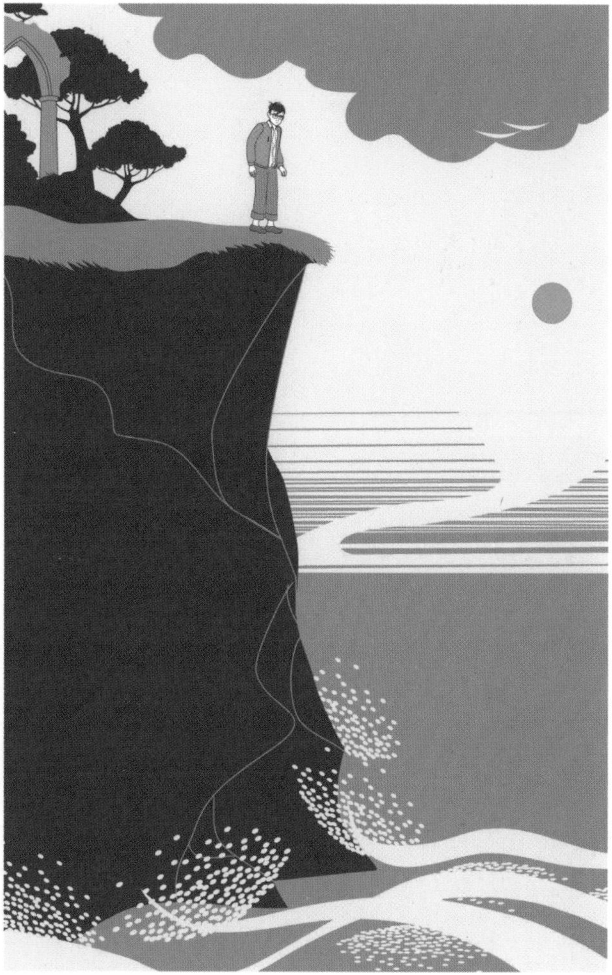

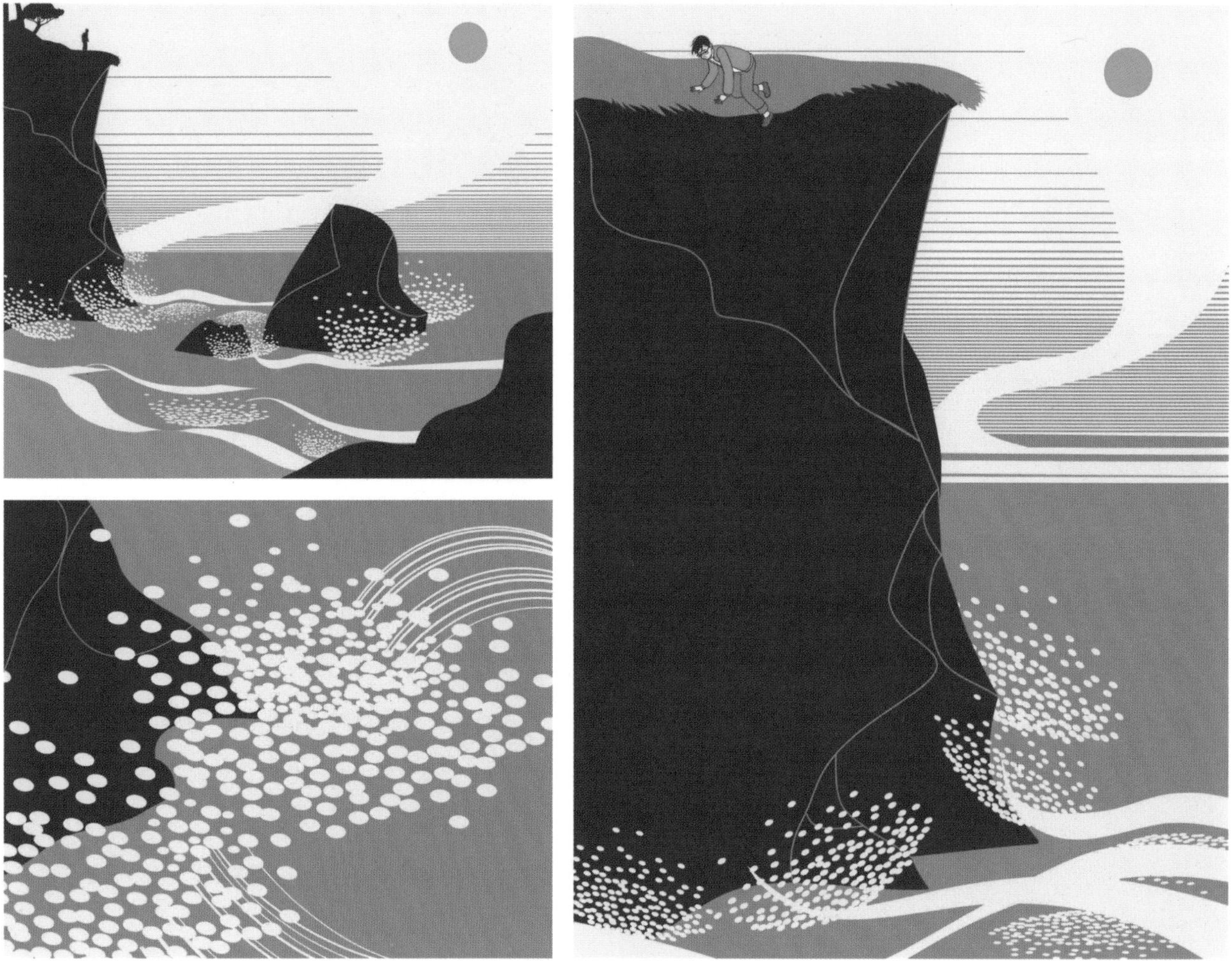

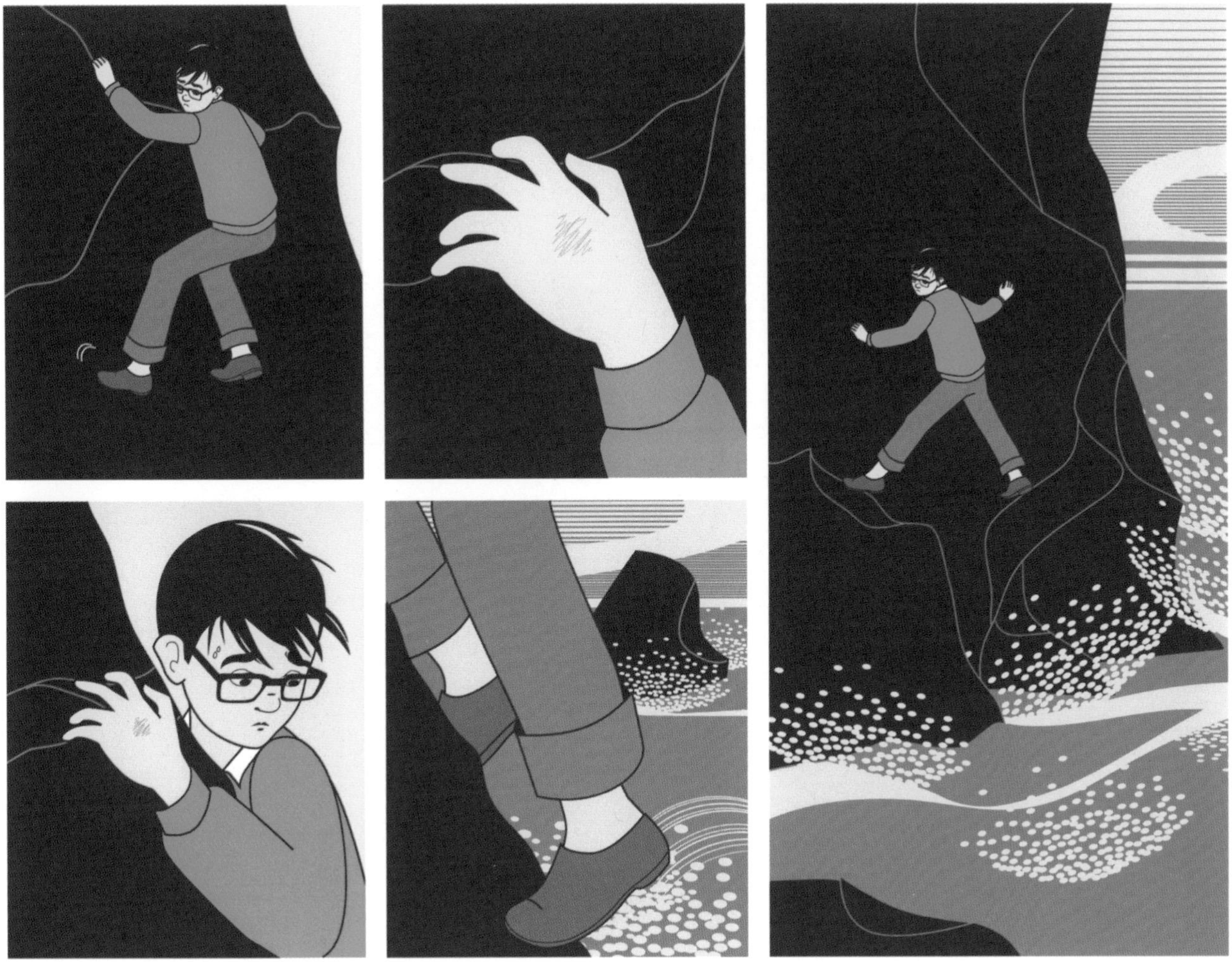

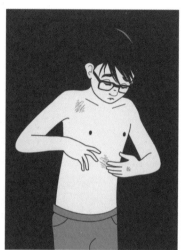

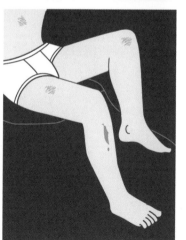

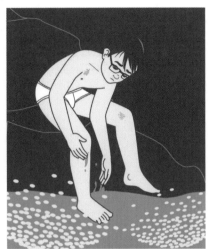

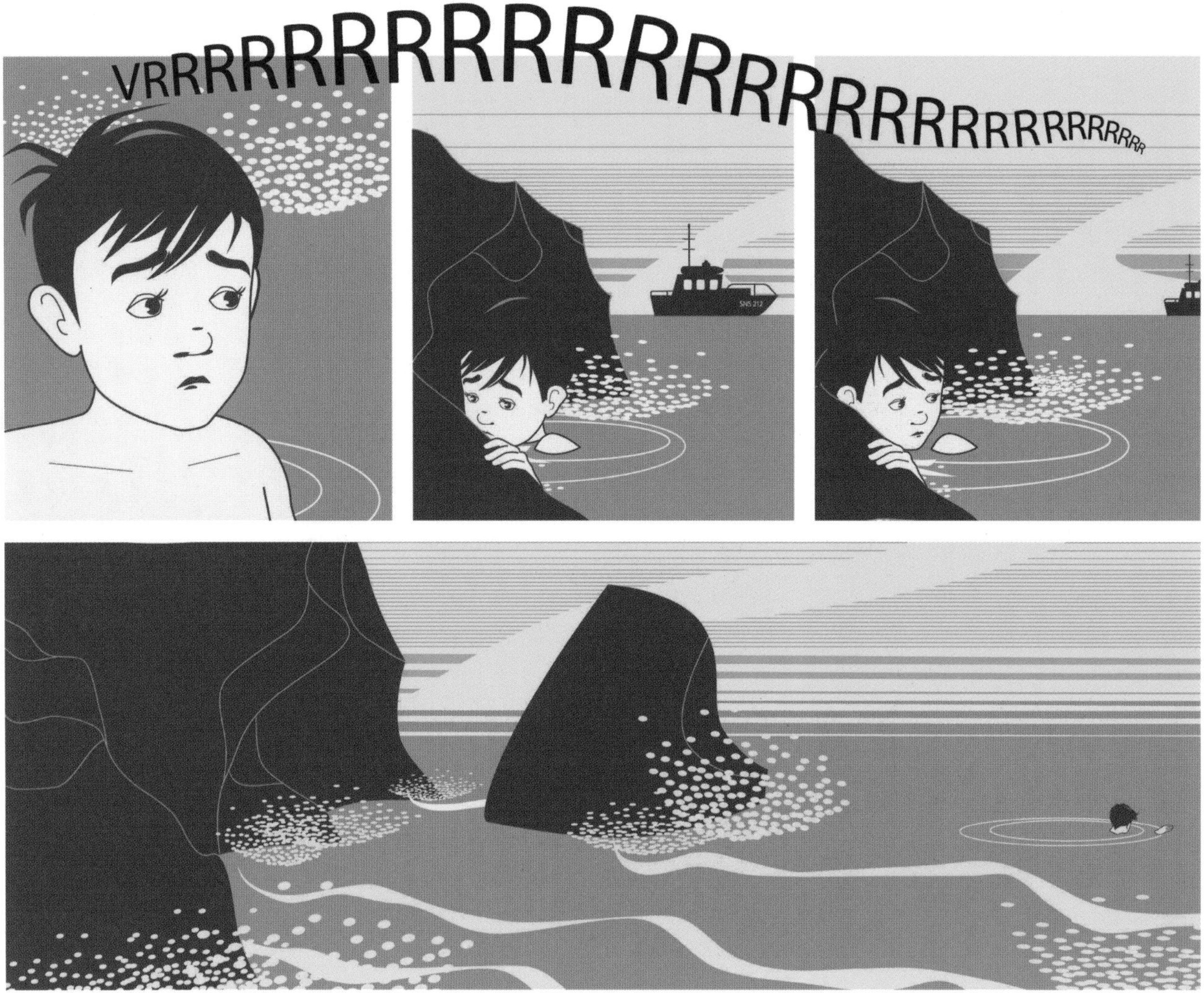
VRRRRRRRRRRRRRRRRRRRRRRRRRR

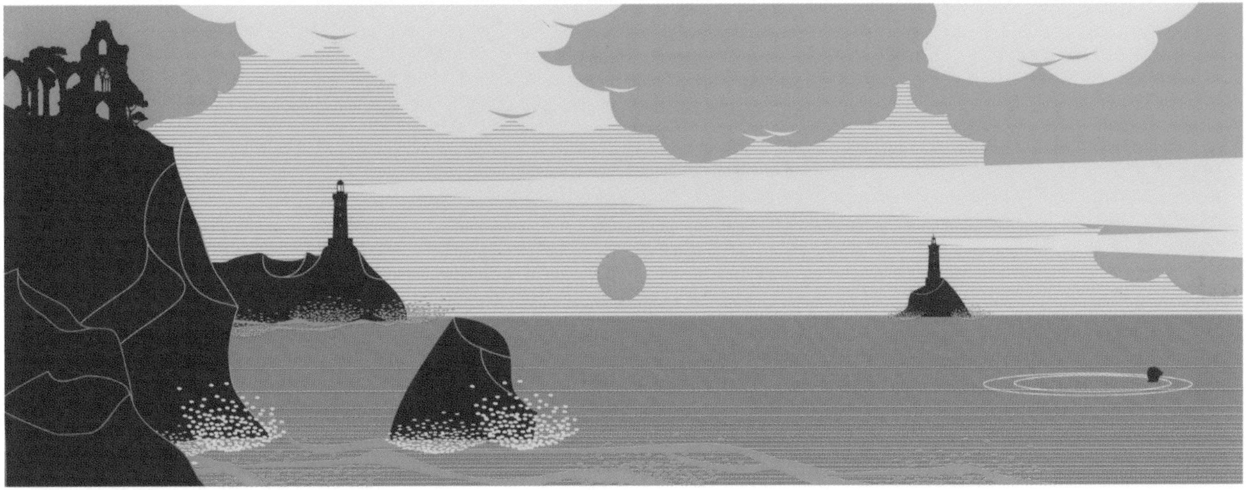

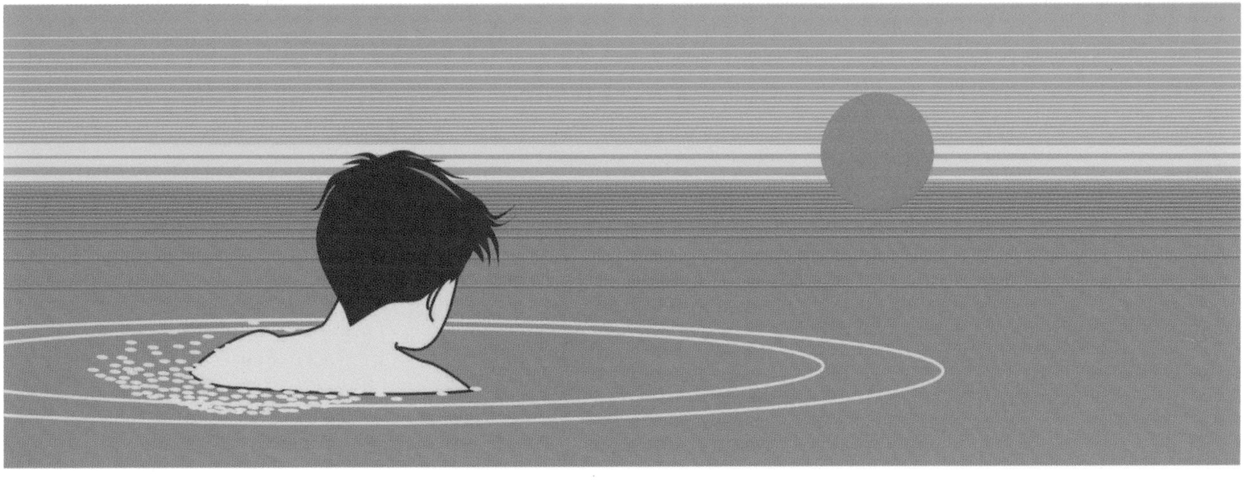

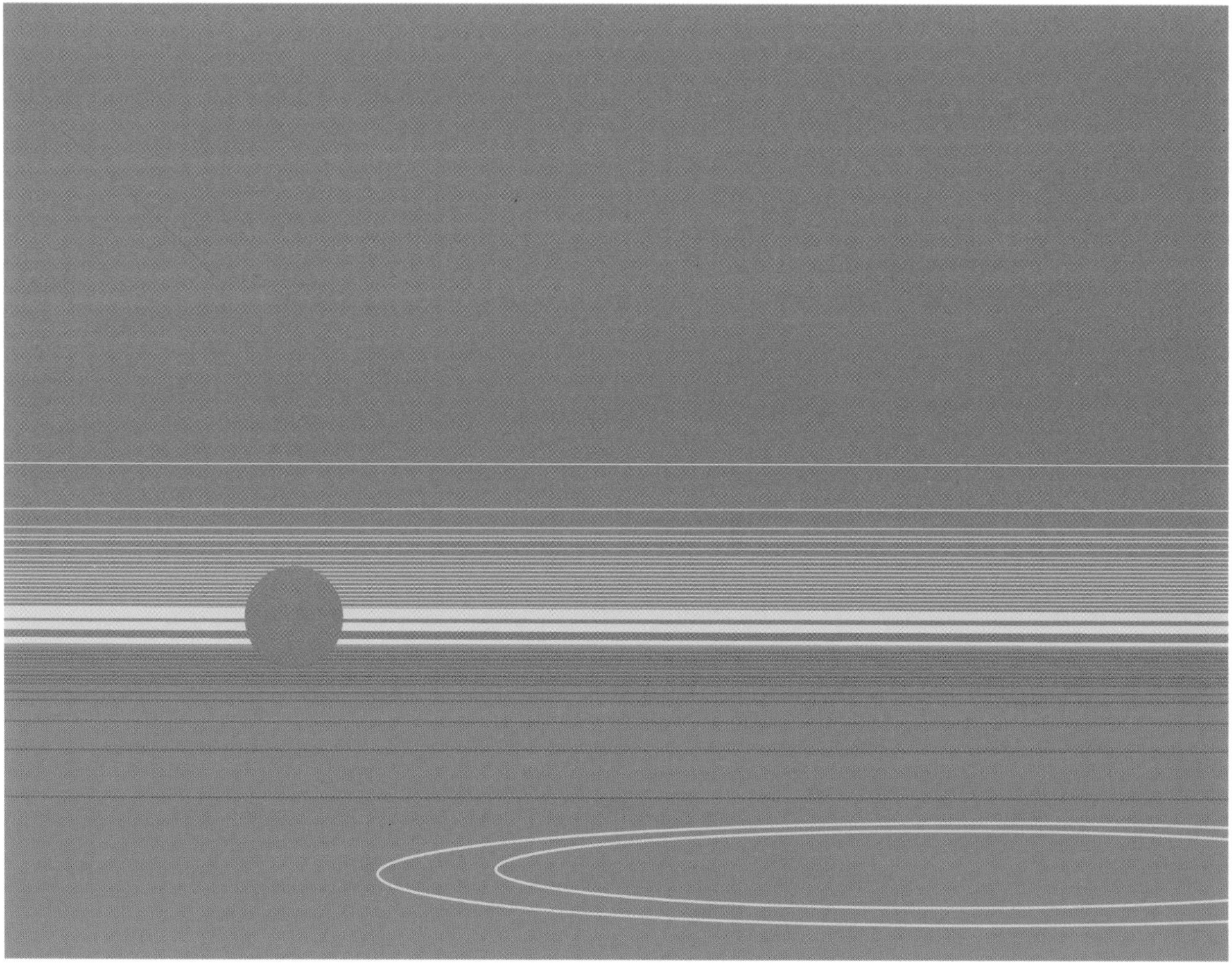

HUBERT studied at the School of Fine Arts in Angers, France, where he first set his career sights on comics. He has written a number of graphic novels and comic series in French, including one that has been translated into English: *Miss Don't Touch Me*, Vols. 1 and 2, a graphic novel series set in Paris in the 1930s. He lives in Paris.

MARIE CAILLOU studied Fine Arts in Strasbourg, France, and then in 1995 went to Brussels to study animation. She has directed short animated films, including a series entitled *Peur(s) du Noir* (Fear of the Dark). This is her first book to appear in English. She lives in Paris.

DAVID HOMEL, born and raised in Chicago, is a Governor General Literary Award-winning translator and writer. His most recent translations include *Kuessipan* by Naomi Fontaine, *The World is Moving around Me: A Memoir of the Haiti Earthquake* by Dany Laferriere, *The Last Genet: A Writer in Revolt* by Hadrien Laroche, and *The Inverted Gaze* by Francois Cusset (all Arsenal Pulp), and his own novels include *Midway* and, most recently, *The Fledglings*. He lives in Montreal.